Pick Six

max monroe

Pick Six
Mavericks Tackle Love #2
Published by Max Monroe LLC © 2018, Max Monroe

ISBN-13: 978-1984368867
ISBN-10: 1984368869

Editing by Silently Correcting Your Grammar
Formatting by Champagne Book Designs
Cover Design by Peter Alderweireld
Photo Credit: Wander Aguiar
Title Font by: Font Forestry

Dedication

To all the curvy girls who love tacos and donuts as much as we do:
You're fucking beautiful.

To delirium: Thank you for making hitting this nearly impossible
book deadline possible and then erasing any and all memories of the
trauma. You're just like childbirth.
Our book baby is fucking beautiful—and not at all weird-looking.

To the music goddess Rihanna: we're so happy you fictionally agreed
to fictionally perform inside this book. You were supersexy, sang
amazing, and your fictional concert was on fire.
We still don't know what words come after work, work, work, work,
work, but we trust you. We're sure they're amazing.

intro

Sean Phillips
The New York Mavericks
#26 | Wide Receiver
Height: 6-3 | **Weight:** 210 lbs. | **Age:** 26
Alma Mater: University of Washington
Last Season Stats: REC: 112 | YDS: 1533 | TD: 13

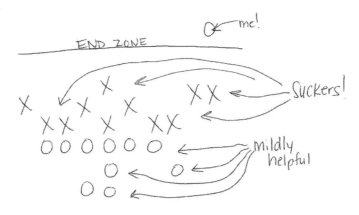

As the best wide receiver in the national professional football league, I'm the envy of almost every man in the United States.

I'm quick on my feet, sure with my hands, and trained to score frequently. You'd think with my expertise, I would have spent my entire young life playing this position, but the truth is different.

I've played almost every position there is to play in the game of football, and *that's* what really makes me good.

I can adapt. I can visualize.

And I sure as fuck can win. That's why I'm in the end zone, and everyone else is standing around holding their dicks.

I go after what I want, and I always get it.

Just wait. You'll see.

Chapter One

Six

Insanely tall steel framing, cement ceilings, and a gigantic mural of NYC painted on one of the walls, the grandeur of my location was hard to miss. It was substantial and important, and it was the kind of thing that made your stomach flip with excitement.

I can't believe I'm officially inside the New York Mavericks' Stadium with an all-access security pass to boot.

I smiled, big, proud, *overwhelmed.*

Today was a *big* day.

Gladiators in the form of professional football gods fought many a battle here, and starting this afternoon, I would be a tiny woman among giants.

Well, not of the scoring touchdowns or kicking field goals variety, but I'd be all up in their business just the same. I was a video blogger who made money from posting all sorts of hysterical videos to the number one personal content channel in the world, YouCam, and the idea of access to things other people couldn't see on a regular basis set my blood on fire.

Popularity on YouCam was all about originality and

never-before-seen content, and I was nothing if not a girl with a lack of societal rhythm. I was outspoken, playful, and I rarely gave much attention to being ladylike. My parents, truthfully, were often horrified by how I conducted myself in mixed company. Curses, insults, and dirty jokes were all staples of my repertoire, and they were first-generation immigrants. Apparently, I didn't do an adequate job of *blending.*

Earbuds in and Rihanna's "Pon De Replay" providing my own personal soundtrack, I walked through the Mavericks' stadium with a little pep in my step.

My hips swayed, my toes bounced, and the bagel and cream cheese I'd eaten before arriving blessed me by sparing me its usual heartburn.

Ready to conquer the world—*aka a room full of huge, muscular, professional football players*—I followed the instructions Georgia Brooks had given to me via email earlier in the week.

Six,

The New York Mavericks organization would like to send you an official welcome. Everyone here is buzzing with excitement over this exclusive series with the very creative, talented, and popular YouCam vlogger, Pick Six.

We have everything set for Friday at noon. I've couriered over a security pass for you. You'll need that to get into the stadium.

When you arrive:
-Park in the back lot marked Staff and use that stadium entrance.
-Take the elevator to the first floor and take a left.
-Follow the long hallway until you reach the end, then take a right.
-You'll see two big doors (they should be open), and that's

the small auditorium/meeting room where we'll do the meet-and-greet with the players.

And I can't say it enough, everyone here, especially me, is thrilled to have you on board! Don't hesitate to reach out to me if you have any questions.
See you Friday!

Sincerely,
Georgia Brooks
Director of Marketing
The New York Mavericks

I scanned through the email on my phone and shrugged my shoulders.

Left, right, big ole set of balls…I mean doors.

Sounds easy enough. Sliding my phone back into my pocket, I hopped onto the elevator and made my way to the first floor.

I was so damn pumped I could hardly contain the frenetic energy coursing throughout my body. Like a kid hopped up on Pixy Stix and Mountain Dew, I did my best to tamp down all of the anxious vigor by listening to music as I walked.

But when I paused to dance it out a bit in the middle of the long and very empty hallway and dropped into position to twerk, I started to rethink my music selection.

Yeah, okay, Six. How about a little less booty popping and a little more professional and focused?

I couldn't take back the dance moves now, but I could replace them with my game face.

Which I did.

Eyes focused forward. Shoulders high. Back straight. Chin up.

Thanks to the *Rocky III* Soundtrack, this girl was ready to knock 'em out with charm and sophistication, and tiger's eye had more meaning to me than its use in my nighttime eyewear. I was ready to win over the crowd, and maybe, if necessary, surprise an attacker with a hard as hell right hook.

Once I reached the end of the hallway, I took a left and saw the two big doors Georgia's email had mentioned, but they were closed.

That's weird...

With a quick glance to the watch on my wrist, I confirmed my early arrival and explained away the discrepancy.

Obviously, Georgia and the players had yet to move on from the last item on their schedule, but that didn't mean I had to wait.

I could just go in and acquaint myself with the room, test out the flow, and prepare myself for the acoustics. I might've been an expert at chitchat, but that didn't mean I was impervious to nerves and occasionally using an outside voice when I should have used one designed for inside. Yeah, a few quiet moments to get my thoughts in order was a fantastic idea.

Hand wrapped around the metal handle, I switched my playlist yet again to Shania Twain singing about feeling like a woman and pushed gently, but the damn door didn't budge.

Thanks to being vertically challenged, this kind of thing actually happened to me a lot.

With an annoyed sigh, I bent my elbows and pressed my hip to the wood, and with all of the energy my five-foot-one body could muster, I shoved. *Hard.*

With a creak and a crank, the doors opened...six inches.

My face was distorted as I took four deep breaths and sucked in hard to make myself skinny enough to slip inside. I keened and wailed a little, but the sounds were muffled by my scream as the doors I'd just come through closed and swallowed me into utter darkness.

Ah, *fuck.*

Light switch, light switch...

The cinder block wall felt bumpy under my fingertips as I scrubbed tentatively along the area to my side. I estimated the switch to be at throat height, but as anxiety crept in, my legs spread and bent, pulling me into a fearful squat.

Arms stretched above my head now, I crab-walked the line of the wall to a corner and then down another wall, but the next corner came too soon.

Jesus flipping Christmas, am I in a closet?

I was going to miss the biggest break of my blogging life because I couldn't get the fuck out of a closet! I panicked then, turning back to the doors and pulling with all of my body weight, but they wouldn't open again. Sweat pooled in my armpits and under my baby boobs. They started to cry at the possibility of facing some of the hottest men on the planet while sporting sweat underlines.

"Hush, little babies," I comforted my breasts. "It'll all be okay. Mama's gonna get you out of here."

Oh God, I was hysterical.

Chill out, Six. You're just nervous because you're about to meet the freaking New York Mavericks.

Surely, the auditorium was just on the other side of this wall. This was an entryway, not a closet.

Yeah, had to be.

I ignored the sense of impending doom and turned back to the other wall in search of another door.

The handle felt cool against my palm when I finally located it, so I took a moment to press my overheated boobs to the surface. They cheered their gratefulness, and my mind cleared, poised and ready to conquer all over again.

This time, the door opened easily, and I pointed at it victoriously as though I'd gotten away with something.

But my momentary confidence skidded to a halt, along with my feet, once I found myself a few inches into the actual room.

The landscape didn't make sense. *At fucking all.*

A shelf of white towels. Bins of dirty laundry.

Football equipment scattered pretty much everywhere.

Unless the Mavericks' auditorium for meetings looked a lot like a locker room, it was safe to say I was in the wrong place.

Ho-lee shit. This is literally a locker room.

Oh. My. God. *Can anyone see me?*

Like I was watching a tennis match at lightning-fast speed, I swiveled my head back and forth to find out the answer, but the adrenaline coursing through my veins made rational thought impossible.

I dropped down to the floor, ninja style, did a roll to put out the imaginary fire, and crawled behind a giant cart filled with white towels.

I was officially reporting from behind enemy genitalia lines. If I were truly lucky, I might actually find the big set of balls I'd thought Georgia had sent me to find.

With my back pressed into the wall and my body hidden behind the towel cart, I exhaled the breath I didn't realize I was holding.

Good God. Had I really just stumbled into the New York Maverick's locker room? Like, the real one? Maybe this was, like, the west wing locker room that they never used.

Well, good news, these are clean towels instead of dirty jock straps sitting right in front of your nose...

As I lifted my gaze from the towels, I realized the cart I was using as my own personal cloaking device was essentially see-through. Like, if I peeked just above the rows of towels, I could see straight into the locker room.

Everything, in the locker room.

Then, as if on cue, a penis walked by...

A *walking* penis. Right in front of my face.

Well, it didn't have legs, but it had balls. *Huge* balls.

Don't worry, Mrs. Brooks. I've located them.

My ears buzzed loudly, and everything around me turned to white noise. Apparently, adrenaline rushes made my brain prioritize penis sightings over actual sounds, and I couldn't really criticize its priorities. I'd much, much rather see penises than hear what someone said if they caught me seeing them.

Speaking of penises, there goes another...

Like Dr. Seuss had trained me for, they came in all sizes and shapes.

One dick, two dicks, red dick, blue dick, and all that.

Okay, so there weren't any blue dicks, but that was beside the point.

With some circumcised and a few sporting turtlenecks, these puppies were out and ready to party.

Men in white towels. Men naked. Men half dressed. Men in boxer briefs.

It was a buffet of delectable muscles, and I was the thirsty weirdo in the corner salivating over sausages.

Holy moly, this is like a hot guy secret convention.

But with dicks. Lots and lots of dicks.

Like my brain flipped the on switch for my ears, all at once, the sounds of the room blared inside my head. Music with deep bass, hearty laughter, and loud chatter reverberated throughout the large space. And the sounds of running water echoed from the far back corner as steam billowed up toward the ceiling from what I assumed were the showers.

Those are the very showers where all of these penises get clean.

Jesus. What was wrong with me? Why was I still sitting on the ground staring at all of the man candy?

Dick-i-pops. Cock-tarts. Shaft-treats.

Fucking hell, now is not the time to come up with penis-inspired candy names.

I had to get it together and get the H-E-double hockey sticks out of here before someone saw me.

It'd taken months and months of persistence and contact with Georgia Brooks, the Mavericks' Director of Marketing, to get this gig of a lifetime. And I highly doubted she'd be too thrilled if she found out, on the day I was supposed to actually meet the team, I'd taken a pit stop into their locker rooms to hobnob it up with the shafts and schlongs of the organization.

Hell, I'd traveled from San Diego, which was literally across the freaking country, just to be here. Not to mention the fact that I'd be living out of my suitcase inside of hotel rooms whenever I was in

New York or at away games for filming.

Thankfully, all travel, including flights, was paid for by the Mavericks' organization, but still, I'd worked my ass off and sacrificed the comforts of home to get this big career chance.

Rare and amazing, this opportunity wasn't the norm, and I couldn't let a little cock bomb distract me from the prize. Endorsed by the New York Mavericks as this season's official YouCam vlogger, I'd scored an eight-episode series with my dad's and my favorite professional football team, and if things went really well, there was even the possibility of seeing this upcoming series on actual television.

Which is exactly why you should rethink your current location...

The longer I sat here, hiding behind a towel cart and staring at dicks, the closer the opportunity drapes got to the fireplace.

Wide-eyed and heart pounding wildly inside of my chest, I peeked over the towels again and glanced around the room to see if anyone had noticed my presence.

Instantly, I sighed in relief when I noted everyone inside the locker room was completely oblivious to the little voyeur behind the linen cart.

Thank God, I thought to myself, but for some unknown reason, I didn't move.

God, I'm so creepy right now, like a little Peeping Tom.

I really needed to get the fuck out of here.

But before I plotted my getaway plan, I saw it.

Well, *him.* Sean motherfucking Phillips. One of my top ten favorite professional football players, and oftentimes, when I watched Mavericks games, the sole recipient of my attention.

Good God, he was glorious.

Gloriously naked.

Him. His body. And his...*Holy peen-asurus-rex.*

As Sean Phillips's penis and I made direct eye contact, all I could think was *no wonder women flock to him like he's some kind of god among men.* It was perfect in shape and impressive in size, and I would swear until the day I died that the snake between his legs had used its one and only eye to wink at me.

Like my own personal mirage, he beckoned from the other side of the room.

That penis deserved headshots and an agent and his own Hollywood film. If *American Idol* looked for the X-factor in future musicians, I'd just found the star among swinging shafts.

Oh, and Sean looked inviting too. Dripping wet, muscular as fuck, mocha-colored skin, and handsome as the devil himself, he looked *good* naked.

And when I say good, I mean lick your lips and you don't even realize you're licking your fucking lips because you're too busy gawking, kind of good.

Get it together, Six! Stop being such a pervert!

I tried to snap myself out of it, but Lord Almighty, it was hard.

That's what she said.

Holy moly. What was wrong with me? I felt like I'd acquired brain damage somewhere along the way.

My playlist was no fucking help. It'd switched from Shania to Lil' Kim and 50 Cent, and they were *so* right about the magic stick.

With a back-and-forth swivel of my head, I shook myself out of the trance and found the strength to discreetly slip out of the magical set of doors that had somehow led me to the Penis Promised Land.

Quiet as mouse and ass fictionally on fire, I moved like my life depended on it.

Once I'd cleared the exit and didn't hear any commotion behind me, I rested my back against the opposite wall and tried to slow my erratic breaths. All the while, my heart attempted to climb out of my body at the speed of a race car.

What in the hell had just happened?

Surely, Georgia Brooks hadn't meant to send me into the fucking locker room…? The bit about finding the two big balls had been nothing more than a Freudian slip.

I took my earbuds out of my ears and pulled my cell phone out of my pocket.

One more glance at her email and I realized where I'd gone wrong. I'd taken a left instead of a right.

With a hand to my chest, I tried to calm myself down.

Holy hell. That was *not* something I'd planned on seeing today.

I mean, I hadn't minded it one flipping bit, but the stress that came from stealing glances at the Mavericks' dicks was nearly too much to bear.

But cripes…the urge to share was *strong*.

I need to tell the girls.

Technically, I still had twenty minutes until Georgia would get here.

Well, not here, but in the actual spot where I should've gone in the first place.

Needless to say, I had some time on my hands, and I needed to use that time to cleanse myself of my penis-seeking sins.

After a brief fight with the door that had gotten me into this mess in the first place, I squeezed my way back out and stumbled into the small ladies' restroom at the opposite end of the hall.

I checked the stalls with little to no shame, bending at the hips to look under the doors and shatter any and all privacy of any people I might find. Luckily, there wasn't an overpopulation of women in Mavericks Stadium on a Friday, and I moved back to the door and locked it.

Phone out of my pocket, I pulled up the YouCam app, but instead of logging in to my public account that had millions of followers, I logged in to my private account—the account only shared with my two best girlfriends, Samantha and Everly.

We'd started private YouCam accounts many moons ago when all three of us had left our hometown of San Diego to head to various colleges across the country.

It was the best way to keep in touch with each other's lives without having to spend hours typing out rambling emails or making trips to the post office for stamps. Letters were the way of the past, and videos were the future. At least, as my entire survival depended on the pay I made from people watching my videos, I certainly hoped so.

Several times a week, we'd upload short videos with updates, and when shit went down and we needed urgent advice, we'd ramble and vent our dilemmas to each other via camera.

One tap to the live video option for **@MySixCents,** I rambled into the camera of my phone.

"Holy fucking shit, I just saw the Mavericks' dicks. So many dicks. Like, they were everywhere. Everywhere, I tell you!"

Lucky for me, my girls were all ears. They must've seen my live notification and logged in right away.

Sammy was the first to comment.

@SammySays: **WHAT?**

Then Everly followed suit a few seconds later.

@EverlyAfter: **What is happening right now? Why are you rambling about dicks?**

Eyes serious, I nodded. "Guys, I accidentally walked into the freaking New York Mavericks' locker room. And I saw *everything*. It was like…I took a wrong turn and then BAM! Penis party."

@SammySays: **DID THEY SEE YOU?**

@EverlyAfter: **Oh. My. God.**

"No. No one saw me. I dropped it like it was hot and hid behind a big-ass cart of clean towels. And, seriously? It probably shouldn't be that easy to get inside their locker room…."

@EverlyAfter: **Well, they probably feel like the people they give**

security passes to won't be wandering around, trying to catch glimpses of the players naked.

"I wasn't trying to do that! It was an accident!"

@SammySays: Just answer us this, how long did you stay in there?

"I don't know…not *that* long…"
Way too long.

@EverlyAfter: LIAR.

"Okay…so…I hung around for a bit, but that was only because Sean Phillips was in there." My cheeks flushed ruby red at the erotic visuals already stocked away in my brain, and I had to fan myself with my free hand. "And…like…I have no words…."

@SammySays: That good?

I nodded again. "That fucking good."

@EverlyAfter: Damn, girl. I'm a little jealous.

I grinned and preened. "As you should be. I just randomly stumbled through magic doors that apparently led to some alternate universe where you get to stare at hot naked guys for as long as you want, and they don't even notice you."

@SammySays: Aren't you supposed to be meeting with them soon?

I glanced at the clock on my phone and saw I only had five minutes until I needed to meet Georgia Brooks.

"Shit. Yeah," I muttered. "I better go so I'm not late, but I just had to tell *someone* about the things I just saw. It was nuts. *Literally.*"

@EverlyAfter: Good luck, girl! You'll be awesome!

@SammySays: And if you get nervous, just imagine them naked...

I giggled at that. "Yeah. *Imagine them naked.* That definitely won't be a problem now."

Chapter Two

Sean

The door to the meeting room swung open, and the roar of noise only a room full of rowdy football players could produce quieted to a rumble.

Wes Lancaster, owner of our team, the New York Mavericks, and Georgia Brooks, head of marketing, were walking single file, and the look on Mr. Lancaster's face said our clever, quirky promoter had talked him into something he regretted once again.

Quite the opposite, the look on Georgia's face said I was going to find it entirely too amusing.

I nudged Cam Mitchell's elbow, and he startled in the seat next to me.

"What do you think she has us doing now?"

He smiled. "Hopefully the adult version of the Miss Teen USA Pageant."

About two years ago, we'd all headed to the Bahamas to judge a beauty pageant in the name of marketing and promotion, and it had been a shitshow to say the very least.

A group of grown-ass men paired with teenage beauty queens?

Yeah, that event had been about as ridiculous as one might assume on the idea alone.

I chuckled *and* shook my head at Cam's libido.

No doubt mine was stronger than his, but I exercised it by using it—*not* talking about it.

"By the look on Mr. L's face, it seems more like Cirque du Soleil."

Cam frowned. "I hope not. I'm definitely not delicate enough to fling myself around."

Quinn Bailey, our quarterback and one of my best friends, laughed from his seat on the other side of Cam.

"Yeah, right, Cammy. Delicate is your specialty."

"Shut up—"

A sharp whistle rang out just as Cam was gearing up to fight back. I patted his shoulder patronizingly but turned my attention to the front. Mr. Lancaster was glaring at us, and Georgia was smirking.

Basically, things seemed to be right on track. Still, I was employed by the guy, so I did my best impression of contrite, clearing my throat to rid it of any lingering chuckles. "Sorry for the disruption, Mr. L."

He didn't look particularly convinced, but he wasn't calling me down to fire me either. I counted it as a win.

Any whispers hanging in the air vanished, and actual silence fell over the room.

"All right," Mr. L started. "I know you're all wondering what we've brought you in for today, and no, it's not another seminar on social media."

A small cheer rang out from the front of the room, and Georgia had to tuck her chin to hide her smile. As best friends with my sister Cassie, Georgia always had a higher tolerance for our bullshit than Wes did. After all, she'd spent nearly the entirety of her friendship with my crazy fucking sister training for it.

Mr. L cut his glare to the vicinity of the sound, and all exuberance died. I smiled.

"However," he went on, "it does have to do with social media and a series of vlogs featuring the team with a popular up-and-coming blogger, so a quick recap of the rules wouldn't be amiss." He surveyed the room cautiously, and as he got a good look at all of our faces, his expression turned gloomy once again. He didn't trust us not to turn whatever this was into a fucking cluster—not even a little.

Knowing what went on in the locker room on a daily basis, I couldn't blame him. We were all a bunch of vagrants.

With a jerk of his head, he stepped back and opened the floor to Georgia. Some of the newer guys sat forward in their seats, eager to listen to our very pretty Director of Marketing speak.

I rolled my eyes and looked to Quinn. We both knew Kline Brooks, billionaire and husband to the fair Mrs. Brooks, and none of these little bullshitters stood a chance.

As professional football players, we liked to think we made good money. The kind that held allure and attracted women when we wanted it to. The kind we could afford to blow on jewelry or a fancy meal in the name of impressing a woman.

But we didn't make jack shit compared to the man Georgia Brooks had legally hooked her star to, and it was funny to watch little rookie, puppy-dog players who had no clue.

"Okay, guys. I know we've gone over this a lot," Georgia said, working the room by pacing back and forth and smiling into each of our faces before turning a brief, frustrated glance over her shoulder. It was obvious and comical, and its intention was clear—to tell Wes Lancaster, boss or not, she thought having her talk about this *again* was bullshit.

"But let's just go over the basics again." Still, he *was* the boss. "No inappropriate comments, no touching, no flirting, and absolutely no sexual harassment. Please, only discuss professional details that have been cleared for discussion, and remember the golden rule I've taught you."

She put her hand to her ear to indicate we should supply it, and we all responded dutifully. "Always assume your grandmother is watching while at Sunday worship with a member of the clergy."

She clapped her hands excitedly. "Exactly! I'm so glad you've all been paying attention. With that, I think we're ready to bring in our guest, a woman you'll be working closely with for the next eight weeks…Miss Six Malone!"

Wes moved to the door and opened it, holding it open gallantly as the woman in question stepped inside.

Pint-sized and packing a smile, Six Malone bounded inside with the energy of a toddler and the body of a woman. A really fucking tiny woman.

Her skin was a smooth, light brown, and her hair stuck out from her head so far it rivaled the length of her short legs. It curled and twisted, ending in perfect spiral ringlets, and the amber flecks in her chocolate-brown eyes shone noticeably despite the distance between us.

A new kind of silence fell over the room as her special something captivated us all immediately.

"Hi, everyone!" she greeted, the corners of her mouth nearly up to her ears.

The more I studied her eyes, the more I noticed how enormous they were. Her features were all that way, actually—bold and beautiful and large. They'd been told her face was their canvas to fill, and they were fighting valiantly to do it, but the job was virtually impossible.

She was petite, especially from up here in the fifteenth row of theater seating, and I wondered lightheartedly if she was actually small enough to fit in my pocket or if the huge room full of unnaturally big men made it feel that way.

"I'm so, so excited for this opportunity, and I'm hoping you'll all view it with the fun and wonder that I do. This could really be something, and I'm going to need your help to make it that way. If not, I'm going to need some of your money to pay my rent."

A ripple of chuckles traveled up from the bottom of the room like a visible wave of sound.

I glanced at the faces around me, wondering if this weird buzz she made me feel was widespread. Seemingly, it was. Smiles abounded, and men who never listened looked to be on the edge of their seats. Immediately, a spark of jealousy flashed in my gut and triggered some unease—I had absolutely no fucking reason to feel anything but annoyed by this woman. All she was doing was adding hours to my already busy schedule.

But I didn't feel aggravated at all. Quite the opposite, really.

"Now, I know your boss wants you to be on your best behavior, and I totally respect that." She glanced to Wes with a practiced smile before turning back to us and turning it into a real one. "But bad behavior gets more views. So, let's do that."

My eyebrows shot up as a bark of surprise filtered through the fifty-three men in the room and slapped Mr. Lancaster into displeasure. Georgia laughed outright, grabbing Wes by the arm and pulling him back. I wasn't sure what he had intended to do—maul her?

"Kidding, kidding," Six said immediately, sensing the room's descent into downright hysteria and the impending risk to her physical safety. "But, seriously, don't be too boring, okay? If you're playful, be it. If you're a big joke maker, tell me some. If you like to collect dolls, I'm officially afraid, but I'm almost certain we'll get some attention out of that."

I raised my hand before I even knew I was doing it. I didn't know that I'd even spoken in the last dozen team meetings, but something about Six turned me chatty.

I just hoped it wasn't a trend.

"What about you?" I asked without waiting for her to call on me, my voice echoing in the cavernous space. A whoosh of sound bloomed as all of the heads in the room swung to find me.

"Excuse me?" she replied, unsure what I was asking.

"What are *you* into?"

She didn't even hesitate. "Being funny and having fun—*not* the same thing, by the way."

I smiled my sexiest smile—the one that *always* worked on women—and her eyes narrowed. I figured she was squinting to see me better. I was far away, after all.

"How *interesting*. I'm into having fun too."

"Sean," Georgia warned, and Mr. Lancaster sank his head in his hands. The rest of the room dissolved into hollers and hoots. Six's calculating eyes never left mine.

"Okay," she said, shockingly loud enough to be heard above the chaos, her eyes never leaving mine. "We'll get started doing our individual introductory interviews, and I'll need you guys in your uniform shirts for these. We'll start with QB himself. And the rest of you...I'll see you soon."

Oh yes, Six Malone... You sure will.

Chapter Three

Six

A sea of burly men exited the meeting room, and I caught the eyes of my favorite camera guy and vlog partner in crime, Joe, standing at the entrance, his wide, captivated eyes watching each and every player leave the room in fascination.

If I was excited about filming the Mavericks, Joe was one rush of excitement away from defying gravity and rocketing himself right into space.

With amusement cresting my lips up at the corners, I walked over toward him and had to tap him on the shoulder with my index finger before he even noticed I was there.

"Oh, hey!" he shouted toward me.

We were three feet away from each other.

I had to open my mouth like a gulping fish to stanch the flow of ringing pounding against my eardrum.

In his defense, the Mavericks football team was making their presence known with loud chatter and boisterous posturing I supposed was common of men of their stature as they dispersed.

My grin grew wider. "Be careful, Joe," I whispered. "Your inner fanboy is showing. Any second, I fear you might pull out a Sharpie and some glitter from your pocket and start making an *I Heart the Mavericks* sign."

"Smartass." He shoved me playfully with his hip.

I laughed and looked down at the black messenger bags sitting beside his feet. "Got the goods?"

"If by goods, you mean video equipment, then yes, I have most of it. Barry and the rest of the motley crew are toting the other shit into the stadium as we speak."

"Fantastic." I glanced down toward the opposite end of the hall and watched in fascination as some of the players started to file back into that magical place known as their locker room. And, trust me, it took a whole lot of willpower to stop my brain from wandering toward visions of man candy land.

Now is not the time for penis pondering, Six.

I cleared my throat and focused on Joe. "Player interviews," I declared. "Let's find a nice, quiet place to set up. I don't think there's much background shit going on today, but Quinn Bailey should be a pretty good leadoff on his own. But, hey, if you can find a secret room of strippers or something, by all means, ditch my request for quiet and fill the background with classic lap dance song choices like 'Pour Some Sugar on Me' or 'Hot for Teacher.'"

Not that I'd been to a lot of strip clubs, but I'd seen *Varsity Blues,* so basically, I was an expert in stripper music selections.

I highly doubted the Mavericks had a secret stripper room, but a girl could wish, she could dream, she could fucking hope.

"Sounds good," Joe said with a laugh and nodded. "I'll do a little scouting and then shoot Barry and the crew a text and let them know where to meet us." Before he could jump into action, his phone started ringing. I rolled my eyes to shame him for his popularity, but he pulled it out of his pocket anyway.

I stuck out my tongue as he studied the screen and then snapped my face back into the glossy graciousness of a debutante when he looked back up. "Hold on, give me a sec. It's Lisa."

Lisa was Joe's fiancée. And she was as sweet as a glass of iced tea in the Bronx. That is to say, *not*. She was a fucking tartlet with big tits and a fake smile, and she was constantly bugging Joe about his schedule. I thought several times about going on a covert mission to switch her nail polishes into different bottles at night, but in the end, I was always too lazy.

I loved Joe, though. We'd been good buddies since NYU, having met at freshman orientation, and he'd been the guy with the plan. A film major with his sights on California, he'd wanted all of the things we were striving for now from the beginning.

I was the opposite—a finance major by my parents' choosing without a fucking clue what I really wanted to do with my life.

Honestly, I probably wouldn't have started my career as a YouCam vlogger had Joe not been cute enough to make me want to hang around him. But he had pretty blue eyes, a sweet smile, and back then, a really tight ass. I'd tagged along to several of his stupid film things for the view. Until I realized Joe's ass in his Levi's wasn't my main focus anymore.

All of the stupid film shit wasn't actually stupid. It was *interesting*. And I wanted to be a part of it.

His filming and video editing expertise took my interest and turned it into a possibility.

And we'd been together since then.

Lisa was a relatively new addition, but Joe Mellow acted like she was the sun and we should all orbit around her.

News flash, Joe. The sun is 4.6 billion years old. Your punk-ass witch wishes she could handle that shit.

I was a good faker, though. And I never wanted Joe to feel like I was judging him based on his shitty girlfriends. I was, obviously, but I didn't want him to *feel* it.

"Tell her Six says hi!" I called sweetly toward his retreating back as he walked down the hall to a place devoid of talkative jocks. He offered a lazy wave of his hand, but other than that, walked several feet down the long hallway and continued his conversation.

Ensuring I wasn't in the way of the team filing out of the auditorium-style meeting room, I slid the messenger bags out of the doorway and squatted down to start unpacking and making sure we had everything we needed.

Since the lighting inside this wing of the stadium was pretty much shit, I silently prayed Joe brought extra light boxes to fix that sad situation.

Raucous laughter from inside the meeting room filled my ears, and I shook my head in amusement. Football players were real fucking loud, and apparently, a few stragglers had stayed behind, enjoying their own personal chat session.

Well attuned to opportunities in eavesdropping, I melded my mind with my ears and used all of my energy to hyperfocus on their conversation.

"I bet she's a feisty little thing," a deep voice said, and my eyes perked up like Scooby.

She! They're talking about a woman. Fuck yeah, I bet this is pure gold.

"She's beautiful."

Beautiful, huh? Fingers crossed they're talking about me.

I wasn't walking around needing ego boosts, but I was as single as a stick of gum.

So, yeah, I'd take all the compliments that were inadvertently thrown my way.

Plus, it'd been a while since I'd dated—*hooked up with*—anyone of substance. And let's face it, sometimes, a girl just needed *and* deserved to hear she was attractive.

I wasn't too proud to admit that. Fuck, I couldn't even find my pride most days. She was prudish and afraid of glitter hair spray. I wanted nothing to do with the bitch.

"Don't get too excited, Teeny," a raspy, sexy as fuck voice responded, but despite its appeal, it was all ego and cocky cajoling. "I call dibs."

"You can't call dibs on the vlogger, Sean."

Oh. My. God. They are *talking about me!*

My eyes popped wide of their own accord, and I had no idea what I was even doing anymore. Pretty sure no one needed to stare at the lens cap for a camera for this freaking long, but surely none of these people had film expertise. I could pass this off as important for a little while longer.

There were professional football players inside that room talking about *me*, for fuck's sake. Mariah who? Beyoncé pssshhh. *Six is where it's at, baby.*

"Yeah, Phillips, you can't call dibs. It's always ladies' choice."

Phillips? As in Sean *the Manwhore* Phillips? The same man whose insanely huge penis I had just been mentally complimenting not even two hours ago while I was giving my best impression of a real-life, female version of a Peeping Tom?

My, my this is getting interesting.

"Just sit back and watch, boys. Six Malone is in trouble." A cocky, confident laugh filled my ears, and this time, I *knew* it was Sean Phillips. "Ladies' choice? She'll definitely choose... *Me*," he said, his voice filled with presumption. "I mean, did you see her playing with me before? So naughty. And naughty girls get the good end of the stick."

My mouth gaped.

"Because when I really turn it on, no woman can resist," he went on. "Especially not sexy as fuck Six Malone."

"You're such a cocky little fucker," someone teased, but Sean just chuckled.

"Cocky? Of course." His voice filled my ears again. "But little fucker? I don't think so, Mitchell."

My jaw tried to unhinge, and my mind whirled.

That motherfucker.

Sean Phillips might have had a penis that deserved rosary beads and an altar, but his self-assurance and cocky as fuck personality did *not*.

His playboy reputation might prove he could charm the fucking panties off of most women, but I wasn't most women. Sean Phillips had a serious surprise in store for him if he thought he could actually schmooze me into his bed.

It didn't matter how awesome his dick was. Or how handsome he was. Or how much I loved watching him play football.

Just, no. Hell to the freaking *no*.

A throat cleared behind me, and I turned on my heels and then looked up, up, up into the baby-blue eyes of Quinn Bailey. In the middle of the hallway, with his uniform shirt covering his toned and firm chest and a mischievous grin smeared across his full lips, he towered above me and winked.

"Interesting conversation in there," he stated and slid his hands into the pockets of his jeans. He rocked back and forth on his heels, and that roguish little smile of his only grew wider. "Sounds to me like someone needs to be taught a lesson."

A laugh bubbled up past my lips at his words. "I agree."

Quinn winked again, and as if on cue, Cam Mitchell, Jorge "Teeny" Martinez, and Sean the assface, cocky bastard, manwhore, motherfucker Phillips filed out of the room.

"Bail-ey!" Teeny shouted and fist-bumped his quarterback.

Cam nodded.

And Sean, well, he nodded toward Quinn, and then his mesmerizing green eyes met mine.

Fuck, he was dangerous. His eyes. His body. His sexy, raspy voice. He was the full package wrapped up into one bad boy, jerk-off with an ego bigger than this fucking stadium, delectable box.

A man with his kind of ego did *not* deserve my attention.

Or any woman's attention, for that matter.

"Hello." I offered Sean a saccharine, far-too-fucking-sweet smile.

"It's a pleasure, Six," he said, sex and hypnotic eyes and pheromones all swirling in a concoction meant to ensnare. "See you around real soon."

Exactly, I mused. *Real soon*, I'd take Sean down a few notches and bring that big old head of his back down to earth.

And I didn't mean the one on his cock.

As Sean and the other guys walked in the opposite direction of

Quinn, I mentally started to plot my revenge.

Quinn smiled down at me like he knew exactly what I was thinking, and I couldn't *not* smile back. I'd been a huge fan of his since forever, and I was probably an even bigger fan of his relationship with his girlfriend, Cat.

A beautiful flight attendant and the sexy quarterback of the Mavericks—in my opinion, it was a fucking fairy tale.

"Ready to get started?" I asked just as Joe walked over to us, and Quinn grinned.

"Ready whenever you are."

"Quinn, this is Joe Mellow, my camera guy and video editor." I introduced the two, and they shook hands. I knew, internally, Joe was probably screaming with excitement like a sixteen-year-old girl.

"I found a good spot for us to film," Joe said as he picked up the bags of equipment. "Everyone else is already in there setting up."

"Fantastic. Lead the way," I said and then smiled at Quinn as we walked side by side behind Joe. "I hope you don't mind, but I don't really have a lot of questions about you."

He quirked a brow.

"I mean, I'm a fan of yours, but I'm a way bigger fan of Cat's."

A soft, amused chuckle left his lips, and his blue eyes brightened at the mere mention of her name. "Well, it sounds like we already have a lot in common, Six. But I should warn you, I'm Cat's *biggest* fan."

I damn near swooned. "Oh my God, you guys are so freaking cute it makes my little heart pitter-patter with joy."

Quinn just laughed, and once we reached the smaller conference room Joe had spotted, our crew quickly finished setting up so we didn't swallow up all of the famous quarterback's time for the day.

I took a deep breath and mentally prepared myself for a very long afternoon.

The Mavericks team was huge, and I wanted to get through all of the key players by the end of next week.

Well, all of the key players but *one*.

Chapter Four

Sean

"Ohh, Sean-y!" Teeny preened, slamming into the locker room like a freight train. Jorge Martinez was a bear of a guy and not in the least bit ironically delicate. He was loud, he was rough, and he was a hell of a fucking football player. "That catch was siiick. How you even get under that thing, son?"

I smirked, thriving under the praise and the pressure to maintain my status, and shrugged. "I'm just good, I guess."

Cocky and confident, I'd firmly established my player personality here on the New York Mavericks. At the end of my college career, I'd had a bad knee injury I feared would be the end of my football career altogether. Dejected and completely convinced I'd never play again, I'd lost some of my fire.

But then my sister, Cassie, brought home one of Wes Lancaster's best friends, Thatcher Kelly, as her new boyfriend. They'd all done their best to convince me I'd been on the list to be drafted before the family connection, but I wasn't entirely sure I believed them.

Still, faced with the option to do what I loved because of a little luck or reject it outright for the same reason, I'd done the smart thing.

You didn't just walk away from a professional football career because of the unconventional way you may have gotten your foot in the door.

But accepting what was given and wallowing in it were two different things. And the Phillipses did their best to stand out.

I trained harder, worked harder, lived football harder than almost anyone I knew, and I made a vow to myself I'd believe I had what it took every day.

So far, it'd done me pretty well.

"Good at running your route," Quinn shot back teasingly. "I'm the one who put the ball in the right place."

My smile curled higher. "Aw, feeling a little left out of the praise, QB?"

His eyes lit up with the fuel to volley some insults back and forth, and I braced. Quinn was one of the best guys on the team—by far. He was one of the best players in the league and had a heart of fucking gold, but he loved to tease. And just like everything else he did, he was fucking good at it.

"Speaking of left out...you think the cute little vlogger forgot about you? Seems like she finished up with everyone else but you," he poked.

"Nah," I said with a smirk. "Saving the best for last."

I'd had the pleasure of stealing glances at her sexy little ass over the past week, and I couldn't deny I was practically salivating over the opportunity to be interviewed by her.

No doubt, it would only take a little taste of the charm I was so famous for, and she'd be eating out of the palm of my hand.

All the guys in the locker room clucked and hooted at our little pissing contest, and my chest swelled. They'd been watching Quinn and me go back and forth for four years now, and it was practically a team tradition. Hell only knew what they'd do for entertainment around here when it came time for one or both of us to retire.

The door to the locker room swung open, and a sharp whistle pierced the air. Fifty heads swung in that direction to find Coach

Bennett just inside the door.

"Listen up! We're about to have a female visitor in the room, so get your shit together. You've got the thirty seconds it's going to take me to tell her she can come in to cover your dicks."

Bodies lumbered into action, pulling on shirts and pants and buttoning all the fasteners. I was still naked, wrapped only in a towel from my shower, so I did the only thing I had time for and pulled on a pair of black boxer briefs.

I'd just settled them on my hips and removed the towel when Six Malone stepped in. She smiled unabashedly, taking in all of us in our various stages of undress. She didn't blush, and she didn't turn away.

Apparently, she didn't feel the need to be anything other than assertive.

It made me wonder if she had experience handling rooms filled with a bunch of rowdy, half-naked football players.

"Hey, guys! Sorry to interrupt, but I've got an announcement to make."

Smiles broke out like a rash across the room. She'd obviously had no trouble winning everyone over.

"The crew is outside packing up now, and we'll be heading out soon."

Groans and boos filled the air, but I was too busy frowning.

What the fuck?

Had she actually *forgotten* about me?

Fucking no one forgot about Sean Phillips.

"I know, I know," she said with no faux modesty. "You're going to miss me. Frankly, I'd miss me too. But my time is up this week, and you were all great! This is going to be one of the best opening segments I've ever done, and I can't wait to see what else we can come up with in the next seven weeks."

Quinn was nearly apoplectic with glee as he leaned over and whispered, "Saving the best for last, huh?"

Six waved cheerily and then exited the sad room. Everyone wanted her to stay, that much was clear, but I'd never even gotten the chance to know her.

What the fuck was going on here?

I grabbed a shirt from my locker, storming after her in just my boxer briefs and trying to put the shirt on as I went.

There was a titter behind me, mostly Quinn if his laugh was anything to go by, but a few others had joined in. I ignored their amusement and lengthened my strides. I'd be damned if the cute little vlogger was going to get away without an explanation.

I was out the door in a flash, and staff looked up and then back down again immediately at the sight of me in my underwear. None of them took out their phones that I could see, but I had more important things to worry about than showing up online in all my hard-bodied glory.

Six startled as I tapped her on the shoulder, and she spun around to find the culprit. Her eyes hit the wall of my chest first, thanks to our stark difference in height, and then climbed their way up to my eyes.

"Oh," she said, "Hello."

Oh, hello. That's it. Like I was the fucking *janitor*.

"Hi there." I smarted, trying to keep the grit of my teeth from making me sound like too much of an asshole. "Heard your speech in there about being done."

"Oh yeah," she cooed. "The guys were great! This is going to be a hit. I can tell."

The guys. *The guys.* Like I wasn't fucking one of them.

I faked a smile, but even I could feel it was a little manic. "That's great. I hope it is a hit."

"Me too," she agreed easily, twisting her feet and shrugging her hands into her pockets. She was the poster child for nonplussed, and I was about to come out of my skin.

"But I know something that could help."

"Oh yeah? What's that?" she asked, completely oblivious.

The painful truth struck me like a sword to the gut.

Good God. She really didn't even know who I was. Worse

than that, she didn't even remember talking to me at the meeting, apparently.

Am I completely losing my touch?

"Interviewing *all* of the guys."

"Oh my gosh!" she gasped. "Did I forget someone?"

And then she looked around me. *Behind* me. Pretty much every-fucking-where *but* at me.

Finally, I lost it, snapping, "Yes! Me!"

"You?" she said, perplexed.

I looked to the ceiling and tried to tamp down the surge of anger. "Yes. Me. Sean Phillips. One of the best goddamn players on the team."

Her eyebrows popped dramatically. "Wow. High praise for yourself, huh?"

"It's just a fact, honey."

"Ohh. Honey now. Interesting. But I'm confused. Are you yelling at me or seducing me?"

I took two deep breaths and talked myself back. Women never responded to aggression. I knew that all too well. Sweet-talking was a much better way to go.

"No seduction, no yelling," I said easily. "Just helping you out with the information that you left someone out."

She bit her bottom lip, cutting into the plump flesh dramatically. Her chocolate eyes flared to life, and my gaze zeroed in. "Oh, well, thank you. I guess we'll have to fix that."

I smiled and crossed my arms over my chest as she turned to the crew and prompted them to stop packing up. "Guys, hold up. We've got one more interview to do."

She turned back to me then, surveying my stance, and her already vivid eyes started to dance. "You planning to do the interview like that?" She glanced pointedly to my barely covered cock and jerked her chin. "Or would you rather wear pants?"

Only then remembering my state of undress, I jerked to full height, and she laughed.

"I mean, I'm sure it'd be a big seller with the ladies. Maybe I should have done all the segments in underwear. Especially the really *big* guys," she said with a wink.

What the fuck did she mean by that? I was a big guy. I had a big fucking cock and had half a mind to show her just how well-off I was—

She smirked.

Well, well. I shook my head. *Someone is a feisty little teaser.*

"I'll go get dressed."

Her laugh was melodious. "Good plan..." The rest of the sentence hung in the air like a lead balloon.

Did she not remember my fucking name?

"Sean," I supplied with a frown.

She snapped and clicked her tongue against her teeth. "Right. Sean."

This girl was one fucking kick to the balls after another.

"Right. I guess...I'll be back," I muttered, a good amount of the wind officially gone from underneath my wings.

"Okay," she said with a smile. "See you soon."

I reentered the locker room to find it a lot emptier than before. Most of the players had headed out, through the back entrance, off to their lives.

Truth was, I didn't have much of one outside of these walls. My sister was at least close, now that I was living near NYC, but I kept a tight training schedule and an even tighter friends list. Any of the guys I hung out with outside of the stadium were ones I saw in it, and any women I gave my time to were on a one-time basis. I wasn't looking for a girlfriend or a wife. That would come later. After I'd done everything I could to make a name for myself as one of professional football's most influential players.

Quinn Bailey, however, had waited for my return, despite having a girlfriend to go home to. I suspected it was all for the pleasure of getting in one more good jab.

"So?" he asked, a mischievous sort of joy lingering in the corners of his lips and eyes.

"We're doing my segment now," I said, avoidance of the facts hidden under layers of camouflage.

"And why is that?" he prompted, unrelenting.

I sighed and rolled my eyes, knowing he'd find out one way or another. I might as well go ahead and get the truth over with. "She forgot about me."

He guffawed. "O-ho! Wow, that had to sting, huh, buddy?"

"Shut up. She just doesn't know me yet. Once she does," I taunted, "she won't be able to forget."

"Sure, sure," he agreed with a laugh. "She's getting your name tattooed now."

"Just go home to your girlfriend already."

He smiled, full of pure ecstasy and adulation as he swung his bag up onto his shoulder. "Don't mind if I do."

He gave me a slap to the shoulder and booked, and I was left alone to get dressed. I hurried through the motions, making sure I got everything in place, and then made my way back out the door to Six.

She smiled sweetly, comically, really, at my new state of cover. I tried not to roll my eyes.

"So where do you want me?"

She held up a hand, a slight shake of her head saying it didn't really matter. "There's good."

Without pausing to brief me, she glanced over her shoulder and nodded to the man with the camera. "Hit it, Joe."

I flinched at the sudden flash of the light in my face, but Six didn't even pause. She dove right in. "We're here with Sean Phillips of the New York Mavericks."

I forced myself to smile as she stuck a microphone in my face. "Say hi, Sean."

"Hi, everyone!" I greeted cheerfully.

With a flick of her wrist, she dragged a hand across her throat, and the camera shut off immediately.

"Wait…What? That's it?" I asked.

"Yep. We're good. Thanks, Sean." She turned to the guys. "Go ahead, you can pack up now."

"You don't want something more?" I asked again, knowing she had to be mistaken.

Her smile was unrepentant. "Nope. I'll see ya next week."

And just like that, it was over. She was gone, and so was my usual cocky confidence.

What the hell had just happened?

Chapter Five

Six

The Mavericks' cheering section boomed with raucous hoots and hollers and applause, and I raised a small handheld camera to capture some of the goodness.

Miami's crowd, on the other hand, was about as interesting as a deflated balloon. Disheartened and unenthused as the visitor's fans celebrated their team's big away-game win, they filed out of the stadium with long faces and broken souvenirs. I, personally, thought it was a bold move to smash a cup that had cost $14.95, but what the fuck did I know? My team had won.

I smiled on the sidelines, scanning the vast, now nearly half-empty stadium as New York supporters started chanting "Phillips! Phillips! Phillips!"

A twentysomething girl in a gold half-shirt and his number twenty-six painted on her toned stomach bounced up and down excitedly, her perky and very large breasts just about smacking her in the face from the movement. I moved my handheld camera over to her just in case I had a chance to capture the damage.

Just to her left, two grown men with beers in their hands hugged each other while their beverage of choice sloshed out of the glasses and onto the red metal seats.

And a little girl holding a "Marry Me, Quinn Bailey" poster smiled big, her homemade memento blowing violently in the Florida wind and almost slipping out of her hands. Thankfully, her mom was there to save the day, gripping the edges of the cardboard sign with her hands and preventing a fan-tastrophe.

The win for New York today stretched this season's record to 5-0, and it was moments like this that made me realize just how fucking lucky I was.

Every day, I lived my freaking dream. I worked for myself, I made my own schedule most of the time, and I got paid for making videos about how many chicken nuggets were too many chicken nuggets. I'd traveled to Mexico to film a segment on the beach in sponsored bikinis, and I'd tasted some of the best-brewed beer in the world when I'd talked a brewery in Germany into doing a fun segment on their flavor development. I never had to worry about evaluations or progress reports, and the only scrutiny I really had to face was from haters online.

And even then, they were doing it from a computer.

And now, with my new assignment doing this series with the Mavericks, my workday consisted of watching an amazing game, from the sidelines, with nothing more than my camera in hand.

Life was good.

But as I followed the team toward the tunnel, filming their raucous laughter, testosterone-fueled cheers, and overall hyped-up reactions, the inklings of fatigue started to set in.

I'd only been working with the Mavericks for a little over a week now, but damn, fitting the busy filming schedule in with my daily vlog content was no easy feat.

Alicia Keys's voice filled my head as it pumped through the stadium's sound system, but instead of singing about being on fire, I switched it up to suit my mood.

This girl is so tired! This girl is soo tired!

"Enjoy the game, Six?" An actual, real-live human voice met my ears, and I looked up to find Sean Phillips walking beside me. Helmet in hand and a few droplets of sweat dripping down his handsome as hell face, he was the epitome of every male athlete fantasy I'd ever had. And, high of all highs, right now, he was smiling at me.

He had played one hell of a game tonight.

Three touchdowns and boatload of passing and rushing yards under his belt, he'd more than helped the Mavericks bring home a win.

I didn't have to check my video footage to know that a lot of it revolved around the cocky manwhore himself in action.

Likely a cool ninety percent.

"It was o-kay." I shrugged to emphasize the mediocre tone of my words, but in the end, I couldn't hide my teasing smile.

Had I mentioned the Mavericks had pretty much blown Miami straight out of the water? If it weren't for a single field goal, they would've managed a complete shutout.

A soft chuckle left his full lips. "Just okay?"

Gosh, he had nice lips. It was too damn bad those lips were connected to a man I would never in a million lifetimes kiss.

I laughed, but before I could respond, Martinez came up from behind me and wrapped a big, strong arm around my shoulders. The man's huge frame made me feel so damn tiny, and his long strides, and my resulting jog to keep up, made the two of us move ahead of Sean. My shoes barely even had time to sink into the rough, green turf as we skated across it.

"You partying with us tonight, little lady?"

"Partying with you?" I questioned in surprise. *Aren't football players supposed to refrain from partying during the season?* "I was just planning on going straight to bed once we got back to the hotel."

"Ah, *hell* no," Martinez retorted and shook his head as we walked. "No bedtime. You owe it to your team to hang out with us for a little while. Have a few beers. Shoot the shit. Celebrate our big win."

"*Beers?* Are you serious?" I asked just as we got to the end of the tunnel.

"Of course, he's serious," Quinn Bailey interjected. I looked over my shoulder to find his blue eyes smiling toward me.

"Don't worry," he responded. "Coach gave them the okay."

Martinez guffawed. "Oh, don't act all high and mighty, Bailey. You're going to be hanging out with us too."

"I thought I was the leader of this team?"

"You are…*most* of the time."

"Suck it, Teeny," Quinn teased before his gaze met mine again. "So, you coming to 'party' with us tonight?" he asked and even used air quotes to drive his sarcastic point home. "And by party, I mean, sit around in the hotel bar with a bunch of football players who will most likely be ready for bed before the clock strikes midnight."

"Well…when you say it like that…" I paused, pretending to ponder the decision like I had a choice. Tired, schmired. The Mavericks wanted to hang out with me, and I could fucking sleep when I was dead.

A big old smile curved the line of my lips. "I definitely can't resist. Count me in."

"Hell yeah!" Martinez cheered. "Now, it's time to hit the showers," he updated and pointed one index finger in my direction. "And I better see you back at the hotel."

I held both hands up in the air like I was being held at gunpoint. "No need to get aggressive, Teeny," I teased, pointing at him directly. "I'll be there, and just so you know, you're buying."

"That's an even better idea." Quinn chuckled, and just as he started to walk inside the locker room with Martinez following his lead, he yelled, "Hotel bar tonight! Teeny's buying!"

The answering cheers were nearly deafening as the locker room door shut behind them.

I shook off the far too erotic thoughts that threatened to spill into my mind at the mere thought of a men's locker room.

Apparently, a girl never forgets her first love of a penis party.

Sheesh. I definitely do not want to go there right now...

But there was one place I would be going tonight. The freaking hotel bar to party with the Mavericks.

I'd only stay for a little while, though.

As I walked toward the exit, I kind of hated myself for glancing over my shoulder to watch Sean Phillips make his way into the locker room.

Man, he has a nice ass.

In fact, I kind of hated myself for even allowing that man to be on my radar. But in my defense, I'd seen his glorious body naked. And trust me, that was not a visual one's mind wanted to scrub from its memory.

You can look, but you will not *touch,* I reminded myself.

Sean Phillips was completely off-limits. I could look. I could admire the view.

But that was as far as it went.

A few hours into hanging out with a bunch of big-ass and boisterous professional football players and I knew it was probably a bad idea.

Or, maybe it wasn't so much the larger-than-life men, but the beers Martinez had peer pressured me into drinking?

I had no answers, but damn, it'd been a hot minute since I'd enjoyed a few beers.

After several in quantity and higher than average in alcohol content, I was feeling the buzz.

But a night out without the pressure and stress of work was well worth the dull headache I'd be experiencing in the morning. No cameras. No thoughts of vlog material or video edits or deadlines.

Just fun for the sake of fun.

Not to mention, besides Quinn's awesome girlfriend, Cat, it was flattering to be the only female surrounded by twenty or so men.

Sure, there were a few other women inside the hotel bar, making eyes at the Mavericks' players from across the room, but for the most part, it was just me, Cat Wild, and the team inside our own little bubble of beer and chatter and laughter.

I was in all my performing glory, and the alcohol had steadily advanced my ability to strut. To the side, to the front, bent over to the back—I'd been practicing hitting all of my best angles, you know, visually, and soaking in the compliments they produced.

I felt pretty and entertaining, and the whole night was entirely enjoyable. Of course, when I was buzzed, every-fucking-thing was fun. I could be stuck in a room listening to a random stranger talk about organic chemistry, and I'd somehow find a way to be entertained by it.

"All right!" I exclaimed and slapped my hands down onto the table of our circular booth. "Who wants to play a little drinking game with me?" Both Martinez and Bailey were sitting near me, and I caught the attention of at least one of them immediately. Quinn, to be fair, was entirely distracted by the really fucking attractive swell of his girlfriend Cat's breasts. I wasn't into women sexually, but I could recognize and appreciate the work of a contouring master. Cat's boobs were a whole lot fuller than mine naturally, but my voodoo sense tingled in indication that she'd also given them an artistic lift. I needed to know her secrets.

"What ya got in mind, Sixy?" Martinez asked, and I grinned, looking away from the best breasts slowly.

My thoughts were a little slow and muted, but I was still in control. I stuck to the simplest of answers just in case my slurring was worse than I realized. "Most Likely."

"Most Likely?" Quinn asked, raising a questioning brow, before his gaze moved right back to Cat.

"Yep," I said, popping the p with an overzealous bottom lip. "Who's ready?"

"Mind telling us what this game entails first?" Sean questioned as he slid into the booth and situated himself beside me.

Like, right beside me.

I inhaled through my nose and was instantly hit with the delicious aroma of freshly showered, clean laundry, and the oh so perfect scent of Sean Phillips. It was seven types of enticing, and if I hadn't already decided he was completely off-limits, I might've been tempted to lick his neck just to see if he tasted as good as he smelled.

Yeah, I'm definitely buzzed...

"Yeah," Cat agreed. "What exactly are the rules of Most Likely?"

"It's super-duper easy," I started to explain. "Someone asks a 'most likely' question, like, 'Who would be most likely to marry a stripper in Vegas?' And then, on the count of three, everyone points to whoever they think would be most likely to do whatever the question entails."

"And when exactly does the drinking come in?" Martinez questioned with a raise of his brow.

"You have to take a drink for every person who's pointing at you."

"Aha," he responded with a nod of his head. "Count me in."

"Why the fuck not?" Quinn shrugged and took a sip of his beer. "I'm in."

"Me too!" Cat exclaimed excitedly.

"Hell yeah!" I cheered, and then I looked directly at the sexy man sitting beside me who, quite literally, smelled like heaven.

I hadn't been there personally, but I'd read the reports.

Rainbows and fresh, airy clouds, that shit was freaking ordained. "And what about you, Mr. Manwhore?"

Quinn coughed and nearly choked on his beer, and Martinez snorted as the nickname came out unchecked by filters alcohol had conveniently taken out of position. Sober me might have been a little mortified for actually saying that nickname out loud, but sober me was only partially here, and honestly, she didn't really have much control over buzzed me.

"Did you just call me Mr. Manwhore?" Sean questioned, an amused smirk covering his oh so full lips.

I giggled and shrugged. "I'm pretty sure I'm not the only one that knows you by that nickname," I expanded. "In fact, I think I read it somewhere in a gossip rag that included a full-page spread of you and your many celebrity women."

Cat giggled. "I think I have a girl crush on you, Six!"

I just barely stopped myself from telling her how much I liked her breasts.

Some other time, maybe.

"Hey, now!" Quinn teased as a result of Cat's widening affection.

"Shut up. You know I love you most," she said back, and I swooned. Hand to chest, I think I even made a little cooing sound out loud.

The guys largely ignored us, instead focusing on the virtual dirty rag I'd thrown at Sean before.

"Dude," Martinez said, slowly dwindling laughter and smile aimed directly at Sean. "She just called you out."

Sean only had eyes for me. His tormenter. His mystery. The only woman on the planet who'd ever challenged him before taking off her pants, I was sure.

Luckily, amusement was his main emotion, even if the green of his eyes danced as he studied me.

"So, what do you say, Mr. Manwhore?" I pushed, taking it to another level by questioning his manhood. "You man enough to play with us?"

He laughed at that. "Honey, I'm always man enough. Count me in."

Always man enough? I wavered for a second, but his penis was the prover. I'd have to agree.

"I'll go first," I announced, more than willing to be the belle of the ball. I wasn't sure if it was the alcohol telling my brain that they were entertained by me or if it was real-life, but that was the thing about alcohol—it ensured that you gave zero fucks. "Who would be most likely to be called Mr. Manwhore?" I questioned with a grin the size of Texas. "Okay…one…two…three…go!"

Even Sean pointed to himself, a sexy smirk engaging the almost dimple in his plush cheek. High and cut but still filled with flesh, his cheeks were something to be envied by fashion models around the world.

"Looks like someone gets to take four drinks!" I cheered, and Sean chuckled.

"You play dirty, sweetheart."

I shrugged. "You mess with the bull, and you get the horns, buddy."

"Did you just quote *The Breakfast Club*?" Quinn asked with a raise of his brow, and I nodded—several times, in fact.

Wow. My brain feels a little swimmy.

I fought the nausea and won. "You bet your QB ass, I did. It's only one of the best movies ever made." I clapped my hands together. "All right! Who's going next?"

"I call dibs." Martinez lifted his beer and took a quick drink. "Who is most likely to have a crazy fucking sister named Cassie Phillips?"

I giggled. Sean sighed. Both Quinn and Cat burst into laughter. And then, on the count of three, we all pointed toward Sean again.

By the fifth round of Most Likely, Sean had been the punch line to nearly every teasing question, and I loved every single minute of it.

I loved his sighs. And the number of drinks he had to consume. And the way his mouth would crest into the sexiest little smirk just before he lifted the beer to his perfect, full lips…

Wait…*what?*

Fuck, what time is it? And how many beers have I had?

I glanced at the clock above the bar and noted that it was nearly half past midnight. *Oh my God! My carriage is a pumpkin!*

I laughed aloud as I realized that was Cinderella.

A quick count of the beers on the table took me to a number I could no longer comprehend, and the answer, no matter my foggy mind, became clear.

It was time to make my grand departure and head back up to my room and get some sleep. If I stayed down here, trying to drink with men three times my size, it was highly likely I'd end up sloppy and slurring—more so than I already was.

"All right," I announced and proceeded to stand up on the booth, grabbing the attention of the other ten or so Mavericks players still left at the bar. "Before I call it a night, I'd like to propose a toast!"

Martinez cheered me on from our booth while a few of the Mavericks sitting at the bar turned on their barstools and gave me their undivided and amused attention.

"This is a toast to winners. My favorite winners. The men who have started this season off with a bang, the motherfucking New York Mavericks!"

I received several hoots and hollers in response, and it only fueled my tipsy fire.

And just before I dove headfirst into the meat and potatoes of my toast, I glanced down at Sean Phillips, who was now sitting right beside my feet, and I smirked.

Yeah. Now is the most perfect time to use some of his "inspirational" words.

Chapter Six

Sean

"**A**ny team you guys face will *be in trouble*. They'll *be yours without a fight*, that's for sure. Because *when you really turn it on, no one can resist* or deny the fact that you are fucking champions! Cheers to the Mavericks! The best goddamn football team in the world!"

Mind running on overdrive, I listened to the ending words of Six's tipsy congratulations speech with my hand frozen around my beer and a hard jaw. Most of the words she'd used had been ones I'd heard before—specifically, when they'd been coming out of my own mouth—and the amount of time it took me to realize was embarrassingly short.

They were instantly recognizable.

The truth was I'd used them more than once, more than about Six, and the taste of their tone felt horrendously rotten when they were coming out of someone else's mouth.

Shit.

She raised her glass, hard, challenging eyes on me, but I stared up at her, refusing to wilt. The thing about being a member of the

Phillips family was that you sometimes put your foot in your mouth. You said things that felt good in the moment, and you owned them completely. You said what you said, no matter the shittiness, and you couldn't take them back.

That didn't mean I couldn't attempt to make up for them.

Knowing I'd committed a wrong against a person who didn't deserve it, I tried to meld my face into something of an apology, but her acceptance wasn't there.

She knocked back the last of her drink and set it gently on our table before climbing out of the booth. She waved her goodbyes, a small smile curving one corner of her mouth with false sincerity, and moved toward the front entrance of the bar.

The rest of the guys were completely over her departure, Quinn especially, as he was enamored with the line of Cat's neck.

A twinge of unknowns rippled through me, but I pushed it aside. I knew the feeling of being skin-on-skin with a woman of Six's physical caliber, but I'd never even attempted something with a woman of her worth.

Not that those women hadn't tried.

I just didn't want it. I was young and successful, and a career in football wouldn't last for forever. I didn't need a family making me homesick and pulling my focus. I didn't need sick kids to worry about while I was away or recitals to miss.

I needed to focus on myself, and I needed to fuck. The two of those together were like a secret recipe for success on the field. The more I philandered in my extracurricular, *ahem*, activities, the more big plays I made in games.

It wasn't a life plan likely to win me any humanitarian awards, but it sure as hell was fun.

I shoved out of the booth and pushed past my lingering teammates as I navigated a course to follow Six and headed for the front entrance. It was crowded with fans and players alike, but I smiled politely and kept moving. Anytime anyone looked particularly eager, I told them I'd be right back, hoping to soften the disappointment of my disappearance.

When I'd first joined the Mavericks, I hadn't cared all that much about fan outreach. The game was about more to me than fame. It always had been.

Something about having injured my ACL in a way that called my future in football into question had changed my respect for the opportunity to play and forced me to dive into it headfirst.

I wanted to make big plays and enjoy myself in every game. I wanted to know how lucky I was but stay focused enough to remember it was a job. I wanted to have absolutely no regrets if an injury took me out of this life I was living tomorrow.

But Quinn's attention to fans had rubbed off on me. Apparently, I'd spent enough time with the bastard that it was unavoidable.

By the time I made it out to the lobby, Six's location was notably less obvious. I felt desperate as I searched the vast space, knowing she could be nearly anywhere by now. My eyes bounced from person to person, searching for her wild curls and tiny little body, and finally landed on her as she stood waiting at the bank of elevators just past the main lobby.

"Six!" I yelled, calling the attention of more than just her, but achieving my objective all the same.

She followed my voice until her eyes locked with mine, and I moved toward her quickly. My legs churned through a jog, and I made quick work of the distance, stopping mere inches from where she stood.

"Everything okay?" she asked.

"Yeah," I said and nodded, but then thought better of it and shook my head slightly. "Well, no... I just wanted to..."

"You wanted to?"

"Apologize."

Her perfectly shaped eyebrows rose high on her forehead. "For what, exactly?"

"You know what," I responded. "I know you overhead me talking to the guys that first day at the stadium."

She shrugged and stepped forward to press the call button for the elevators. "It's fine."

"No." I shook my head again. "It's not fine. I shouldn't have said that."

"I shouldn't have eavesdropped."

I smiled knowingly. "Pretty sure you were eavesdropping for a good reason, though."

She grinned in response. "Well, I have to admit, it was kind of hard not to when I heard my name leave your lips."

"I'm really sorry about that."

"Sorry you said those things?" she questioned and then put a defiant hand on her little hip. "Or just sorry that I heard you saying those things?"

She didn't back down, and she didn't mince words. The honest challenge was so refreshing.

"Both."

The elevator dinged its arrival, and my lips turned down at the corners before I could stop them. I wasn't sure what I was disappointed about, but the emotion was strong and swirling about in my stomach.

I stared at her pouty, pink lips for a moment too long, but I couldn't help it.

I wondered if they felt as soft and perfect as they looked.

"Consider your apology accepted," she said and took one step into the elevator. "Anyway," she said with a shrug and dropped her voice to a sexy, silky rasp that seemed to have a dedicated path straight to my cock. "You need to understand one thing."

"And what's that?"

"You couldn't handle me," she whispered, and my back snapped straight.

I couldn't handle her?

Fuck, I wasn't sure if I wanted to get on my knees and worship at her feet or hop into the elevator, carry her to my room, and spend the next eight hours proving her wrong.

She took two steps into the elevator cart, and I heard her finger tap the button for her floor.

All the while her mesmerizing gaze stayed locked with mine.

Just as the doors started to close, she smiled, winked, and said, "Goodnight, Sean."

The big metallic doors closed with a thud, and without hesitation, I fell to my knees and brought my clasped hands to my chest.

Sure, it was over the top, but I gave zero fucks.

I'd never in my life had a woman challenge me like Six Malone just had.

"Dear Lord in Heaven," I prayed. "Tell her to get ready."

She was going to need God on her side from here on out. A gauntlet had been thrown, and there was no turning back now.

Get ready, Six. You'll be mine.

Chapter Seven

Six

"How was Miami?" Joe asked, and I looked up from my laptop to meet his eyes. "Not gonna lie, I was a bit jealous I didn't get to watch the Mavericks bring home another win from the sidelines."

I pushed out my lips into a faux pout. "Aw, does it hurt your little football-loving heart when I get to do all the fun stuff and you get stuck in the office working on video edits?"

While I'd been in Miami last weekend, getting drunk and rowdy and telling professional football *gods* that they couldn't handle me in bed—*cue the red-cheeked embarrassment*—Joe had been back in San Diego, working on piecing some of our early footage together. I'd invited him along, but *Lisa* had kept him in town to cut up her meat or something.

We weren't planning to post the first episode for another couple of weeks—essentially a month after filming—but a lot more editing and tweaking went into these kinds of videos than most people realized, so his having a demanding shrew for a girlfriend was actually helpful in this instance. He stayed behind and worked, and I didn't have to be the bad guy.

Joe was a master at altering lighting and sound and overlaying some of the coolest effects you'd ever seen. I liked to think they helped the Pick Six YouCam videos stand out in an overwhelming sea of up-and-coming stars videoing audition reels in their basement.

"You better watch yourself," he teased. "I hold all the power when it comes to the finalized Mavericks' episodes. I'm sure there's a way to Photoshop a giant wart onto your nose or alter your voice to be more screech and annoying than anything else."

A soft laugh left my lips, and I raised the white flag by holding my hands in the air. "Okay. Okay. No need to get vengeful."

I could understand his frustration, though. I mean, last weekend, I hadn't had to sit at home with a mountain's worth of video edits to scour through while he hung out on the sidelines and then went drinking with my football heroes.

Though, he didn't actually know about the drinking yet, and it was probably a good idea to keep it that way. No need to rub salt into the already open wound.

Joe's grin was bigger than the stadium we were currently sitting inside—good old Mavericks headquarters. We were back in the meadowlands of New Jersey, only thirty or so minutes from the Big Apple and a bit of a confusing twist on where you would think a New York team would be located, and we were prepping for another episode. They'd played another home game yesterday—and won, *Go Mavericks!*—but thanks to an unfortunate scheduling conflict with another segment I'd promised the San Diego Cupcakery, I hadn't been able to be here.

"Phillips played one hell of a game last week. Fuck, yesterday wasn't bad either."

I couldn't deny that. Hell, I didn't even want to. The cocky fucker was single-handedly carrying my favorite fucking team toward a league championship. "If he keeps up this pace, he could very well break league records for rushing yards *and* touchdowns."

"Was that fifty-yarder he caught in the third quarter as fucking amazing from the sidelines as it was on TV?" the excited puppy formerly known as my friend asked.

"Better," I said with a knowing smirk, and Joe groaned.

"Remind me again why this Pick Six partnership is beneficial for me?" he questioned, seven shades of amusement highlighting his voice. "I'm having a hard time wrapping my mind around it right now."

"Because it makes you a lot of money." I fluttered my eyelashes at him. "And you have the time of your life. And there's no one you'd rather spend all of your time staring at." I leaned forward dramatically. "Me, by the way. I'm talking about me."

"Time of my life? At home? While you're on the fucking sidelines watching my favorite team in the league?"

"Yep." I nodded. "Plus, I should remind you that you were invited to make the trip to Miami, but you declined."

"That's because I'm currently suffering through engagement party hell," he muttered and moved to the opposite end of the room to set up lighting. "How many parties do two people need to attend to announce their plans for marriage?"

"As many as the *lovely* Lisa wants you to attend."

He just chuckled and shook his head. "I guess it's a good thing I'd walk through fire for that woman."

My tongue rolled with the urge to point out that being with Lisa was more like being *in a fire*, but I stopped myself. Men didn't make statements like that about women who didn't give world-class head. The deep-throat had sealed her deal just as sure as she'd sealed her lips around the top of his balls.

Before I could picture Joe's penis—a serious casualty of my encounter with the locker room—Barry walked into the room, holding a tripod and an additional camera. Small ones, tall ones, black ones, brown ones, dicks were the only thing I seemed to be able to picture anymore.

"Where do you want this?" he—Barry, *not a penis*—asked, eyes directed at Joe.

"Let's utilize that corner so we can have footage of both Six and the guys."

I nodded actively, trying to pretend I had any say in the matter. "Good plan, guys."

Neither of them even bothered to look up at me.

Fuckers.

While they busied themselves with preparing the room, I moved my focus back to my laptop and proceeded to do a final run-through of the PowerPoint presentation I'd created for the segment we'd be filming for the series today.

Honestly, I'd never had more fun creating a PowerPoint presentation in my life. The photos were a gold mine all their own, and the jokes I'd thought up weren't bad either.

The hell of learning how to create those little fuckers in college hadn't felt so horrible once I was actually able to put those skills to use for what I had in store for four of the Mavericks' star players.

Lunch and Learn with the Mavs.

Not half as serious as it sounded—fuck, not even a quarter—this short segment in our eight-episode series was sure to be filled with nothing but laughs.

We'd found the perfect location inside one of the stadium conference rooms, and in another ten minutes or so, we'd be all ready to go.

With both cameras set up and Joe and Barry ready to catch all of the soon-to-be footage on digital cards, I was more than ready to get this show on the road.

As if on cue, Quinn, Sean, Cam, and Martinez strode through the doors of the room.

"Little Six!" Martinez bellowed in amusement once his eyes met mine.

Quinn offered a soft, amused smile. Cam nodded his arrival.

Sean's hazel green eyes looked at me a little too closely. His smile was too handsome. His body was too defined. His presence too damn captivating. It should've been illegal to look that good after a workout.

I was lucky if I looked like a cute drowning mouse after I'd put in an hour of cardio at the gym.

"Come on in, boys," I greeted and pointed toward the empty seats across from me.

"Uh oh…" Martinez nodded toward the cheeky grin on my face. "That smile looks ominous, Sixy. Should I be scared?"

"Of course not." *Well, at least, not you,* I silently added. *But Sean Phillips? Yeah, he should probably be a little scared.*

Having just completed a two-hour session in the weight room, they were dressed in workout gear—sweats, T-shirts, gym shoes and had just the right amount of glistening sweat to appeal to the female contingent of my fan base.

The only thing that would have been better was having them completely naked, but that was an adult film angle neither Wes Lancaster nor my parents would be comfortable with me tackling.

Sean Phillips sure would make a good porn star, though. Not skeevy or creepy or anything.

Unable to stop the visuals as the guys sat down and made themselves comfortable, I let my mind drift off to dirty and erotic thoughts.

White towel slung over his shoulder.

Droplets of water sliding down his toned and defined abs.

Toned body naked. Every single inch of him bared for my inspection.

"Excuse me, sir," I'd say, my hair in pigtails. "I'm lost, and I need your help finding my vagina."

"I'd be happy to help," he'd say. And then he'd take out his cock and go on an exploratory mission.

Fuck, I had to get it together.

Quickly, I refocused my gaze to my laptop and mentally reminded myself now was not the time or place to start fantasizing about naked wide receivers and their penises, porn-style voyage of discovery or not.

"So, what do you have for us today?" Quinn asked innocently. He couldn't know my plans, obviously, so he had no idea just how fun his question was. I grinned at him from across the table.

"Well, first, I've got lunch," I announced and nodded toward the opposite end of the room at a hearty display of sandwiches, chips, drinks, fruit, and whatever else the team's nutritionist allowed. "So, help yourselves to some food, and then we'll get started."

Bribing people with food was always a good idea. It mellowed the mood and settled nerves, and if I was really lucky, it turned people into pliable pawns. I knew sandwiches didn't really say bribery, but it was the best I could do. I'd requested pizza, but apparently, that wasn't an appropriate in-season meal.

The team's nutritionist would probably have a coronary if he knew my daily meal rotation consisted mostly of coffee, donuts, and tacos.

While I hooked up my laptop to the large, flat-screen television hanging on the wall behind me, the guys grabbed some grub and sat back down.

I gave them a few minutes to gain some food energy, and with cameras now rolling, I dove right in.

"Welcome to Lunch and Learn with the Mavs," I announced, and Cam looked up from his sandwich. Once he noted the PowerPoint slide on the flat screen, his brow rose and the corners of his lips followed suit.

"Lunch and Learn?" he asked suspiciously, sensing he'd been trapped by the food.

I nodded as I spoke in a comforting tone. "Don't worry, it's not as serious as it sounds."

"Well, thank fuck for that," Teeny chimed in between bites of grilled chicken, and Sean smirked.

"This short segment is meant to let your fans get to know you on a more personal level. But, you know, in a fun and playful way," I explained.

"So it's not a round of twenty questions about my cock size?" Teeny asked, and I laughed.

"Well, not today."

That would be a huge seller, though, if I could ever make it work. I'd just have to bleep out every time he said cock with a picture of a rooster. Immediately, I started picturing a segment called *Measure My Rooster*. I doubted I could swing it with the Mavericks, but I could definitely pull it off in personal content. And the people would love it, trust me. If anyone was an expert in what kind of content people wanted to see these days, it was me. You didn't reach several million followers without understanding what got views on YouCam.

The biggest key to it all? Be yourself. Even if it meant allowing yourself to be the butt of the joke.

"And I just know," I continued, "that when intertwined with all of the practice and game footage, it will be a *touchdown*. You thought your fans were rabid for you before? Just wait until after this series goes live."

Sean chuckled softly. "Love the confidence *and* football lingo, honey."

Of course he loved confidence. The man had it in spades. Hell, he had so much cocky confidence, he should've considered scheduling a neighborhood garage sale and downsizing.

"Today's focus is social media training."

Three of the guys groaned audibly.

"You're going to train us on social media?" Sean, the only non-groaner, questioned with a quirk of his brow. "I should warn you. The last time Georgia Brooks attempted this, it didn't go well."

"Have no fear, Sean," I responded and couldn't fight the smile from my face if I tried. "I have a feeling you, especially, will get a lot out of this."

Quinn burst into laughter over a mouthful of a turkey sub. He covered his mouth, and once he swallowed down the food, he looked around the room until his eyes locked with Sean's. "Oh man," he finally said through soft chuckles. "I haven't felt this excited about something since you were on Jimmy Kimmel's Mean Tweets."

Middle finger in the air, Sean silently tossed back his response.

"All right," I announced and stood up from my seat. I positioned myself beside the large flat screen, and I even had a little metal pointer in my right hand for comedic effect.

"I took the time to review your social media accounts. And I can't deny, some of you do a fantastic job of really giving your fans what they want to see."

"Just some?" Cam questioned, and I nodded.

"Don't worry, Mitchell. You're included in that." I clicked to the first slide, and it was an Instagram post by Quinn Bailey. It was a photo of him and his lady love, Cat Wild. They stood underneath the summer sun, sunglasses covering their eyes and beautiful smiles stamped on their faces. He had his arm wrapped around her, and she was nestled into his side. The tagline: *This woman makes everything better.* #bae #WildCat #mine

"This is a great example of perfect social media content. Awesome job, Quinn."

I clicked to the next slide, and it was a video from Cam Mitchell's Facebook. A short clip of him walking his four-legged best friend. Lucky, a little meatball of an English bulldog, was the star of the show.

I was a sucker for cute animal videos, as were most internet surfers, and Lucky did not disappoint.

"Love this so much, Cam. And, for the love of God, call me if you ever need someone to watch Lucky."

Cam grinned. "Deal."

The next slide was a picture Martinez had posted to Twitter a few weeks back. It was a photo of him holding his brand-new baby niece, Mya. Chubby cheeks, a ton of jet-black hair, and a little pink romper, she was a pint-sized heart stealer.

"Same goes for you, Martinez. If your sister ever needs someone to watch Mya, I'm your girl."

He winked. "Get in line, Sixy. My sister has a whole list of babysitters she's bribed with overpayment and free food."

God. Now I *really* wanted to babysit. Before, I'd kind of just said it for effect. I pouted, and Teeny laughed.

And the fourth slide? A photo from Mr. Manwhore's Instagram.

He was on the beach, his sexy, toned body shirtless, and his full lips were wrapped around the spout of a bottle of water.

The tagline: *Who is feeling thirsty?*

Plus, a winky face emoji to bring the sexual innuendo on home.

It was a hot fucking picture.

But I sure as hell wasn't going to tell Sean that.

I bit my lip to tamp down the laughter that wanted to bubble up from my throat and forced my mouth into a flat line.

"And this," I started and turned my lips down into a little, half-disappointed frown. "Well, this tells me that there's a lot of room for improvement."

"Room for improvement?" Sean questioned, and a smug smile covered his mouth. "I completely disagree, honey. That looks like perfection to me. Plus, look at all of those likes and comments."

I shook my head. "But it's not nearly as good as Cam's video. Think about the other guys' posts for a moment," I said, and he looked at me like I'd asked him to translate my words into Chinese. "They all showed some personality," I explained. "They showed tiny pieces of themselves without giving too much to their fans. They showed heart."

"And what does mine show?"

"Abs."

"What?" His lips parted in surprise. "What's wrong with my abs?"

I shrugged and forced my expression to remain neutral. The instant I cracked, he'd know I was merely fucking with him.

Obviously, Sean Phillips's social media was on point. Besides Quinn Bailey, he had one of the highest followings in the entire league. And trust me, the man knew exactly the kind of content his followers wanted to see.

Including *me*.

But again, he didn't need to know that. At least not until after I had the opportunity to razz him a bit.

"It all just comes across as…well…*vain*…"

Quinn, Martinez, and Cam burst into laughter at my words.

And damn, it was a Herculean effort not to join them.

"Ho-ly shit!" Martinez howled. "This is the best social media training I've ever been a part of!"

Sean's head shot up and his eyes narrowed, but he took it all in good spirits.

Which made it even easier for me to continue on into three more rounds of social media examples, each one ending with the same variation on photos of Sean.

Abs under the sun.

Abs at the gym.

Abs behind a protein shake.

Each picture of his that appeared on the flat screen only urged his fellow teammates' laughter to get louder and louder.

"All right," he said after the last photo. A sexy, amused little smirk stayed fixed on his oh so full lips. "You *have* to be screwing with me right now."

"Yeah." I nodded and dropped the act, a big old smile kissing my lips. "I'm definitely screwing with you."

"Wait…" He paused, and his eyes narrowed. "So, this social media training…it was all just a prank to pull my leg?"

I shrugged. "Pretty much."

Martinez's laughs bellowed inside the room, and he slapped his hand down on the table in hilarity. "Goddamn, this was so good."

"What's wrong with my abs?" Cam repeated, mocking Sean in a high-pitched voice. *"My abs are amazing. Ladies love my abs!"*

Quinn laughed, and Sean flipped them all the middle finger.

"You can all just fuck right off," he said, but his words held no real threat. He enjoyed the teasing, and most likely, the attention. He was a good-natured guy with a strong self-awareness, and he fucking knew how good he looked. A little mocking only enforced it.

"Before I officially end our first Lunch and Learn with Mavs session, I need to acknowledge the fact that Sean took my little prank like a man. And because of that, I've got a little present for you." I reached into my bag resting beside my feet and pulled out a plastic, golden trophy I'd had made just for him. "Today, Sean Phillips, I present to you the award for best abs."

He grinned and stood up from his seat, taking the trophy from my hands.

"Speech!" Quinn shouted in a low, deep voice. "Speech!"

"Wow. I don't even know where to begin," Sean said, clutching the award to his chest. "I have so many people to thank…" He turned toward me and grinned. "First, I'd like to thank the lovely Six Malone for creating such an amazing highlight reel of my abs. I know it probably took a lot of work to scour through each and every one of my photos to find the very best ones. And I'm sure, at times, you were so torn over the plethora of amazing options."

I laughed at that. He had a point. It'd taken me more than a few hours to stalk all of his social media. And most of his photos were straight-up eye candy that might as well have been sent from hot guy heaven.

But, obviously, he didn't need to know that.

"I'd like to thank God for creating the perfect specimen of a man that is me. And I'd like to thank my teammates for all those times they stood by my side and only made me look better."

The guys clapped and chuckled, but before they could get too carried away with razzing each other, Wes Lancaster peeked his head inside. "Sorry to interrupt the party, but Coach Bennett just called a team meeting downstairs."

Quickly, they pulled it together and stood up from their seats. All about a good time when they had the freedom, but serious when duty called. At the end of the day, this was their job just as much as these videos were mine.

None of them would even be talking to me if the team weren't paying them to.

I nodded toward Barry and Joe to cut the cameras and waited patiently for the guys to make their way out of the room.

"Thanks for lunch, Six," Quinn said as he picked up his empty lunch plate and cup and tossed them into the trash. "I thoroughly enjoyed this."

"Dude," Martinez chimed in. "Me too. Any time you need me to participate in fucking with Phillips, count me the hell in."

With Sean at the rear, the guys filed out of the room, but he paused before his feet passed the threshold. Two steps, then three, he moved closer to me, until we were standing nearly chest-to-chest.

Quiet as a whisper, he leaned down and said, "Just so we're clear, I'm one hundred percent all man."

"Is that so?" I questioned back on a murmur.

He nodded. "Yeah, and just like today, I *take* everything like a man."

Take everything like a man?

Like everything *everything*?

Am I included in this scenario?

I hated that I had the urge to cross my fingers and toes.

"Oh," he added, "and you should probably watch your back, honey. I've heard paybacks are a bitch."

"You planning on retaliating?"

He shrugged. "I always keep my options open."

Of course, the manwhore always kept his options open.

His never-committed relationship status was proof of that.

"Bring it on, Phillips," I whispered back, but my words sounded way too dirty just to be referring to teasing pranks.

Was it bad that my brain started imagining beds and a naked Sean and a naked Sean's penis?

That wasn't bad, right?

Yeah...keep telling yourself that...

Shit. My gut instinct told me Sean Phillips just might have become an itch I needed to scratch.

Sean

F resh off a home game win against Minnesota, we were officially the leader in the league with overall wins. Seven and fucking 0, baby.

If we kept playing like this for the rest of the season, that championship trophy we were all vying for wouldn't be just a dream anymore. No, it would be a reality.

With every win we slid under our belts, the greedier we all became. Especially me. A championship was starting to feel so close I could taste it.

And now, after a forty-eight-hour rest from our last game, we were balls deep into practice.

The practice squad was present, challenging their active roster teammates on every play during scrimmage. And they weren't holding back. Not one fucking bit. They hit hard. And scrapped harder. They fought us like gladiators, unwilling to settle for defeat.

It was exactly what we needed.

No doubt, if we ended up hitting our season's end goal of bringing the championship trophy back to New York, these guys would be a monumental part of that.

Coach stood off to the sidelines chatting with Bailey, while the rest of us stayed huddled up at the fifty-yard line.

When QB jogged back over toward us, I could see the anticipatory grin smudged across his lips underneath his helmet. "You ready for a little Razzle Dazzle?" he asked, eyes locked on me.

Instantly, excitement spilled into my veins, and my heart pumped faster. Feet light, I did a little dance on the turf and wiggled my fingers in the middle of the huddle.

Razzle Dazzle was a play our offensive coordinators had created, and it packed one hell of a punch with its creative choice in routes. Executing a zig and a zag, I had to run from one side of the field and then back across to the far corner of the end zone. It was a test of foot skills and athleticism, and it almost always caught the other team off guard, nothing for their hands but the balls between their legs as I danced into the end zone to add six to our tally.

"Let's do it."

"All right, Razzle Dazzle," Bailey said into the huddle. "Martinez, hold your line. I'll need every second I can get in the pocket. Williams, keep your routes quick and snappy to pull the defense. And Sean, well, do what you do best."

I smiled around my mouthguard and put in a wink for pizazz before breaking apart and heading to my position on the outside.

We lined up, toes to the lines, and the practice squad matched our power and size on the other side of the coin.

"Hut!" QB shouted for the snap. I watched the ball as it left the line, hard and swift in Sam Sheffield's hand as he pitched it to my man and busted up to block. From one heartbeat to the next, his words were the starting shotgun to my race.

Off like a rocket, I sprinted forward for ten yards before switching my route and dropping my defensive opponent like a bad habit.

Five more yards and I looked over my shoulder to find Bailey still confidently in the pocket, his gaze laser-focused toward the opposite side of the field.

Until it wasn't.

One quick look toward me, and he visually confirmed the opportunity the play was designed to create.

Me, unmanned, and yards of open field.

Quinn sent the ball to the air, and I watched it soar through the sky, increasing the long strides of my legs as I followed it toward the end zone.

Hands up and ready, I jumped to meet the line of Quinn's well-placed pass, prepared to bring it back down for the groundwork. Once the skin of the ball kissed my fingertips, I snagged it from the air, cradled it to my chest, and kept running until my feet crossed into the end zone.

Fucking Razzle Dazzle, babbbbby!

Coach's whistle blew as I did a squat and whirl, a signature celebratory dance move I'd spent years perfecting, and then turned toward the field. QB's eyes were on me, and a shit-eating grin was on his face as he jogged toward me.

"Hell of a throw, QB!" I exclaimed, and he laughed, lifting his arm in the air for a fiver. We slapped palms loudly, and Coach Bennett blew the whistle again to get our attention.

"Hell of a catch," Quinn congratulated back, making sure to give me glory where glory was due.

"Razzle Dazzle, motherfuckers," I agreed with a laugh.

Quinn grinned, and we headed for the sidelines.

As we jogged across the field to grab some water and regroup, I caught sight of the pint-sized, sexy as fuck woman standing beside one of her camera guys.

Her gaze was focused directly on me, and a secondary wave of satisfaction rushed through my body. She made a big show of acting like I was the last thing on her mind, but that didn't change the facts now. She was watching closely, and she was aiming at *me*.

It's only a matter of time, I mused. *Only a matter of time before sexy Six Malone is mine to devour.*

"All right, boys," Coach announced inside the huddle of our entire team. "Since I'm happy with what we've accomplished today, and you've been playing your asses off, I'm giving you the rest of the night off, *and* I'm even letting you sleep in. Be back here tomorrow at noon."

The cheers that accompanied his words were damn near deafening.

"But…" He held up both hands. "If you guys come back tomorrow and look like dog shit warmed over, you can guaran-fucking-tee this will never happen again."

"That means no drinking," QB chimed in, and his eyes met everyone's before he looked back to Coach.

Always the mother hen of our team, Quinn was a leader through and through. And it was a known fact you couldn't get shit past him.

"What about eating?" Martinez asked on a shout, and Coach just grinned.

"Of course, you're concerned about food."

"You gotta eat big to be this strong and powerful, Coach B," Teeny retorted. "If anything, you should be thanking me."

"Yeah," Coach responded through a chuckle. "The only thing I'm thankful for is that I don't have to foot the bill to feed you."

Martinez was a beast. There was no denying that.

But it wasn't fat. It was one-hundred percent muscle. His power, his strength, was what kept our star quarterback protected inside the pocket.

In my opinion, Teeny could eat as much as he fucking wanted as long as he kept playing the way he did.

"All right," Coach said with a grin. "Go home, take a load off. Someone make sure Teeny gets his tenth meal of the day, and I'll see you back here tomorrow."

As the team parted ways, I stayed back to chat with Bailey and

Mitchell while I guzzled a bottle of water.

It didn't take long for Martinez to make his way over to us, a big old grin on his face. "Which of you ladies is taking me to dinner tonight?" he asked, and I chuckled.

"I'll be your date, Teeny, but only if we hit up that little Mexican restaurant across from the stadium."

"Cancun's?" he asked, and if it was possible, his grin got wider.

"Yep."

"Oh, hell yeah!" he cheered. "Count me in. I haven't had their chicken enchiladas in a long-ass time."

I looked at Quinn and Mitchell. "You guys wanna go?"

Quinn shrugged. "Cat's out of town on a work trip, so, yeah, sure. Count me in."

"You're so whipped it's not even funny," I teased, but he just grinned. He apparently liked the sting of leather.

"Thank you."

"Nice practice, boys." An all-too-familiar voice filled my ears, and I turned to find Six, without her camera guy, walking toward us.

"Thanks, little lady," Teeny accepted the compliment with literal open arms and a smile. And before she could stop him, he picked her straight up off the ground and tossed her over his shoulder.

My stomach tensed at the sight. And I wasn't sure if it was out of fear he'd drop her or the fact that she was in his arms and not mine.

"Oh, dear God!" she squealed. "Put me down, you big sweaty man!"

He just laughed and turned around so Six's face was looking toward us.

"Having fun?" Quinn asked, and she rolled her eyes.

"A little help would be nice, you know."

"I'll help," I chimed in. "But only if you agree to come eat dinner with us tonight."

"What are you guys eating?"

I waggled my eyebrows. "Only the best fucking tacos and enchiladas you'll ever taste in your life."

"Meh," she said with a shrug of her little shoulders. "I think I'll pass."

"Oh, come on!" Teeny bellowed and, eventually, put her on her feet. "I won't take no for an answer, little sister."

She smiled up at the big brute of a man. "Well…okay…maybe… But only if you ask nicely."

Teeny got down on one knee and took her left hand into his. "Please, pretty little Six Malone, come eat dinner with me and these other bastards who don't really matter."

Her smile grew. "All right, count me in."

Wait a minute…she said no to me, but yes to Teeny?

What the fuck?

As everyone filed off the field in the direction of showers, I watched on from behind as fucking Martinez finalized our dinner plans with Six.

Quinn wrapped an arm around my shoulder, and I looked over to find him smirking like the devil. "I think he stole your girl," he whispered, and I shrugged him off with a laugh.

"I have no idea what you're talking about."

"I bet it stings a little being the third wheel and all," he feigned sympathy and patted my shoulder. "It'll be okay, buddy. Promise."

"Just for that, you're buying my dinner," I retorted. Quinn just shrugged.

"Hey, anything to make you feel better." He winked and walked through the locker room doors first, but not before he tossed over his shoulder, "I got your back, boo."

Fucking Bailey, the shit stirrer.

Chapter Nine

Six

Tacos and enchiladas at Cancun's had turned into watching *Game of Thrones* and eating takeout from Styrofoam containers at Martinez's house.

All occurring on Quinn's suggestion *and* insistence.

When it came to the famous quarterback of the Mavericks, he stayed true to his leadership role, on *and* off the field. Even if that meant keeping his boys out of a Mexican restaurant where pitchers of margaritas and tequila shots might have been too damn tempting to avoid.

At first, I'd been disappointed by the turn of events. The idea of watching Sean surreptitiously seemed easier in a public place than during a quiet night at one of the players' houses. There were distractions, both alcoholic and otherwise, at a restaurant, and if I got really creepy, I could blame it on bad beef and make a getaway through the bathroom.

As it was, I figured people would notice if I jettisoned in a hurry.

But it'd been better than expected, and I had a feeling it was all of the laid-back, sexy-times vibes in the air.

Those vibes were probably more related to me—*more like, my obsession with Jason Momoa*—than the guys, but I sure as fuck didn't care.

I was late to the *Game of Thrones'* party, but holy moly, after watching Khal Drogo and Khaleesi together for one episode, I'd officially added a new series to my must binge-watch list. It was hot. It was tender. I was willing to let Jason Momoa defile me in all fifty states and the District of Columbia.

Hopped up on what I would forever refer to as Momoa-itis, I pulled out my phone to send a quick text message to my long-distance besties, Sam and Everly.

Normally, I would've logged in to my private YouCam account and sent them a long diatribe revolving around the one million reasons why they needed to watch *Game of Thrones*. But considering I was currently sitting inside a house full of football players, one of whom's penis I feared I *might* talk about specifically, I figured it'd be safest to keep my conversation to text.

Our group chat was only three spots down, just below my mom and dad.

With one tap of my index finger, I was in like Flynn.

Me: Why haven't one of you fuckers told me about Game of Thrones? Are we not really friends? Is our friendship an elaborate hallucination on my part?

About a minute later, my phone vibrated in my hands with a response. I smiled.

Everly: At least one thousand people have told me I need to watch it, but I haven't. I'm just as in the dark as you are. Or were. And no, getting drunk in Cancun and almost getting thrown in Mexican jail WAS NOT an illusion. I can only assume that means our friendship is real.

Me: Oh. My. God. How many times have I told you NOT to bring up Mexico? He seemed like he was propositioning me, okay? I didn't know he was a cop and all he wanted was for me to calm down.

I shuddered at the memory and typed out another message.

Me: Anyway, we're done talking about that. Right now, we're talking about Game of Thrones and how much YOU NEED TO WATCH IT. Do it. Do it now.

Everly: Geez. Bossy, much? Some of us can't just drop everything and watch Game of Thrones.

Me: Shut up and listen. You will fall madly in love with Khal Drogo. Who, by the way, is played by Jason Momoa.

Everly: Jason Momoa? Fuck, Six. How many times do I have to tell you to lead off with the important information? What channel is that shit on?

Me: I'm rolling my eyes at you for asking about a "channel." That's so two years ago. You can STREAM it on HBO Now. Ask your hot brother for help.

Everly: STOP CALLING MY BROTHER HOT.

A hearty, raspy, sexy laugh sounded across the room and pulled my attention from the text message screaming match with Everly.

Standing by a high-top table next to the pool table, Sean was laughing and backslapping with a couple of guys I recognized from the practice squad.

More and more guys had been arriving with each minute that passed, a turn of events Mother Hen Quinn had no control over, and the lower level of Martinez's house was filling up fast. I wiggled into the white leather of Martinez's basement sectional and tried to blend into the material.

Sudden and powerful, Sean's gaze found mine and held it.

Fuck, I don't think the blending is working.

Instinctually, I wanted to avert my eyes, but it was too late to save face. I'd already been caught in the act, gawking at him like a fool.

He smirked and then winked, and I rolled my eyes in response.

The fucker. I kind of hated how fucking attractive he was. How well he carried the weight of his big-ass ego and how I couldn't stop looking at him.

My phone could apparently sense my distress. With a wiggle and a vibration, it danced in my hands and called my attention back.

Sammy: My ears are ringing from all the yelling the two of you have been doing about hot brother and Mexico.

Me: Don't bring up Mexico!

Everly: My brother is NOT hot.

Sammy: You're both in denial. Maybe that's why I didn't tell you about Game of Thrones. As punishment.

Quickly, my mind refocused on my new *Game of Thrones* fandom, and I typed out a message.

Me: You've been watching this shit and never told me?! I don't know if we can be friends anymore.

Sammy was shameless.

Sammy: Yep. I've seen all seven seasons, and I'm desperately waiting for the eighth. It's so freaking good!

Me: I no longer love you, Sammy. I'm transferring everything I once felt for you to Jason Momoa. He's much more deserving. Khal Drogo and his beautiful Khalessi. Sigh. They make my little heart pitter-patter with all the fucking feels.

Sammy: HAHA. Too bad you don't love me anymore. If you did, I might be willing to save you from heartbreak.

Me: What? What are you saying, Sammy?

Sammy: How many episodes have you seen?

Me: Like, two and half. Why????

Sammy: No reason. Just wondering.

Everly: Isn't Game of Thrones known for killing off like every-fucking-one?

My eyes popped wide of their own accord.
Hold the fucking phone...

Me: Oh. My. God. Sammy... Does Drogo die?!?!?

Sammy: ...

I jumped from the couch violently and screamed. All eyes came to me.

"Oh. Whoops. No worries, guys."

Everyone but Sean laughed it off and turned back to their regularly scheduled programming. I could feel the weight of his eyes on me, though, long after I sat back down on the couch and moved my focus back to my phone.

Me: *Thanks a lot, hooker. Now the Mavericks think I'm a psychopath.*

Everly: *They don't already think that?*

Sammy: *It was only a matter of time.*

Me: *You're both assholes.*

Sammy: *I'm sorry, but are you seriously texting us about Game of Thrones right now? While you're hanging out with the Mavericks?!*

I furrowed my brow and tapped my fingers across the keypad.

Me: *Is that a bad thing?*

Everly: *Consider this text conversation over. It is now time for Six to be a normal human being and go mingle with the sexy AF football gods.*

Sammy: *Yep. Agreed. We will resume our GoT conversation another time.*

Six: *GUYS! Don't be dicks. I need to know more details! I mean, does Drogo die? Tell me he doesn't die, Sammy! I don't know what I'll do if he dies!*

But my desperation didn't matter. My friends gave zero fucks.

Everly: *Let us live vicariously through you. Go have some goddamn fun with the freaking Mavericks!*

Me: *Live vicariously through me? What exactly does that entail?*

Everly: I think you should experience at least one of the penises you managed to see several weeks ago. And, personally, if I were you, I'd be calling dibs on Sean Phillips.

Of course, she just *had* to mention him.

I mean, there were only approximately one million players on the team, and still, Everly mentioned the one man I was bound and determined to stay the fuck away from.

Me: He's a total manwhore.

Everly: Which means he'd be absolutely perfect for a no-strings-attached hookup. You talk like you're Mother Teresa.

Sammy: Plus, you've already seen his penis. You'll know how many jaw exercises to do prior to your rendezvous.

She had a point. But I refused to let it become anything of substance inside my stubborn brain.

Me: Gah. All this penis pressure. You guys are the worst best friends ever.

Sammy: Love you! Bye, Six!

Everly: Stop thinking about Game of freaking Thrones and go enjoy yourself! Anyway, we all know it's been a while... Your vagina needs a cleanout.

Six: My vagina isn't fucking old and crusty.

I waited for their rebuttal, but it never came.

After a good minute of staring at the screen had gone by, I gave in and sent them a text message.

Six: GUYS. Come back. Please?

Six: EVERLY…SAMMY…COME BACK!

Six: Hello?

Six: God, you're such bitches.

I knew from experience, when they ended a group chat for the night, they meant business. No doubt, they wouldn't respond until tomorrow.

And that would most likely be to ask me if I'd managed to get down and dirty with a Maverick.

My old, cobweb-filled vagina tingled at the thought.

Goddammit.

With a heavy sigh, I finally threw in the towel and shoved my phone back into my side pocket, dug my body out of the butter of the couch, and occupied my time by watching as Quinn and Cam played a game of pool. All the while, my mind couldn't stop thinking about what my stupid best friends had ridiculously suggested.

Hooking up with Sean Phillips?

What a terrible fucking idea…*right?*

"Uh oh, Mitchell," Quinn teased after he missed his first shot of five. With only one solid and the eight-ball left, the odds of a win were looking pretty damn good from where he stood. "Looks like you better shit or get off the pot."

Cam chuckled, then flashed a quick glare. "Slow your roll, QB Pie. I'm only a few shots behind you."

I giggled at the nickname. "QB Pie?" Cam smiled triumphantly.

"Georgia Brooks gave him that one. Personally, I think we should use it more often."

"Pretty sure she calls you *Hammy Cammy*," Quinn chimed in, and I giggled some more.

"And what does she call Sean?" I found myself asking. It didn't matter what lies I told myself on the regular—my interest in the cocky son of a bitch was potent.

"The man. The king. The dual threat." A deep, raspy, sexy as fuck voice whispered into my ear.

I turned my head, tucking my chin into the hollow of my shoulder to look back at him.

"Are you sure those aren't just your nicknames for yourself?"

"She calls him *Sealami Roll-ups*," Cam kindly added before leaning down into the table and lining up his next shot.

Sealami Roll-ups as in Salami Roll-ups?

His Georgia-given nickname literally revolved around meat.

Which, recalling the size of his…yeah…*that*…it was quite ironic.

I bit my lip to fight my perverted giggles, but I couldn't swipe the grin from my face.

"That's pretty fucking hilarious."

Sean shrugged and smiled. Apparently, it'd take a lot more than a ridiculous nickname to bruise his confidence.

God, he was dangerous. And hot. Quick on his feet and sure with his hands, he lived up to his dual threat position.

Don't forget about his huge penis.

Shit. If there was one thing I really needed to do, it was forget about *that*.

Like, it was becoming a real fucking problem. If I, all of a sudden, decided to take up golf, I'd have to claim the cocky fucker's penis as an actual handicap on my score.

Oh, sorry, fictional golf partner, but I have a ten-inch handicap. Which means, I can't go fifteen minutes without thinking about Sean Phillips' penis, and therefore, I completely suck…

Suck…Sean's penis…

Oh my God! Stop thinking about it!

God, if anyone was ever actually inside of my head, hearing these ridiculous fucking thoughts, I'd honestly think they'd need therapy.

Despite my scattered, schlong-focused thoughts, our gazes locked for a long moment, but before either of us could say anything, a football version of bulls on parade came barreling down the stairs.

It was only then that I realized I'd been the only female at this shindig…until *now*.

Behind the ten or so football players came a handful of very pretty females. Hemlines at crotch level and boobs set to spillage, they were more than ready to give their all to the occasion.

Most were blondes, but one was a brunette. All were white.

Instantly, I glanced down at my hoodie and yoga pants and mauvy-brown skin. One of these was definitely not like the others.

Meh. Oh, well. I mean, I'd come here to fill my belly with tacos, which meant I'd needed something cozy, otherwise known as my official "eatin' pants," and I couldn't change the fact that one of my parents was from India and the other from the Philippines—more than that, I didn't want to.

Not only did my special pants accommodate food babies, but they also kept my legs surprisingly warm in the cool fall weather. And as weird as it was, the combination of my parents' traditionalism and my wackiness worked for me.

It was a total win-win, and if anything, when I really looked at the ladies with full makeup, wearing skirts and dresses over bare legs, I only felt sympathy.

For them—not me, obviously.

I might've looked like a hobo, but *I* was fucking comfortable.

Before I knew it, more bodies came downstairs into the basement, and the little "get-together" had turned into a damn party.

"Teeny, if the team looks like shit tomorrow, I'm sending Coach's wrath and fury directly to you," Quinn called over the now bass-pumping music that bumped and bounced throughout the house.

Homeboy had one hell of a sound system, that was for sure.

I wonder if he minds if I snoop around to figure out what brand it is? Clearly, finding his sex toys and snapping pictures would be purely on a bonus basis.

When a glass filled with what I assumed was a margarita was

pushed into my view, I stopped worrying about my covert mission on Teeny's belongings and cooed.

"Ooh," I said, smiling. "Pretty alcohol."

Sean grinned.

"Trust me, you'll need this in about twenty minutes when Teeny pulls out karaoke."

Evidently, Sean had somehow developed the impression he needed to convince me. That wasn't the case, but I was a kind woman. I could live without correcting him. If he was like other men, there'd be plenty of other opportunities to prove I was the superior being.

Accepting gallantly, I took a sip of the cool, refreshing beverage that was, in fact, an ice-cold margarita and moaned. "Mm. That's really good."

"That's because I made it." He waggled his brows. "You'll eventually learn that I'm a man of many talents."

Slowly, we found our way back to the couch, Sean moving some of the groupies out of our way with just a jerk of his head.

I curtsied and took a seat. The cushion beside me jostled a bit as Sean sat down, and instantly, my senses were assaulted with how fucking good he smelled.

His scent was sweet and spice and everything sexy and erotically nice, and just about every cell in my body stood up and took notice.

Hot damn. I wonder if he tastes as good as he smells?

Instantly, déjà vu assaulted my thoughts.

I'd been down this whole *Sean Phillips smells fucking amazing* route before. But for the life of me, I couldn't pinpoint when it had occurred...

"Having fun?" he asked, and I couldn't stop myself from searching inside the depths of his hazel gaze. I had no idea what I was looking for, but goddamn, he had the most mesmerizing eyes.

I just offered a little shrug in response. "I'll never complain about a party that serves tacos and allows me to drool at Jason Momoa for two hours."

"Jason Momoa," he repeated through a soft chuckle. "I never

would've guessed it."

"Guessed what?"

"That he's your type."

A laugh bubbled up from my lungs. "I'd love to meet the woman whose type *isn't* Jason Momoa."

Pretty sure this delectable, smells like heaven, with the body of a fucking mocha-skinned Greek god man sitting next to you is also your type…

It was moments like this I wished I possessed the power to turn off my brain.

But it was useless. The wheels of my mind had started to turn, and with every rotation, I categorized all Sean Phillips's most irresistible traits.

His body. His eyes. His sexy voice. His contagious laugh. The way he had the power to say all of the most charming things followed shortly by something completely egotistical.

It was an attention-grabbing combination, and I lived for everything noteworthy.

He was undeniably powerful on the field and one of the best players in the league, but I wondered endlessly what lived below the surface.

A person is almost never *one* thing. They're an onion of layers, deep fried in secrets.

Wow. That makes everyone sound like a popular appetizer at Texas Roadhouse.

Sean shifted, his hand doing the discreet adjustment dance all men did with their cocks, and another kind of appetizer took over my thoughts.

Ah, fuck. Everly and Sammy's pervy suggestion about fuck buddies and hookups was starting to sound like a good idea.

Oh, sweet summer wine, I had to stop the crazy train of bad ideas.

Because Sean Phillips was a very bad idea.

But he'll probably feel so good.

With the rim of the glass to my lips, I guzzled down the rest of the margarita in one gulp.

"Thirsty much?" he teased, and his eyes sparkled with amusement.

Yeah. For you.

Oh, dear God.

Maybe the margarita was also a bad idea?

Alcohol led to loosened lips and zero inhibitions, and the last thing I needed right now was to blurt out something ridiculous like, *Oh, hey, Sean, do you want to go upstairs and fuck my brains out?*

Visions of the craziest words flowing out of my mouth like water consumed my mind, and I knew I had to get up off this couch before I did something insane.

Too lost in my thoughts, too tempted by his presence, I stood up from the couch and strode away without offering a goodbye or an explanation for my sudden muteness and inability to carry on a simple conversation.

Up the basement stairs, my feet paused momentarily on the first level while my eyes searched out a quiet reprieve. But the music was too flipping loud, and there were too many people scattered throughout the main living area.

So, I did what any insane woman who couldn't seem to stop thinking about the biggest manwhore she'd ever met would do, I walked through Martinez's house like I owned the place.

Once I reached the second level, I found a quiet guest bedroom to recollect my thoughts.

But the peace and quiet only lasted for a moment or two.

"Six?" a sexy voice I couldn't scrub from my brain asked from behind me. "You all right?"

"Uh-huh."

"You sure?" Sean asked, but I couldn't find the strength to turn around and meet his eyes. All I could do was stare out the guest bedroom window into the endless, nothing landscape that was the dark of night.

Only the glow from the moon and a few scattered stars provided anything of substance for my eyes to latch on to.

"Yep. I'm sure."

"Did I say something to upset you?" he asked, and the sounds of his feet taking a few steps into the room filled my ears.

"Upset me?" I turned on my heels at his words, a sarcastic laugh on the tip of my tongue.

Upset me? No. Upset my hormonal balance? Yes.

His eyes were like light green lasers, and the power of his gaze was more than I was prepared to handle.

"Yeah…" He paused as he stepped all the way into the room. "You just kind of up and left, and it felt like I'd said something to piss you off." He shut the door behind him with a quiet click to give us some privacy.

Privacy that I knew was dangerous.

Being closed away in a room with Sean Phillips was not good for my willpower.

My libido was a screaming lunatic, and closing out all the other voices in the house made it easier to hear her.

"No," I said on a near whisper, trying to duct-tape Libby Libido's mouth shut as she begged me to take off his pants and ask him to come all over me. "I just needed some fresh air."

He quirked a brow. "Fresh air? Inside the house?"

God, I sounded like a lunatic.

And honestly, what was the point in all of it?

So what if I was attracted to Sean?

So what if I wanted to know what he tasted like?

So what if I wanted to know what he felt like inside of me?

I was a single lady, and Sean's bad boy appeal had short-circuited my brain. Wires smashed together and hot-wired into business, little Six's engine was officially off and running.

I flashed the bat signal, looking up from under my eyelashes with coy seduction, but all I got in return was a squint.

I worked my body harder, pushing out my chest and sighing a

heavy, hot breath.

Still nothing.

I turned on the charm even harder and danced my eyes, willing him into submission like a snake trainer with a cobra.

"Uh. What are you doing?" he asked.

Ah, shit. Fuck subtlety. I apparently wasn't any good at it.

With a charge in and a leap, I closed the distance and forced myself into his arms. Finally, he got the fucking message.

Our lips found one another quickly, fusing into a battle.

And good God, Sean Phillips knew how to fucking kiss.

His lips guided and demanded while his tongue teased and tasted.

His kiss, his touch, held some kind of live wire straight to all of my erogenous zones.

My nipples grew hard and sensitive beneath my bra.

My pussy throbbed, and I clenched my thighs together to lessen the ache.

Goose bumps peppered the skin of my arms, my neck, and back.

And my heart, well, it flew like a hummingbird's wing, each *thump-thump-thump* coming faster and faster.

Libby was fully in control now. I *wanted* him.

And by the thick arousal sheathed beneath his jeans and pressed into my belly, I knew the immense need wasn't one-sided.

Strong hands to my ass, he lifted me up, and I wrapped my legs around his waist as he moved us two steps and pressed my back against the wall.

All the while, he never stopped kissing me.

"Fuck me, Sean," I whispered against his mouth on a soft moan.

He stopped for the briefest of moments to look me deep in the eyes, his free hand brushing a few loose curls out of my face and tucking them behind my ear. "Are you sure?" he asked, and I nodded without hesitation.

"Yes. Please."

The begging, the fucking needy words that were coming out of my mouth went against everything I'd promised to myself when it came to this man, but I'd handle the backlash after the fact.

I was incapable of focusing on anything besides *feeling* him. All of him.

My fingers to his jeans, I undid the button and managed half of the zipper, all the while, my eyes stayed locked with his. "Fuck. Me. Sean."

With his guttural groan and nip of my bottom lip, it was clear my words goaded him into action, moving us toward the bed in two long strides. My back hit the mattress with a soft bounce and a brief ricochet before I could process his movements.

We locked eyes for a moment, just a quick, quiet stretch of time to feel safe with one another, and then he turned primal.

I watched with rapt attention as he slid off my yoga pants and panties, pulling them down my legs and tossing them to the ground.

Soft, needy whimpers fell from my lips as he kissed from my toes upward.

Slowly, so fucking slowly, he kissed a trail up my bare skin as his hands led the path up my legs, always just a little higher than his kisses.

My back arched in anticipation, and my head rocked back against the mattress as his lips placed fluttering kisses against the one spot where I throbbed and ached relentlessly for him.

"I knew it," he whispered and circled my clit with the very tip of his tongue. "I knew you'd taste even fucking better than I imagined."

His lips. His tongue. His mouth. His fingers.

I was on pleasure overload.

God, he's good. So. Fucking. Good.

Within minutes, I was coming hard against his mouth.

My thighs shook. My heart raced. And pleasure assaulted all of my senses.

By the time I'd managed to regain my focus, Sean was sliding his thick, hard cock out of his boxer briefs and jeans, and I'd never seen anything that erotic in my life.

Well, except for the first time I saw it.

His hand on his cock, he stroked it up and down, up and down, while his gaze stayed fixated on my spread thighs, my wet pussy. His eyes drew a slow path up my body until they locked with mine.

"You want my cock, Six?" he asked.

Shame long and truly gone, I nodded and begged.

"Yes. *Please.*" I was beyond caring. I wasn't too proud to plead. I just wanted to feel him inside of me.

Condom out of his pocket and sheathed over his dick, he gripped my thighs and slid every inch of his thick shaft inside of me.

I moaned. He moaned.

One thrust. Two thrusts. And I felt delirious with how good it felt.

By the time he pushed himself in to the hilt, the world just up and melted away, and our priority turned to fucking each other's brains out.

Deep, pulling kisses accompanied by clutching hands and a pounding rhythm, and I was done for, lost to the intense feel of it all.

Each drive forward stayed steady and persistent, and it didn't take long before another climax started to build deep within me. Beginning at my toes and working its way up my trembling thighs, my orgasm taunted until it found its path up my spine.

My heart rate tripped into an erratic rhythm, and my breath came out in short, desperate pants as I felt the pleasure build and build and build.

God, I am so close.

But all at once, he slowed his pace, turning his hard, deep thrusts to slow and easy, and I whimpered.

The toying bastard leaned forward to press a heady kiss to my lips, his tongue sliding in and out of my mouth in sync with the pace of his cock.

I writhed beneath him, desperate, greedy—*needy.*

"Do you want to come again, Six?" he asked, his voice laced with pleasure and satisfaction, and this dominant, alpha control that only seemed to intensify my arousal. "Does that perfect little pussy want to come around my cock?"

"Yes," I whispered against his lips.

"Beg me for it," he said. I was wanton and unashamed and ready to comply, but he picked up his pace again, and all I could do was moan.

Fucking me harder. Faster.

Taking me just to the edge and then slowing again.

Eyes locked with mine. Demanding. Powerful. Fucking mesmerizing.

"Say it," he whispered. "Tell me what you want."

"Fuck me," I said, forcing the words out between my needy moans. "Make me come."

Ordinarily, I was a woman of my own mind and power. But now, I was a simple slave to the pleasure he so generously gave.

Thighs shaking, heart pounding, and breaths a staccato rhythm of moans and pants, I came hard, and it didn't take him long to follow my lead. With his strong fingers gripping my thighs and a guttural groan, he found his release deep inside of me.

I had no idea how long it took me to come back down to Mother Earth, but the instant I became fully aware I'd just had sex with Sean inside a guest bedroom at a party filled with his teammates, it felt like the walls were closing in on me.

Ho-lee mother-flipping shit. I just fucked Sean Phillips.

I'd had sex with Mr. Manwhore, and I'd be a liar if I said it wasn't some of the best sex I'd ever had in my fucking life.

A mindfuck of epic proportions.

Quietly, we disentangled ourselves and put our clothes back on, and my mind whirled with the consequences of my actions.

I'd been the one holdout in Sean's life, and I'd just willingly given up my role. I'd thrown myself into the moment, and I didn't regret it.

But goddamn, I wasn't ready to face the living nightmare of his growing ego.

The answer, albeit a little cruel, came to me in an instant of clarity.

I needed to save face.

I needed to go back to the façade where I acted like he wasn't one of the most irresistible men I'd ever met.

I looked up into his big hazel eyes and patted his shoulder with my hand. "Thank you for that," I said, voice easy breezy. "That was pretty good."

A surprised little smirk brought his smile into check as his gaze searched mine. "Just pretty good?"

"Yeah. It was pretty good." I shrugged. "Better than I thought it would be."

Liar.

His stare was manic and searching, and I shielded myself against it. Libby bounced in the background, begging me to give up the ghost, but I stayed stalwart and strong. This would be for the good of both of us in the end.

Because Sean Phillips would never settle for being mediocre. No, now, he'd be determined to prove me wrong.

I patted his big, muscular shoulder again, forced a big-ass smile to my lips, and walked out of the guest bedroom.

Ready for the onslaught.

Sean Phillips would be back. Of that, I was sure.

Chapter Ten

Sean

A long week of practice and a game-free weekend had come and gone.

Now rested and rejuvenated from a few days off, we were deep in the trenches of a Monday afternoon practice.

From where we were huddled up on the forty-yard line, Quinn called the play.

"Sweep and switch," he instructed. "Ready! Break!"

One loud cohesive clap and we separated, lining up against the practice squad.

This weekend we'd be playing Pittsburgh, on their turf.

They were just behind us in the league standings, and no doubt, they would step onto the field Sunday with every intention of ruining our winning streak.

They could aim for the win all they wanted. I called bullshit.

Even though Pittsburgh was a powerhouse of brutes and savages, they were no competition for us. We'd outplay them. We'd outsmart them. And we wouldn't allow their overaggressive defense to stop us from shoving touchdowns down their fucking throats.

But in reality, my brain wasn't one hundred percent on our opponent—or this practice, for that matter. Six had gone back to California the day after we'd had sex, and I hadn't heard from her since.

We hadn't exchanged numbers, she hadn't attempted to hunt me down online, and I absolutely had *not* watched six hours' worth of old YouCam videos of her to pass the time.

Toes on the line, I searched the sidelines for the vlogger. She was due back today, I knew, thanks to the scheduled question-and-answer session Georgia had told me about two days ago. And as much as I knew searching Six out wouldn't make her get there any faster, I couldn't help it.

It'd been a week since I'd found out what it felt like to be inside Six Malone, and I couldn't get her out of my fucking head. The undeniably gorgeous, pint-sized woman with the mane of black curls and eyes that drove me wild was a manipulator and a con artist.

Saying I was unexceptional in bed? Please.

Just pretty good? Give me a fucking break.

I had the experience to know that wasn't the case. I was a gracious lover, attuned to the needs and signals of a woman's body. I knew they weren't all the same, and I *listened*.

I fucking dared her to find a man more perceptive of her needs than I was.

My skin pulled at my cheeks as my face dropped into a scowl.

She'd begged me to fuck her. She'd come on my mouth. On my cock. And at one point, I'd seen those gorgeous eyes of hers damn near roll in the back of her head.

She'd caught on fire when I'd slid inside of her. Her hands had clawed at my chest, her lips moaning words of insistence.

More. More. More, she'd begged.

I was a sex expert, for fuck's sake. A *sexpert*.

Quinn shouted the signal, and the ball was snapped into his hands. Action sped into motion, and I had to get my mind right, and quick.

Get your head out of your ass and fucking run your route.

I locked eyes with my opponent, Billy Willis on our practice squad, and prepared to outmaneuver him until I found nothing but open field and free hands ready to catch Bailey's rocket of a pass.

Forward and to the right, I sprinted over the line of scrimmage and ran parallel to the sideline for ten yards, all the while Billy stayed beside me, shoulder-to-shoulder.

He was quick on his feet, but he wasn't quick enough. For as good I was in bed, I was even better on the field, and that was saying something.

With a stutter step and a turn, I switched up my route and sprinted diagonally across the field, and my opponent couldn't keep up.

I was just a few feet out of his reach, but he couldn't stop my forward progress, and the instant Quinn saw the opening, he sent the ball soaring into the air.

Five yards.

Eight yards.

Ten yards.

I followed the ball's lead until it dropped from my sky and straight into my hands on the twenty-yard line.

I felt the defense's presence behind my back, but they were no match. I was just too fucking fast. Twenty yards flew beneath my feet, and I came to an unscathed stop just inside the end zone, the ball still cradled like a baby in my arms.

Coach blew his whistle, and I jogged toward the bench with the rest of the team, offering QB a modest celebratory high-five just before we crossed the sidelines.

"Your routes are on fire," he said, and I smirked, lifting a water bottle to my lips and taking a long swig.

"My routes are *always* on fire."

"Not like this." Quinn chuckled, and his assessing blue eyes locked with mine. "Something's different. But I can't quite put my finger on it."

"Don't be so fucking dramatic, QB," I retorted, focusing on him intently to avoid letting my gaze stray into searching for someone again. "I'm just playing the way I always play, which, let's face it, is always fan-fucking-tastic."

He shook his head, not impressed. "Nah, not like this. Something's different…"

I started to tell him to stop being such a mother hen and mind his own fucking business, but that retort stalled before it even got going. My gaze was a traitor.

She was petite, gorgeous, and fucking beautiful, and I couldn't have missed the woman walking out of the tunnel and onto the field if I'd been blindfolded.

Her hair was as wild as ever and her clothes relaxed, but the way she held herself was so different from every woman I'd ever encountered.

Coach Bennett started rambling about something, but for once in my life, I couldn't hear a fucking word he was saying.

I was too busy watching her walk toward us.

The way the curve of her hips moved subtly with each step. The way her toned legs looked beneath her tight jeans. The soft little bounce of her breasts.

Fuck. I wanted another taste.

And even then, I wasn't sure just one taste would suffice.

Six was self-assured and outspoken, and she didn't make decisions based on other people. She was authentic to herself instead of deferential to anyone else, but the truth was, I couldn't think of anything that would draw people to her more.

She was unlike any woman I'd ever met.

She fucking challenged me. Made me work for every little inch.

The fight turned me on.

"All right!" Coach B shouted. "Everyone head inside and hit the showers. Meet me in the conference room in an hour."

Our team started to disperse, but I remained on the field, watching Six talk to one of the camera guys on her crew that had been filming snippets from today's practice.

"Now, it's starting to make sense," Bailey whispered into my ear. "She's the something that's different."

I turned to meet his eyes, heart kicking up in my chest that he knew about us sleeping together, but his face was amused.

And I doubted very much he'd find anything enjoyable about me potentially breaking the heart of someone professionally involved with the team.

"What do you mean?" I asked cautiously.

"I'm sure this is a difficult situation for you," he said, and his fucking smirk grew wider. "You're used to always getting what you want. Until *her*."

Normally, I wouldn't hesitate to tell my best friend to fuck off and provide the actual facts, the ones that included me fucking Six's brains out at Martinez's house last week, but this wasn't normal.

She was a professional contact, sure, but it was more than that.

I just wasn't quite sure what it was.

Regardless, I'd continue to keep the secrets of our sexy fucking rendezvous to myself, even if it meant getting razzed by my teammates.

"Quinn Bailey, quarterback of the New York Mavericks and professional gossip queen," I retorted through a soft chuckle.

"What can I say? I'm a man of many talents." He grinned and wrapped an arm around my shoulder. "Come on, boo, I'll take you out for some ice cream once we finish up here. Cat tells me chocolate chip cookie dough makes everything better when you get rejected. I, of course, wouldn't know."

I shrugged him off with a laugh, and together, we walked off the field and through the tunnel, until we reached the inside of the stadium.

Before I headed into the locker room, I made a pit stop in Matt's office, our personal trainer on staff, and gave him a quick update on my ankle.

"How'd it feel during scrimmage?" he asked as I stepped into the small space of his office.

"Felt a lot better. More stable. No discomfort."

Injuries were common in football. Hell, my list of battle wounds was a fucking mile long. But when you played at the professional level, when football became your livelihood and career, you had to take each injury, no matter how minor, seriously.

And I'd sustained a minor right ankle strain at the start of the preseason.

I could definitely play without problems, but it wasn't the kind of thing you didn't monitor.

The biggest concern was doing something in practice or in a game that would change its status from minor to something much worse.

"Good to hear," Matt responded with a grin. "Let's keep the training sessions and massage schedule the way we've got them, then. Sounds like it's helping. And next week, we'll have Dr. Winslow evaluate you again and possibly grab an MRI."

"Okay." I nodded and patted the palm of my hand against the doorframe. "See ya around."

The locker room and a shower calling my name, I wasn't expecting to run into Six as soon as I stepped out the door.

Walking straight toward me, she smiled, but it didn't feel right. It wasn't the kind of knowing, secret smile I'd expect to receive from a woman whom, just a week ago, I'd had my cock inside. It wasn't teasing or inviting, and it didn't beg me to do it again.

I frowned.

Her big brown eyes flared as she noticed.

"Hey, Sean," she greeted despite the tiny hint of emotion, and I started to wonder if I'd imagined it. Her cheeks weren't rosied with a hint of a blush, and her lips were sealed tight. The amber flecks in her eyes didn't sparkle with erotic memories, and her legs didn't churn with unspent arousal.

She was flawlessly affable, and I was officially fucking mystified. *What the fuck?*

My cock was half hard, and I could taste the sweetness of her honey as though I'd just licked it. The feel of her skin on mine, the rasp of her moan as I'd slipped inside her—I was tortured by all of it.

Either she was made of steel, or I really was a second-rate asshole.

Neither option sounded exceptionally appealing.

"How's it going?" I asked, leaning forward and brushing a finger along her arm to try to stir some hormones into awareness. Friendly and mocking, her smile remained unchanged.

"Pretty good."

Pretty good.

Jesus Christ. I've completely lost my touch.

"Pretty sure I've heard those words before," I said, bitterness coloring the edges of my tone. She *laughed.* Satisfied and rich, she was *enjoying* my misery.

"Yep. Me too." She dropped her voice to a whisper as she stood up on her tiptoes and added, "Thanks again for the *pretty good* night at Martinez's house."

And then, with another fucking pat to my goddamn shoulder, she resumed her walking path toward the conference room, only offering a simple, "See ya around, Sean," over her shoulder.

I stood frozen in my spot, watching her ass sashay as she disappeared into the conference room at the other end of the hall.

My blood surged, and my cock saluted me as I ordered the mission.

If I had been determined to make her mine before, I'd reached a whole new level after hearing the words *pretty good* for what felt like the one hundredth time.

Pretty good? Yeah, I'd blow her pretty good right out of the fucking water.

The next time I slid my cock inside Six Malone, she wouldn't be saying the words pretty good. She was going to lose her fucking mind. Words wouldn't be possible. Just moans. And orgasms. And her incoherently begging for more.

Game on, Six.

Chapter Eleven

Six

"We ready?" I asked, glancing back at Joe as Quinn, Sean, and Cam Mitchell took their places in front of me. We were doing a group question-and-answer session to use in any of the segments we needed filler for, and the three of them had volunteered for the job.

I'd briefly considered turning Sean down, just to get a rise out of him, but the fans really did love him. Plus, I'd probably done enough damage to his self-esteem with the way I'd just left things in the hall.

I imagined if I'd ever kicked a puppy, it would have looked something like Sean did as he stood waiting for me to keep tearing him apart.

I felt a little bad about his state of emotional duress…but not enough to switch places.

Women were always making themselves feel bad for the well-being of another person, and I just wasn't about it. I was intelligent and worthy, and if it took a little reverse psychology to get there, Sean would eventually know those things about me too.

Big picture, Sean was smart and charismatic, and he had a lot to offer. In fact, I knew he'd be a big part of the success of the entire series if I could harness his cocky confidence and use it in the right way. He just needed a little taste of humility. And I certainly wasn't too proud to walk a mile of orgasms to give it to him.

Joe nodded and gave me a point of his finger, and the red light on the front of the camera illuminated.

I quelled my fluttering nerves with a swallow of breath and reminded myself that being anxious was a part of my process.

Even though I felt pretty strongly that I was called by some higher power to be a performer and blessed with the personality to back it up, I never did it without fear. Fear that I'd be enough, fear that I'd do my best, and fear of how my audience as a whole would receive it.

I'd built an extraordinary level of vlogging success for myself, for which I was exceedingly grateful, but that didn't mean I stopped dreaming. No, I had stars in my eyes, and no matter the distance, the reach never seemed too much.

"Welcome back, Mavericks fans and drooling women who know nothing about football. Today we're back for another session with three of the New York Mavericks' most promising players—and hunkiest hunks." Quinn's, Sean's, and Cam's smiles grew instantly, and my own lips curved to match with a wicked twist. "Go ahead, guys. Lift your shirts and give the viewers a look."

Cam and Quinn glanced at each other uncertainly, but Sean didn't hesitate, lifting the royal fabric of his uniform shirt and flexing his muscles with a wink. I laughed at his willingness and shamelessly used it against him.

"Well, I'd say we know who the brazen one of the bunch is, don't we, ladies?" I asked, turning to address the camera directly.

Sean was getting used to my digs at this point, though, and he used the insinuation as a compliment rather than an insult.

"Why, thank you, Six."

I smiled widely. My puppy was being good, so he deserved at least a *little* bone.

Not to mention you actually want to bone *him again...*

Damn. And I had been doing so well up until this point.

Eyes toward the camera, I refocused on the task at hand.

"Today, we're getting down and dirty and personal with these three. Their likes. Dislikes. How many times a day they shower. All the questions they'd normally be too afraid to answer, we're going to do our best to force out of them. Saddle up, viewers. There are a couple of broncos in this mix."

I smiled at my own line and looked to my cheat sheet of questions, but I didn't get even the first word off my tongue.

Blaring and screeching like a banshee, the most obnoxious of noises catapulted itself from the speakers at the ceiling of the conference room. Lights flared and people scattered, and I caught a peek of even the grounds staff running down the hall outside.

Quinn and Cam moved immediately.

"Come on," Quinn ordered as the two of them made it to the door. "Let's go check the locker room. Make sure the guys get their asses out in a timely fashion." With a twist of the top of his abdomen, he turned the other direction. "Sean, you get Six and the crew out of here and into the evacuation zone."

Sean nodded and came my way, putting a hand to my back and gesturing toward the hall behind us to Joe.

"Go that way," he ordered. "Follow signs for the east parking lot."

Joe and Barry both packed up and turned tail, leaving Sean and me to follow behind them dutifully. Sean's hand felt warm and reassuring on the small of my back, and it heated my skin all the way through my thick sweatshirt.

"What the hell is going on? Is someone storming the stadium?"

"What?" Sean laughed, turning his mesmerizing eyes on me and lifting the corner of his mouth. "Haven't you heard a fire alarm before?"

"I have, obviously," I defended with a roll of my eyes. I'd attended several schools, all of which conducted monthly fire drills. But I swore the teasing lilt of this alarm sounded different. "But fancy, professional football stadium alarms sound different from poor people alarms."

I wasn't exactly poor, but I hadn't grown up far off. Living in Southern California, I'd watched as my immigrant parents struggled to make ends meet. We had food to eat, but not much pop and pizazz. This alarm sounded like it was encrusted in eighteen-karat gold.

"What?" Sean scoffed, laughing a bit while the top half of his face turned down at the edges. "What are you talking about? What's different about it?"

"I don't know," I mused, searching for the words to explain. It was musical, vibrant. The kind of thing I didn't normally associate with a call to evacuate or face certain death. "It kind of seems…upbeat."

"Upbeat?"

"Yeah. Like in *Titanic* where they play music for the rich people while they load the lifeboats."

"Wow. Your take on a classic movie has me questioning how closely I watched it before. And if my hearing is the same as yours. But, hey, I've been hearing it about once a month for the last six months, so maybe I'm just used to it. They can't seem to get all the kinks worked out of the new system. Alarm, sprinklers, that fucker keeps going haywire at the blink of a hat."

I laughed at his mixed metaphors and hurried toward the daylight at the end of the hall.

Sunlight flooded back into my eyes and warmed the skin of my cheeks as we finally stepped out the door that led to the east parking lot. A crowd was gathering a hundred or so feet back from the building—some distance of regulation, I was sure—and the owner of the Mavericks was pacing the front of the group like a caged lion.

Some of the guys' voices carried easily over the closing distance.

"Fuck, I'm a little cold," Martinez announced. Big as a tree and normally jovial, the man was standing in only royal blue boxer briefs and shower flip-flops, shivering and running one hand up and down his other arm while a baggie of carrots dangled from that hand.

"Dude," Sam Sheffield added and nodded down toward his black boxers, bare legs, and half-tied Nike trainers. "Fucking same."

I stifled a giggle and moved my eyes back to Wes Lancaster. His pacing had turned to a scary combo of stalking and bristling and I did not envy the guy in charge of the fire alarms.

"Wow. Mr. Lancaster looks pissed."

Sean dropped his voice to a whisper as we reached the group and walked by the man-turned-animal himself. "Ha. He was pissed five months ago. Now, he's…well. *That.*"

"Gene! Get over here!" Wes shouted. "What do we have to do to make this goddamn thing stop going off? I've got players out here in their underwear for shit's sake and a sprinkler-soaked office. My patience is running out."

A man I assumed was Gene jogged over toward him.

"So sorry, Mr. Lancaster," he said. "We thought we had it fixed last time, but apparently, it's not fixed."

"Christ, you think?" Wes retorted.

I'd really been rooting for Gene to come out with something Oscar-worthy. Something that would bring Wes back from the brink and save the man from having to search the classifieds for a new job. But it was pretty apparent good old Gene kind of sucked at explanations, and from what I could see, fire alarm systems, too.

Get your highlighter ready, Gene. I see mind-numbing searching and ink-stained fingers in your future.

A part of me wished I'd had my camera, but the smarter, more rational side of me knew it was for the best. All signs pointed to Wes Lancaster flipping his fucking rage-filled top if he caught me filming footage of this circus.

But good God, I could see visuals of the most perfect segment clips and the *dundt-dundt-dudda-dundt-dundt-dudda* music playing in the background.

Martinez in his fucking underwear and flip-flops.

Sam Sheffield faring no better.

Son of a bitch, it would've been gold.

"Gene, let me level with you," Wes stated. His lips were set in a firm line, and a little vein on his forehead popped out and started pulsating. "I'm one fire alarm without an actual fire away from taking a sledgehammer to the whole damn system. So, you need to fix it, or you might as well get ready to replace the entire fucking thing."

I bugged out my eyes, turning casually to show them to Sean without calling attention to myself. The spectacle was completely mockable, but I was a guest, and I'd learned the hard way serious hosts didn't like when you overextended your welcome.

Sean laughed at the overdramatized expression on my face and pulled at the end of one of my ringlets. I'd always been self-conscious of my hair and its endless exuberance growing up.

Most of the other girls had hair that fell below their breasts in straight, strategic lines, but mine went wherever it wanted. Of course, now I understood how well the hair fit my personality and embraced it.

It was vibrant. It was loud. It was nonconformist, and it was me.

Half-distracted by trying to hide my mooning face from Sean's discerning stare, I moved my focus to a point in the distance, well above his shoulder.

And found comedic gold.

"Oh my God," I breathed at the sight of the people moving from the building hand in hand.

"What?" Sean asked eagerly.

I indicated the direction of my gaze with a jerk of my head, and Sean spun to face them.

Georgia Brooks, the woman who'd hired me, and a deliriously handsome man, clutching each other and soaked from head to foot, were exiting the building in a tangled human web, wreathed in smiles.

Lost in each other, they ignored the crowd easily. Georgia's dress was torn in the front, and the man's pants were unzipped, but perhaps the funniest aspect of all was the way Georgia's bra hung from the front of his crotch, obviously caught in the teeth of his zipper.

Apparently, his pants were left unfastened for a reason.

"Oh my God," I repeated, this time choking out the words with a laugh.

Sean joined in, and soon, the whole group was turning to discover the culprit.

Wes maintained his ignorance for a while, but by the look on his face when he finally caught on, it wasn't nearly long enough.

"Jesus Christ!" Wes shouted, and I had to cover my mouth with a hand. "Kline!" Wes shook his head and sank it into his hands, patience obviously tried.

"Georgia," Wes said through gritted teeth as Georgia and Kline came to a stop in front of him. "Do you want to explain to me why you and your husband are just now making it out here, soaking wet and barely wearing any clothing?"

Georgia giggled, and Kline's smile grew even bigger. "I'm guessing you don't want either one of us to explain that, buddy."

"How many times do I have to ask you to stop coming here for conjugal visits? You've got six thousand square feet of big-ass house to sully with your depravity. Spare my offices!"

Georgia's smile was unrepentant, and I instantly liked her even more. Women with balls were *so* my style. "Please. You're trying to tell me you and Winnie don't have sex on Mavericks' property? Sell it to someone your wife doesn't drink margaritas with."

Chapter Twelve

Sean

As the crowd dissolved into hysterics over Georgia and her husband Kline's office disaster, I pulled on Six's hand and dragged her discreetly toward the far side of the parking lot. Georgia, Kline, and Wes's extremely public conversation had set the tone for my thinking and served pretty conveniently as a distraction. To say I hadn't been thinking about getting inside of Six since the moment she'd arrived back in town would be a lie, but the suggestion that others were acting on it at work only strengthened my brazen resolve.

My Jeep sat waiting, and we had the time.

One-on-one attention seemed like the best way to make use of it.

"What are you doing?" Six asked in a panicked whisper, her tiny legs churning at a nearly alarming rate as she tried to keep up with me. The height discrepancy between us was alive and real, but I didn't let that get in the way of logistics. I'd bend, I'd stoop, I'd turn myself into a pretzel. There wouldn't be any connections of a sexual nature that I wouldn't attempt.

A siren whined in the immediate distance, bleating into the

open swampland around the stadium with overzealous enthusiasm. It called into the wind and signaled its arrival, but most importantly, it made everyone who had gathered outside of the stadium turn to look.

"Just come on," I told Six as I used the distraction to my advantage, picking her up to span the distance between me and the line of all of our cars more quickly, and opened the back hatch of my Jeep.

Her glance was wary and her eyebrow challenging, but I bit my lip and winked in promise. *Climb inside*, it said. *And I'll show you all the reasons why you're doing it then.*

I gave her a small boost, assuring she didn't knock her legs as she hoisted herself up, and I followed dutifully.

The silence of the privacy I created by closing the hatch behind myself settled over us and changed the hum in the air. Her breathing sped up, and mine soon followed, eager to touch and taste and explore.

Navy blue and fuzzy, a blanket I kept in the back for emergency winter roadside situations beckoned. I grabbed it with ease and spread it across the entire space, laying the back row of seats forward flat to give us even more room.

"Fire-drill sex?" she asked on a whisper as I leaned my weight into her body and forced her to lie back.

"I couldn't think of a better way to use the time," I admitted. The smell of her perfume was like warm roses as I nuzzled her neck.

She smirked naughtily. "I mean, you do kind of need the practice."

I narrowed my eyes at her game. She'd *had* to be playing with me. The connection between us was palpable—electric. Larger than goddamn life.

I sucked on her neck and licked a line around the shell of her ear before moving around to nibble each of her lips. Her coos and moans filled the tight space quickly, wrapping me in their cloak and hardening my cock at an exponential rate.

"No time for foreplay this time," I whispered, shoving a hand into the front of her pants and pulling moisture from the center of her pussy up to her clit.

"Mmm," I moaned at the feel. "Good thing you don't need it."

She giggled a little, excitement bleeding from her movements as she matched my fervor and stuck her hand down my pants in kind. The feel of her fingers wrapped around me was heaven, and I was a transplant from hell. Her gift would be torture, and I'd take it to the brink of soul-selling.

"Oh, shit," she breathed as our pants came off and neediness took over. I poised above her, and my cock was rubbing through the wetness coating the skin between her legs. "I don't have a condom. My bag is inside. And I doubt you have one in your uniform."

I glanced down the line of my jersey with a smirk and laughed when I got to the end of the fabric. I didn't keep condoms in my uniform, and I certainly didn't keep them in the half I had left.

"You're right, baby. No condom here. But I have one in the console."

She froze momentarily and then rolled her eyes. "Of course you do."

"What?" I asked seriously. "You'd rather I weren't prepared?" I rubbed my thumbs across the bare skin of her hips for emphasis. "Where would that leave us now?"

"Blue," she remarked easily. "And balled. But together."

I laughed at her and climbed forward enough to open the hatch to the compartment in between my two front seats. The condoms were easily accessible and numerous, and I pulled one off the strip and ripped it open with my teeth. She watched as I went and smiled when I gave my covered shaft a couple extra jerks for her enjoyment.

Her eyes sparkled. "You like that?" I asked.

She nodded, the lids of her eyes falling down to hood them.

"I'll have to remember that for another time," I promised.

She nodded and watched avidly as I settled my hips on top of hers and pushed inside. My blood raced faster and faster with every inch I sank, urging my cock even harder as a result.

Delicate and shapely, she was miniature in so many ways compared to me. The length of her legs only just passed my knees, and she could barely make her hands meet around my back.

But her enthusiasm was greater than her size, and her willingness to take me until we were fully connected amazed me.

"You feel so good," I murmured into the skin of her neck, breathing in the ragged edges of her sigh. "Hot and wet and tight... *God, Six.*"

"Harder, Sean," she ordered urgently, but I shook my head.

"No, baby. Get used to me first. I don't want to hurt you."

"We don't have a lot of time," she argued, forcing her hips toward me.

With two easy hands, I grabbed at the smooth skin of her hips and pulled her to a stop. "We've got plenty. Just relax. Let me make you feel good."

She nodded then, easing the tension in her muscles and giving herself over to me.

I made an internal promise not to let her down and got to work. Teasing. Swirling. Curling my fingertips into the skin as each burning stroke ran higher up my spine.

With a thumb at her clit and my tongue on her neck, I worked them both in the same painstaking circles until her breathing turned tattered. One breath came out at double the pace of the next, and on the very end of each stroke, she had to gasp to take in enough air.

Sweat poured down my back and the windows turned opaque with the fog, but my mind was clear.

This was bliss, finding a rhythm inside her and keeping it until she came out of her skin. I'd find a way to do it as much as possible, for as long as she let me.

Her moan got higher at the end and her eyes closed, and all the tension in my back eased. She was close—I could feel it in the rhythmic pulse of her pussy, and I was free to let go.

Easy, steady, I pushed us higher and higher until both of our balloons burst.

Heat, fiery and delicious, spread through my body and forced me to close my eyes, and the strength of her cry pierced at the insides of my ears.

Tenuous and gentle, I gathered her in my arms and breathed her in, fighting to hold on to the high for as long as I could. Because when we went back out there, in front of the prying eyes of my teammates, I knew she wouldn't let me come within a foot of touching her.

Chapter Thirteen

Six

"**N**o!" I said, panic making my inflection go up at the end.

Sean paused, the ballistic noise had caught him so off guard, and I used the opportunity to fill him in with an explanation. "If we go back together, everyone will be wondering where we went, and I can't handle that kind of an inquisition."

"Six—"

"No. I will not waste that kind of interrogation on mediocre sex," I snapped. I didn't choke on the lie, but it was close.

Sean's eyes widened almost impossibly as he stuttered.

I was beginning to enjoy shaking his confidence. With his man-whore, cocky as fuck reputation, he kind of needed the reality check even if he really didn't need the practice, and I liked reaping the benefits—*pleasure-filled orgasms*—of making him try so hard.

Clearly, with each passing time we got together, he tried even harder. Harder to make me come faster, harder to make us do it together. He tried different things and invented brand-new techniques gleaned from, I knew, studying all of my bodily reactions. It was as fun as it was evil, and honestly, I didn't really feel all that bad about it.

Maybe I should have, but the orgasms. Good God, the orgasms.

Plus, I was all for female empowerment and it was about damn time women held some of the power.

I leaned forward quickly and touched my lips to his to ease the sting, and then I slid out the side door.

I left him behind and moved quickly across the parking lot, eager to put a great deal of distance between us, should we come under scrutiny upon our arrival.

I knew I didn't exactly look well put together, but my clothes were all in their proper places—I'd checked and double-checked—and my hair was always wild. My skin was too dark to really show a red glow, and I was good at talking my way out of things that were awkward. Hell, half my videos on my YouCam channel were just one-woman disasters as I tried to talk my way out of some kind of trouble I'd gotten myself involved in.

Firemen swarmed the crowd, and radios screeched as security placed everyone in a single file line.

I winced at what that could mean and hurried my pace when Cam spotted me in the distance. "There she is!" he shouted, turning the heads of everyone there. My step stuttered, but as security ran toward me, I tried not to be such a coward.

"What's up, fellas?" I asked casually as they closed in like SWAT. "Have I done something wrong?"

"Ma'am, we need you to confirm your name for us and join the line. It's protocol in an alarm situation like this to exit to the evacuation area and stay put until a proper count can be confirmed."

Yikes. Sounded like Sean was going to be in big trouble. Me? I wasn't worried. I wasn't an actual employee, and no one had given me a notebook with a written notice of instructions. I had the whole pretty and dumb thing working for me in a big way.

"Sorry, Officer." I batted my lashes. "I wasn't aware."

"I'm not an officer, ma'am. Just search and rescue. What's your name?"

Eek. "Oh. Sorry. Six Malone."

He pointed over his shoulder and sighed. "Go join the line."

I did as I was told and followed the indication of his hand, squeezing beside Teeny when he beckoned me. He was munching on a bag of carrots. "Hey, Teen."

"Hey, Li'l Shawty. Where you been?"

I shrugged and grappled for a second before landing on a tried and true female response. "I had to pee. Needed to find a private spot."

Teeny laughed and nodded. "You got one of them little fucking bladders, huh?"

I bobbed my head dramatically. Anything to get him to believe me. "Yeah. Something like that."

"You see Sean while you were out there?" Quinn asked from my other side, a suspicious brow raised. I didn't like the look of it, and I didn't trust Quinn. He was too smart, too invested, and just cunning enough to pull off following me without my knowledge.

He might have known the truth, but he also might have been trying to get me to admit something, so I went with the old standby of lying my ass off. I shook my head and gave my best face of plausible deniability. "Hmm. No. Haven't seen him. Is he missing too?"

"Yeah," Teeny confirmed, munching away on the orange crunch. "Mr. L's losing his shit too. You guys were the last of the count, and we can't go back into the building until we have the whole number. Funny as hell."

"Mr. L losing his shit is funny as hell?" I questioned.

"No," Teeny denied. "But thinking about him taking it out on Sean is."

As if on cue, Sean came jogging up to the group, a wide smile on his face. I winced and turned, trying not to look directly at him for fear I'd give my guilt away. But looking toward the pavement didn't take away my ability to listen. No, that sense was keen and willing, and I opened my ears to full volume.

"Phillips!" Mr. Lancaster yelled over the din of excitement as everyone noticed who'd finally arrived.

Teeny offered me a carrot, and I declined but asked, "Where'd you get those anyway?"

"Gotta be prepared, mama. I keep a stash in the office fridge right near the exit. You never know, you know?"

I laughed and discreetly turned my attention back to listening as Mr. Lancaster laid into Sean. "You know the process! We've done it enough in the last six goddamn months, haven't we? Jesus Christ. It's like starting all over again every time."

"I, uh, saw a…"

"You saw a what?" Wes questioned. "It better have been a mirage of Jesus Christ himself calling you home if you open your mouth to finish that statement."

"No, sir," Sean said as seriously as possible. "Not Jesus Christ."

I had to bite my lips, fully sucking them into my mouth, to keep from dying.

Wes's voice drifted out as Sean's eyes came to mine, and despite the distance, I could see everything he had to say as clear as though I'd heard it.

I might not have seen Jesus, but Six sure was calling out for him.

And I had. Several times and without prompting, I'd called out to Jesus Christ to help relieve me of my orgasm.

It wasn't religious, but it sure was something.

Fucking hell, I was in trouble.

Chapter Fourteen

Sean

At third and twelve with two minutes in the fourth quarter, I chewed on my mouthguard and tuned myself to the subtle feel of sweat rolling down my back.

It quieted my other senses and calmed the pounding of my heart to focus on something simple and finite, and fucking hell, the sun was strong. We'd been playing night games for the last few weeks, and the midday sun felt surprising. It was winter and relatively cold out, but the pressure of the game mixed with the pitch and swell of the overpacked Pittsburgh Stadium went a long way toward heating it up.

I scuffed at the grass and poised my muscles as Quinn clapped his hands twice before snapping the ball.

Hard and fast, I ran after my yard line and hit my mark, grunting as the defender got in my space from the beginning. I kept my hands to myself and focused on the ball, a perfect spiral of bliss headed for my mark courtesy of the best quarterback in the league and my best friend, Quinn Bailey.

With sure feet and fast hands, I beat my cover to the mark and came down with the ball, tucking it tight to my chest with one arm and boxing out the coverage with the other.

My feet were moving as soon as I hit the ground, and the howl of the wind and the crowd as I jumped over another defender and set my sights on the end zone was all the motivation I needed.

Twenty, fifteen, ten, five, I counted down as I approached the land of salvation. It was the dream-maker, the place of rest, and an insurmountable task all in one.

Any given game challenged you in different ways, and each play had its own set of rules.

You didn't get six points by magic. You had to take them.

I took mine, crossing the sweet benchmark of the goal line under a bone-crushing tackle, but coming up able to tell the tale. My muscles ached and my flesh was bruised, but overall, I just felt alive.

The pile of limbs of my team came down on me in a crush as the roar of the crowd went wild. We weren't the home team, but we weren't too far from home, and the welcome as winners at an away game was more than we deserved.

"Fuck yeah," Quinn congratulated, slapping me on the helmet and bringing me in for a game-style hug. Our heads met and our minds aligned, but that was all we needed from one another. We didn't linger, and we didn't grasp for more.

I'd done all I needed to for him by catching that ball, and he'd done his job by putting it where I had a chance.

Sam's congrats came in the form of a pat and a shove, and Cam bumped me with a shoulder. We headed for the sideline, but in the end, the sideline met us.

The crowd was a crush of familiar faces, and I pulled off my helmet in order to get a better look as every single one of the Mavericks' fans in Pittsburgh Stadium emptied wildly onto the field.

"Sean!" a reporter shouted, shoving a microphone in my face. "How's the win feel today?"

I put on my most professional hat and turned up the charm as I did the other part of my job. I'd thought originally that it began and ended on the field, but that was a naïve man's dream.

Professional football was more than that in so many ways, and the hours that went into the game itself were just the beginning.

We sold our soul to the Mavericks and everything the franchise had to offer. Luckily for us, we had an owner worthier than the devil.

"It feels great," I mused, pushing some of the sweat off my face with a towel handed in by a sideline attendant and slipping on a hat as they took the towel back. "All of our guys really hustled to give four quarters of great football, and that's what makes the difference in getting a team to the championship."

"Four quarters and a receiver like you," she teased. I smiled, eating it up for the camera.

"I'm just out here having the time of my life, Melissa. That's the perk of playing for a living."

She smiled at that and preened, hoping I'd notice her as a woman now that our interview was done. I gave her a wink and a smile, but no more. I was a manwhore, but I wasn't an idiot. I never fucked the press.

Three more interviews took place before I made it to the sideline and into the tunnel to head to the locker room.

I scoured the crowd looking for Six, knowing she'd been filming more material for one of the episodes during today's game, but she wasn't anywhere to be found.

"Earning your keep," Teeny teased as he passed me on the way to the locker room and body checked me. "Keep it up, fucker."

I laughed and flipped him off, teasing, "I never have a problem keeping it up."

A tiny throat cleared behind me, and I spun, startled.

Six was covering her mouth and laughing, and Teeny was damn near rolling on the ground. Apparently, he'd seen her approaching.

"I didn't see you there," I defended, and she rolled her eyes.

"Don't worry about me, Seany. I've seen the *hard* evidence."

Her innuendo caught me off guard, and my laugh came out choked—and turned into a snort.

"Did you just snort?" she squealed, absolutely gleeful.

I shook my head, but she kept at it ruthlessly.

"Man, I wish I hadn't sent Joe and Barry on their way. That's pure gold."

I shook my head and shrugged my shoulders, secure in the fact that she could tease me all she wanted, but she didn't, in fact, have the snort on film.

"I have a reputation to uphold," I told her.

She laughed. "I heard. A reputation for keeping it up, as it were."

The hall quieted slightly as people found their way, and I took the opportunity to step into her space. She glanced around herself and only settled into the feeling of her body against mine when she was certain the coast was clear.

But a tentative brush in the hall of a random away-game stadium wasn't enough for me.

It'd been almost a week since I'd seen her, and I wanted more. More skin, more kissing, more everything. And I wanted to do it without fear of discovery or a need to rush.

My voice was quiet as I made the offer. "Come back to the hotel with me?"

She smiled and shook her head, turning me down without shame. "No dice."

I paused for a moment as I pulled myself out of the rejection and turned all the disappointment into a last-ditch effort. "Are you sure?"

She laughed.

"Yeah," she remarked, the cruel, cruel woman. "But *you* can come back to the hotel *with me*."

A play on words and a play for power, and I accepted it for what it was—an invitation to spend time exploring everything Six Malone had to offer.

Chapter Fifteen

Six

Nestled into a gloriously naked Sean's side, I looked up from the bed and checked the time on the clock hanging above the television.

7:05 p.m., it read.

We'd only been inside my hotel room for all of two hours, but for the love of all that was right with the world, we'd made damn good use of our time.

After the game, he hadn't wasted a moment with a shower in the locker room.

Instead, the instant we'd discreetly slipped inside my room, we'd engaged in naked, shower-related activities…*together*.

Kissing. Licking. *Fucking*.

By the time the hot water had run cold, I'd come more times than my pleasure-gorged brain could count. And now, clean and sated and lying naked together beneath the sheets of my hotel bed, I savored the feel of being wrapped up in his arms.

With soft and lazy strokes, I traced imaginary swirls and circles across Sean's bare chest with my fingertip. Once the path of my index finger slid to his belly, the muscles of his abdomen tightened and rippled.

"Ticklish?" I questioned. "Or are you just trying to show off and flex your muscles for me?"

He chuckled softly. "We both know I don't need to flex, baby."

Point made. And I'd be a big fat fucking liar if I tried to deny the truth in his words.

Sean Phillips had the kind of body most men would kill for, hordes of women fantasized about, and young, impressionable teenage boys prayed like hell they'd develop.

Firm and toned in all of the right places, and delicious mocha-colored skin to boot, he ticked off all the hot guy checkboxes. And considering I hadn't even mentioned anything about his fan-fucking-tastic cock, that said a lot.

And, apparently, it was the kind of body that made my brain short-circuit and go back on my word. Sean Phillips started out as the one man I'd sworn off, yet here I was. Naked. In bed with him. *Again.*

"Just admit it," he whispered into my ear. "You love fucking me."

"Aw, is someone feeling a little insecure?" I asked and rested my chin on his chest to meet his gaze. "Do you need me to boost your already huge ego?"

He smirked and moved his fingers to the skin of my ass. Cupping and squeezing and kneading my curves with a big, strong hand. "I'm not asking for an ego boost. I'm asking you to state the facts," he retorted and sent a sexy little wink my way.

"And what exactly are the facts?"

"You. Love. Fucking. Me," he answered.

"And what about you?" I questioned and pinched his right nipple...*hard.*

"Ow! Fuck!" He chuckled and gently swatted my hand away from his chest. "What do you mean, *what about me*?"

"If I supposedly *love* fucking you, what are *your facts* in this scenario?"

"The same as you."

I raised a challenging brow, and he didn't hesitate to respond. With his hands gripping my hips, he pulled me on top of his big, strong body and adjusted me until we were nose-to-nose. "Your pussy was made to take my cock," he whispered, and his lips just barely brushed mine. "And my cock sure as fuck doesn't mind the feel of your pussy."

One kiss. Two kisses.

"I want to keep fucking you."

Three kisses. Four kisses.

"We're both having fun, and we both know we should keep fucking until we aren't anymore."

He took my mouth in a deep, heady kiss, and by the time he pulled away, his cock was hard and I throbbed between my legs. Hell, my hips were already moving against him like they had a mind of their own.

Sean's gaze locked with mine, and a self-satisfied smile lifted the corners of his lips. "So, yeah, those are my facts."

He was so fucking cocky. But good God, he backed it all up.

A master of the female body, Sean knew all of the right places to kiss me. Touch me. Lick me. Fuck me.

If I was being completely honest with myself, sex with him was the best sex I'd ever had in my twenty-five years of existence. Not that he needed to know that. If his ego got any bigger, it'd need its own jersey and shoulder pads just so he could play on the field.

It was no wonder, though, that he'd earned the reputation of being Mr. Manwhore.

It was also no wonder his playboy reputation had no effect on the supply of women ready and waiting to experience a night between the sheets with him.

How many women are there waiting in the wings, ready to score a night with him?

Hundreds? Thousands?

When my brain started hitting seven-digit numbers, my chest

tightened up with discomfort, and I had to force a calming breath in and out of my lungs to ease the pain.

No matter how much I wished I could deny it, it bothered me.

Which was ridiculous, I knew.

We weren't dating. We weren't in a relationship.

Hell, we weren't anything besides two people who appeared to enjoy fucking each other.

I couldn't and wouldn't expect Sean to be committed and monogamous, and he shouldn't expect those things from me either.

We were purely having fun together. Enjoying each other's company.

And don't forget having a lot of O-worthy, amazing sex.

Yeah. That too.

"Well, those are…*interesting* facts," I finally said and pushed a small smile to my lips. "Got any other facts you think I should be aware of?"

"Hmm…" He paused and grinned down at me. "Let's see…the very first time I laid eyes on you, I was fucking mesmerized. It was want at first sight."

"Yeah." I snorted. "I do recall you telling a few of the guys how I *wouldn't be able to resist you.*"

His lips turned down into a little frown. "I was a dick."

"Ya think?" I questioned on a giggle. "You might as well have just whipped your penis out and come all over me."

He smirked. "In my defense, I was just trying to stake my claim. Also in my defense, that actually sounds pretty good right now."

"*Your* claim?" I questioned and moved my fingers across his chest to pinch his left nipple. But he was too quick, grabbing my wrist and smiling down at me victoriously.

"I didn't want anyone else to have you," he added and kissed the top of my forehead. "But I'm pretty sure you got me back for being a macho asshole. More than once, actually."

"I have no idea what you're talking about." I feigned innocence with a slight furrow of my brow.

"Oh, so you don't remember pretending to forget about me on that first day? Even acting like you didn't know who I was when I approached you?"

I shook my head and bit my lip to hide my smile.

"What about the social media training?" he asked, and amusement brightened his eyes. "You don't remember that?"

I pretended to mull it over, but eventually, I responded with, "Nope. I don't remember any of that."

He pinched my ass.

"Ow! Shit!" I squealed and squirmed, but he just smirked down at me.

"That's what liars get," he said, and his voice was all raspy and sexy. "Do you know what happens when liars keep lying?"

"What?"

"Those pinches turn to spankings, and if the lies keep flowing, little liars get fucked...*hard*."

Well, hot damn, who needed the truth? Sure as fuck not me.

"You dirty little girl," he whispered. "You're tempted to keep poking the bear with lies until he breaks and fucks your brains out."

"I am not."

"Yeah, you are," he said through a soft, knowing chuckle. "It's written all over your pretty face."

"Well, next time, maybe don't make your threats sound so appealing." I waggled my eyebrows, and he grinned before pressing a soft kiss to my nose.

"So...what about you?" he asked. "Do *you* have any interesting facts to tell me?"

"Not really." I shrugged. "I mean, that first day I came to the stadium to meet the team, I had an impromptu meet-and-greet with most of the team's dicks first." I shrugged again. "But other than that, no, nothing too interesting."

"I'm sorry...*what*?" His brow furrowed in confusion once he processed my words. "You met the team's dicks...?"

"It was all very informal, but yeah." I nodded and bit my lip to hide my laughter. "Ironically, I actually met your cock before I met you."

"You do realize how fucking crazy this sounds, right?" A shocked laugh bubbled up from his lungs. "How about a little context?"

"Before I tell you, you have to promise not to tell a single soul."

He nodded. "You have my word."

"Well…that first day…when I met the team…I kind of accidentally walked into the back entrance of the locker room instead of going to the auditorium."

"Seriously?"

I nodded. "Seriously."

"Did anyone see you?"

"No, thank God."

"Wait…so you mean to tell me you were just peeping in our locker room, staring at everyone's dick?"

"It was an accident!" I exclaimed, and his smile grew wide and amused. "And I didn't see *everyone's* dick. Just a few. Mostly yours."

"You were staring at my cock?" he questioned. "You really are a dirty little girl," he said and punctuated that statement by grinding that glorious hard shaft of his against me. "A sexy little voyeur… *Fuck*, that turns me on."

I giggled at his words, but those giggles quickly turned to moans when the head of his cock kept sliding across where I was already wet and aroused. He did it over and over again until I throbbed and ached and my hips urged him to push inside of me.

"I need inside of you again, baby," he whispered against my mouth. "Let me feel that tight little cunt wrapped around my cock."

I whimpered. "Yes."

Quick as a whip, he grabbed a condom from the top of the nightstand and had it wrapped around his shaft.

The instant he pushed himself inside of me, a deep, raw, needy moan escaped my lips.

"Ride me, baby," he whispered, and I obeyed.

Lifting myself up and keeping my hips straddled over his cock, I braced my hands on his chest and took control.

Up and down, circling my hips, then up and down again, I worked his cock.

"God, Six, you drive me fucking wild," he said through gritted teeth. "So beautiful. So sexy. So. Fucking. Perfect." He gripped my hips and guided my movements until we both became too impatient.

With a twist and a turn, Sean flipped me onto my back and proceeded to fuck me.

Like, *really* fuck me.

He drove in and out of me with the deepest of strokes, and hell if I didn't love every single second of it.

The speed, the rhythm, the feel of it all was too much. Too good. Too *everything*.

It didn't take long.

I came *hard*. And my pussy milked his cock as he buried himself to the hilt and found his release.

God, he was dangerous.

When it came to Sean Phillips, I felt like I was playing with fire.

Chapter Sixteen

Sean

"What time is it?" Six asked, and I loved the raspy, sex-drained tone of her voice.

Her naked, soft as silk body was curled up beside me, her head resting on my shoulder. She was so perfectly close, I could feel the soft thump-thump of her heart vibrate against my skin.

We'd been at each other ever since we'd tumbled inside her hotel room. And fuck if it hadn't been the best damn sex I'd ever engaged in.

"A little after eight," I said after a quick glance at the clock.

Normally, I'd be out celebrating our big win against Pittsburgh with the guys, but I couldn't have cared less about my usual postgame routine.

I was one hundred percent fully invested in this new one. With Six.

Hell, I was mentally plotting ways to convince her we needed to make this a tradition. Create by-laws. Sign oaths in blood to keep doing this until the end of time.

Jesus. Blood oaths? What's wrong with me?

I studied Six's face a little harder, trying to see exactly what was making me think so crazy.

Soft, creamy, brown skin and wide, honest eyes, she stared at me unabashedly, and my heart did a karate kick in my chest.

Most women played coy, downturning their eyes and looking up through long, fake lashes. Six owned her actions completely.

Is it because she's so different? Is that why I can't stop thinking about her?

"God," she muttered. "I feel like you've fucked me stupid."

That spurred a laugh from my lungs and a victorious grin on my lips.

"God isn't here, baby. Just Sean."

She snorted and rolled her eyes. "It's not funny," she said and gently kicked her foot against my leg. "I feel like I've lost brain cells. Important brain cells, at that." She sat up and rested her back against the headboard.

But before I could respond, she was adding to her diatribe.

"I'm also hungry," she said as she scrubbed a hand over her eyes. "And I'm pretty sure we need to do something else besides have sex, or I'll end up bowlegged and need to rent a wheelchair tomorrow."

"Damn, you're a bossy little thing." Another chuckle left my lips. "What exactly do you have in mind?"

"I don't know…just…" She sighed and then sighed again. "Feed me and tell me I'm pretty and then feed me some more."

I sat up on the side of the bed, my shoulders resting against the headboard, and I locked my gaze with hers. "You're pretty," I whispered and pressed a soft kiss to her lips. "The most uniquely beautiful woman I've ever seen."

She scowled, but I ignored it, because fuck, she *was* the most uniquely beautiful woman I'd ever seen. The truth hit me straight in the chest with a sharp pain.

And it wasn't just her pretty face or mesmerizing eyes or sexy little body.

It was *her*. Her mind. Her humor. Her words. Every single piece that made up the quirky, gorgeous, wild little creature sitting beside me was different—better—than I'd ever encountered.

"Now, could you be a little more specific about the *feed me* part?" I grinned at her over my shoulder. "Any food preferences?"

"Anything," she whined, and her full lips pushed out into a little pout. "Everything. Just fucking feed me food before I waste away from too much sex and starvation."

"So…the whole room service menu?"

"That'd be a good start," she said, and her words held more sass and attitude than a sixteen-year-old girl.

Any other woman acting like this probably would have driven me fucking crazy, but not her. Grumpy, demanding Six, in my eyes, was fucking adorable.

"Any other special requests?" I questioned as I pushed to my feet to grab the hotel's menu off the coffee table in front of the small lavender sofa.

"If you could find a way to make watching *Game of Thrones* possible, that'd be perfect."

"So, eat room service in bed and watch *Game of Thrones*?"

"Oh my God!" Her eyes widened with excitement. "Yes! All the yesses!" She clapped her hands together briefly before sliding back down onto the bed and curling up beneath the blankets. "Tell me you love *Game of Thrones* as much as I do."

"I'd love it even more if they'd get season eight finished and released," I said as I opened up the room service menu and started browsing the dinner options.

"Wait…" She paused and sat herself back up. "You've seen all of the episodes?"

"Yeah," I said and lifted my gaze to hers. "You haven't?"

She shook her head. "The only ones I've seen were the ones we watched at Martinez's house."

"No shit?" I questioned. "Well, you're definitely missing out, then."

"Well, that sucks," she muttered. "Now we're going to have to find something else to watch."

I raised a confused brow. "Why?"

"Because you've already seen them all."

"So?" I said. "I'll rewatch them with you."

Her big brown eyes went wide with surprise, and it made my chest ache.

It might have seemed small, but I didn't like that she might think I was that big of a selfish bastard that I wouldn't even rewatch episodes of a TV series with her. I mean, I knew I was known for being a cocky son of a bitch, but that didn't mean I was thoughtless, too.

"We're sticking to the original game plan, baby," I said and forced a smile to my lips. "*Game of Thrones* and room service."

"That sounds perfect." I could've gotten a suntan beneath her bright and beautiful responding smile. As an African-American man, that was really saying something.

I browsed the room service menu once more before walking over to the hotel phone on the nightstand and picking up the receiver. But just before I could hit the speed dial button for the restaurant, the sound of my phone ringing filled my ears.

"Is that yours?" Six asked, and I nodded, eyes searching for the damn thing.

"Shit. Yeah," I muttered. I hung up the hotel phone and started scouring the room for my cell.

"Do you remember where you put it?" she asked from the bed, and instantly, a flash of memories filled my head.

Six and me tumbling into her hotel room.

Kissing. Touching. Clawing greedily at one another.

Stumbling into the bathroom as we damn near tore each other's clothes off.

Fucking in the shower... Aha! The shower.

With four long strides, I walked across the room until I reached where my Mavericks sweats lay haphazardly on the tile floor of the bathroom.

Pulling my phone out of the side pocket, I checked the screen.

Incoming Call: Cassie.

My sister.

But the call ended just before I had the opportunity to answer it.

And the five missed calls and five unread messages from her proved this wasn't the first time she'd tried to reach me.

Damn, how had I not heard her calls or texts?

The reason is currently lying naked between the sheets of the bed.

I grinned at that thought and scrolled through Cassie's texts.

Cassie: Sean? Where are you? Call me back.

Cassie: SEAN. CALL ME BACK PLEASE. This is your amazing, gorgeous, beautiful sister Cassie, by the way. Just in case you forgot about my existence because YOU WON'T ANSWER MY FLUFFING CALLS.

Cassie: Sean. You. Mother. Fluffer. Answer. My. Calls.

Cassie: I will murder you in your sleep.

Cassie: Okay. I take that back. No murder. I need someone to watch these kids from time to time, and you're our top choice. But that's not why I'm calling, and I will fluffing hurt you if you don't call me back. CALL ME BACK. CALL ME BACK. FLUFFING CALL ME BACK!

With one tap to her contact, I did as requested, and she answered on the first ring.

"What the fluffing fluff, Sean?" she said by way of greeting. "I've been trying to get ahold of you for, like, an hour!"

Obviously, I'd been so lost in Six I hadn't even heard my goddamn phone ring.

That's a fucking first.

"Sorry. I had it on a silent," I lied by way of avoiding her inquisition. "What's going on?" I asked. "Everything okay?"

"We're here."

"Here?" I questioned and furrowed my brow. "Where is here?"

"In fluffing Pittsburgh," she retorted, and my brother-in-law Thatch's voice boomed in the background. "Fantastic game, dude!"

"You guys were at the game?" I asked. "Why didn't you tell me you were coming?"

Cassie sighed. "Because we decided last minute, and my big-ass ogre of a husband thought it would be a grand idea to drive instead of fly."

"Makes sense considering it's not that far of a drive from NYC. It's what, like, four or five hours?"

"See!" Thatch shouted from the background. "Even Sean understands!"

"Well, Sean didn't have to sit in a car with your giant fucking ass listening to you sing along to Britney Spears!" Cassie yelled back at him.

"Don't you dare start talking blasphemous things about Britney!" Thatch shouted back.

Cassie snorted. "Pretty sure the internet is filled with a shitload of blasphemous shit about 2007 Britney."

"How dare you bring up 2007?" Thatch retorted in outrage. "It was a bad year. She was going through some serious shit."

Jesus Christ. I needed to change the subject and fast before I just ended up a third wheel in their verbal tug of war.

"So…uh…are you guys still in Pittsburgh?"

"Yep," Cassie responded. "We're at your hotel, and we want to grab some dinner."

"Dinner?" I repeated, and my gaze locked with Six's. She was still gloriously naked and sitting on the bed. "And you're at my hotel? Like, right now?"

Fucking hell, my sister had the absolute worst timing in the world.

"Yes, Sean. I want *dinner*, and I'm at your fluffing *hotel*."

Cassie's voice muffled slightly—but not fully—as she stopped speaking into the phone and started talking to Thatch. "God, I think he took too many hits to the head, T. He's having trouble with simple words."

I rolled my eyes. "I didn't take any hits to the head, Cass. And I can sure as fuck hear these words just fine."

"I think he heard me," she said to Thatch, and the big fucker laughed, commenting, "You think, honey?"

"Whatever," my sister dismissed quickly, never one to wallow in embarrassment. "Since I had to drive a million hours in the car with Thatch singing 'Hit Me Baby One More Time,' you're going to fluffing eat dinner with me."

I sighed internally.

"What room are you in?" she asked. "We'll come up."

"I…I'm not in my room."

"Where are you?" she asked, completely oblivious. "We'll meet up with you."

"I'm at the hotel, but I'm not in my room."

"You're…" She paused. "Ohh…you're in someone *else's* room…"

"Something like that."

"So, you're busy fucking someone."

I grimaced. "Jesus, Cassie."

"Don't act like such a prude. Everyone in the whole fluffing world knows you're quite the little manwhore."

Manwhore. There was that fucking nickname again.

And for the first time in pretty much forever, I kind of hated the fact that my reputation had that moniker attached to it.

Of course, my sister didn't think of it in the same way someone else might, musing, "I'm hoping my little brats are manwhores too. Better than me having to wash basket loads of crusty socks."

Thatch's laughter boomed. "Little sperm factories like their daddy," he added proudly.

Jesus. I had to cut this off at the pass.

"Just sit tight in the lobby," I said. "Give me, like, fifteen minutes, and I'll meet you guys down there. We can just eat at the hotel restaurant."

"Okay. See ya soon," she said, and just as I hit end on the call, she added, "Oh, and bring your lady friend slash fuck buddy along!"

My crazy, blunt as fuck sister, ladies and gentlemen.

"Everything okay?" Six asked, and I nodded.

Instantly, as I stared down at her looking all cute and sexy in the hotel bed, I decided I wanted her to come with me. Not out of obligation or because I felt like I had to, but because I just loved spending time with her.

In everything she did, in every word she said, Six never failed to be a good time.

She just…made everything fun. *Better.*

"Yeah, but there's going to be a change in plans," I updated. "We're going to have dinner with my sister and brother-in-law in the hotel restaurant."

Her eyes popped wide as saucers. "Dinner? With your family?"

"No, not my whole family. Just my sister and her husband."

"Which would equal *your fucking family*!" she exclaimed. "I can't meet your family right now. Look at me," she added and glanced down at her sheet-covered body. "I'm a freaking mess, Sean."

"It's just dinner, Six. And it's not the whole family. Trust me, Diane and Greg are in Portland." I offered a reassuring smile. "And, anyway, you said you were starving…"

"Starving for *room service*," she retorted, and I just grinned. "Diane and Greg?"

"My parents."

Her eyes bugged out at the mention of the p-word, and I laughed. "Who are *not* here, so stop freaking out."

"Do you seriously want to bring me along to dinner with your sister?" she asked, and I didn't miss the weight of her words.

"Yes," I responded immediately, gaze locked with hers. "I want you there."

She stared at me, her eyes searching mine.

"Six, baby, just go ahead and come to terms with the fact that I'm not going to take no for an answer…" I paused and glanced at the time on my phone. "Oh, and you have about ten minutes left to get ready."

"Ten minutes!" she shrieked and hopped off the bed. "Oh my God!"

"Just throw on some jeans and a shirt, and you'll be good to go."

Six sighed but immediately started rummaging through her suitcase.

And I headed back toward the bathroom to toss my after-game sweats back on.

"Hey, Sean?" she called from the other side of the room.

"Yeah?"

"Remind me later tonight I need to strangle you."

I laughed and smiled at that.

Remind me later tonight.

That meant she'd already planned on spending the entire night with me.

Yeah. I'd remind her, all right. Most likely, when my cock was buried ten inches deep inside of her.

Chapter Seventeen

Six

"**A**re you sure about this?" I whispered to Sean as we waited for the elevator.

He just grinned. The bastard.

"This isn't funny," I said, my voice growing loud enough to catch the attention of the older, sixtysomething couple standing a few feet away from us. "I mean..." I paused and glanced down at my clothes with a sigh. "I'm hardly dressed to impress."

The woman couldn't *not* stare at my clothes after that. Her gaze moved down my body, and her lips pushed out into a disapproving frown once she saw my shirt. She smacked her lips together, the way only old ladies with disappointment do, and shook her head as she brought her eyes back to the elevator doors.

Cool it, lady, I shouted internally. *I'm wearing this out of desperation.*

"Are you hearing anything I'm saying right now?" I asked Sean and looked up at him with narrowed eyes.

"I'm hearing you, baby. Loud and clear," he said and shot a little wink in my direction. "But you have nothing to worry about."

I scowled at that. Nothing to worry about. I looked down at my outfit one more time. Yoga pants and a freaking T-shirt with a doodle of a cat holding up two middle fingers and the words *fluff you, you fluffin' fluff* written on it.

The judgy old lady's reaction was correct.

Dressed to impress? Not likely.

I cursed myself for thinking it was a victory to travel to Pittsburgh with just a carry-on. I'd brought only the essentials. No backup outfits. Only a goddamn shirt with a cat on it and yoga pants that had seen better days.

"Are you sure this is a good idea?" I asked, cowardly pointing out the pink elephant in the room. Meeting his sister and brother-in-law seemed a bit odd considering we weren't in a relationship. We weren't even dating, really. I didn't know what we were, but I knew it wasn't serious. Sean Phillips didn't do serious. He did friends with benefits, fuck buddies, one-night stands, but serious? I honestly doubted that word was in his vocabulary.

"I think it's a fantastic idea."

"What in the hell are you going to introduce me as?" I questioned, and he lifted one thick, muscular shoulder up into a shrug.

"What do you think I should introduce you as?"

"Nuh-uh." I tapped his big bicep with my index finger. "Do not try to turn this around on me. I asked you first."

"You have nothing to worry about." He offered a toothy grin. "Thatch and Cassie aren't the type to get too caught up in labels. Hell, they started off their relationship pranking each other, and Cassie pretty much hated Thatch."

I figured this was his typical brush-off when any woman asked him to put a label on what they were. I couldn't really blame him, though. It's not like I had a label for us either.

That old lady smacked her lips together again, and I glanced around Sean to see her staring right at us, her arms crossed over her chest. Her husband was still oblivious, but I had a feeling it was the hearing aids shoved inside his big ears more than anything else.

This old bat really needed a lesson in humility.

Now, that's an idea…

"I think you should just be honest, baby," I cooed, and Sean's brow furrowed.

"Be honest?"

"Yeah," I said in a fake foreign accent that sounded more Eastern European than anything else. I let my voice carry a little too far considering we were standing right beside each other. "I think you should just tell your sister what you are to me. My American mail-order groom."

The old lady gasped, and I had to swallow my smile.

Sean caught on quickly, glancing over his shoulder to find our audience.

"Nice one," he muttered, and I just grinned wider.

"I'm so glad I found you on the interwebs, baby. And I'm so glad you accepted my hand in marriage. And to think, I almost didn't send that email," I said, keeping up the fake accent. I stood up on my tippy-toes to wrap an arm around his shoulder and stare deep into his eyes. "I'm so happy I did. These last twenty-four hours have been the best in my life. Especially…" I dropped my voice to a whisper, but it was a fucking loud whisper. "All of the s-e-x."

Another gasp from the old lady and I had to bite my lip to fight my laughter.

"We are going to be so happy together when we go back to my homeland. You're going to be the happiest husband in all the lands. Our village is small, but my father is very rich. He has the biggest hut, and he will shower you with gifts of gold and goats and wine."

"Gold *and* goats?" he asked, playing right along with me.

I nodded. "And wine. Lots and lots of wine."

I pressed a soft kiss to his cheek. "I can't believe you were a virgin," I added quietly, but don't worry, my voice was still loud for my audience. "And oh my gosh, my family and our village will be so glad to hear you have a big penis. That is very important to them."

Sean nearly choked on his own saliva, but that only fueled me further.

"Although, they will be a little disappointed that you're circumcised. You'll probably get fewer goats because of that."

I pressed a soft kiss to his cheek again, and he looked down at me with a wide grin. He wrapped an arm around my back and playfully pinched my ass.

"Remind me later to pay you back for that," he whispered discreetly into my ear.

I quirked a brow. "Pay back?"

"Yeah." He nodded and leaned in real close to add, "I'm going to show you exactly what this *big, circumcised cock* is capable of after dinner."

Oh boy.

The elevator dinged its arrival, and Sean pressed a gentle hand to the small of my back and led me inside.

And on the ride down, I continued to make a show out of whispering things about our fake nuptials—the ceremony in the river, the penis exam he'll have to undergo before the wedding, and a whole bunch of other shit that mostly revolved around goats.

By the time we reached the lobby level, the older couple practically had to pick their jaws up off the floor just to exit the elevator.

"You're a little minx," he said once the old lady and her husband were out of earshot. "That woman is probably going to pull me aside and ask me if I feel safe or need her to contact the authorities." He pinched my ass again, and a half giggle, half groan escaped my lips as I rubbed at the smarting skin.

I retaliated with a discreet elbow into his abdomen.

"Ow, fuck," he muttered through soft chuckles. "For a tiny person, you sure pack some power."

A big smile covered my lips. "Serves you right."

He wrapped a big, strong arm around my shoulder and started to lead us toward the hotel dining room. "Next time," he whispered, "You'll be the mail-order bride."

I shook my head and glanced up at him. "Nuh-uh. You can't just switch up a bit that I created. You have to come up with your own."

He chuckled softly. "Come on, you little shit stirrer, let me introduce you to my sister."

Like a rock dropped into my stomach, anxiety felt heavy in my gut.

Meeting his sister and brother-in-law felt like a pretty big fucking step for two people who didn't even know what they were. But I did my best to push past the discomfort and follow his lead.

I mean, what was the worst that could happen?

You could meet his family and love his family and start falling for the one guy you should never fall for.

Jesus. I shook those crazy thoughts out of my mind and forced a smile to my face as Sean led us toward the table where his sister and brother-in-law sat.

"Sean!" His sister hopped up from her seat and wrapped her arms around her brother. "I should kick you in the fluffing balls for ignoring my text messages, but I'll let it slide because I've missed you, you asshole."

He chuckled and disentangled himself from his sister. "Give me a break, Cass. I've been a little busy."

A mischievous grin crossed her lips as her gaze moved to me. "I can see that."

I felt oddly calm underneath her scrutiny. It was calculated and clever, but it wasn't completely unwelcoming either.

Besides that, I couldn't miss the stark contrast between Sean and his extremely beautiful sister. Where she was creamy white skin, he was smooth mocha. But I'd done my research and already knew Sean was actually adopted. Although there were no familial traits in common between the two, it was obvious they shared a close bond.

Cassie stepped forward and stuck out a hand for me to shake. I took her hand—and the opportunity of being up close to study her further.

Her features were exaggerated and bold, and the blue of her eyes was startling. Smooth curves and firm lines, her body was unbelievable. And holy shit, *is she not wearing a bra?*

"Hell of a game," a voice boomed, interrupting our introduction. I looked *up, up, up* to find a giant of a man towering over us, a wide, toothy grin on his lips. "That catch you made in the fourth made ESPN's top ten."

"No shit?" Sean said with a smile, and a half bro-shake, half hug commenced between the two.

"And who is this beauty?" the incredibly good-looking giant asked, and his wife nodded.

"That's exactly what I'm wondering."

"Cassie, Thatch, this is Six," Sean introduced us, and I reached out to take Thatch's hand and complete the greeting ritual.

"It's so nice to meet you."

His sister's smile stayed mischievous as she glanced discreetly at her husband. They both shared some sort of secret look before Thatch gestured for us to sit down.

"I hope you don't mind, but I went ahead and ordered for everyone because Cassie was getting hangry."

Sean chuckled at that and helped me into my chair.

"And what did you order?"

"A little bit of this. A little bit of that." Thatch shrugged, and Cassie smirked.

"He pretty much ordered everything off the menu," she offered, and her eyes met mine. "I hope you're hungry, Six."

I nodded. "I can definitely eat."

"Six and I were just about to order room service right before you called," Sean said and wrapped an easy arm around the back of my chair. "She was also having quite the hangry moment."

That's because three hours of sex would make anyone starved.

I rolled my eyes, but I kept my thoughts to myself.

"So, Six," Cassie said from the across the table. "Besides Sean, we have another mutual friend."

"Oh, really?"

"Uh-huh." She nodded. "Georgia Brooks."

"Oh my gosh, I love her! And I owe her so much. She's pretty much changed my life because of this huge opportunity with the Mavericks."

"She's one of the best," Cassie responded. "But she took a chance on you for a reason. Your vlogs are hilarious. Both Thatch and I are huge fans."

"Really? You know who I am?" My brow rose. When they'd introduced themselves, they'd given absolutely no indication that they knew anything about me.

"Oh. Yeah," she said, waving an unbothered hand in front of her face. "We just wanted Sean to feel uncomfortable by having to actually introduce you."

Sean's glare was only minimally serious.

"Of course, the fucker didn't even stutter or anything. It was a little disappointing, to be honest."

Cassie's smile smoothed over Thatch's words as she brought the conversation back around to the beginning. "Anyway. We can't wait to see what you're about to do with this Mavericks series. I'm sure it's going to be fantastic."

"God, I really hope so," I answered truthfully. No doubt I was working my ass off on this series, but it was a huge deal. And it was hard to push insecurities out the door with something that meant this much and had so much hype built around it.

She leaned forward and rested her elbows on the table. "So, what are you two?" she asked, glancing between Sean and me. "Friends? Fucking? Dating?"

Sean nearly choked on his water. "Jesus, Cass."

"What? It's an honest question." She just shrugged. "And don't think I haven't picked up on the fact that my manwhore brother is actually introducing me to one of his *lady friends*. Pretty sure that's never happened."

"Sure, it has," Sean muttered, and both she and her husband shook their heads.

"Sorry, dude," Thatch said through a chuckle. "I've been around for a while now, and yeah, it's never happened."

Sean glanced at me and then back at his sister.

He obviously wasn't sure how to answer her question.

So, I did what I did best and chimed in with my brand of humor and sarcasm.

"Oh, we're definitely not dating. I'm just mentoring him."

"Mentoring him?" Cassie asked, and I nodded.

"Yeah, I'm his sex mentor," I explained with a straight face. "We've got a lot of work ahead of us, but so far, he's shown great progress."

"Jesus Christ," Sean muttered, but both his sister and brother-in-law had already caught on to my lie.

Thatch slapped one big hand on the table and burst out into laughter.

And Cassie, well, her smile couldn't have gotten any bigger.

"You're such a little troublemaker." Sean's lips crested up in hilarity as he leaned into me. His gaze was soft and affectionate, and I felt myself melting helplessly into it. "No fucking wonder you and my sister are getting along so easily."

"Why?" I asked delicately, pretending to be a lady for once. "Your sister doesn't seem like a menace."

His laughter was soul-shaking, rolling through my body in delicious waves, and I felt myself sink. Into the chair, into him—into oblivion.

God, I like him so much.

"Oh yeah, T," Cassie said on a near whisper and looked at her husband. "You're totally going to lose this bet."

"Wait… What bet?" Sean asked, pulled rudely from the trance of my beauty, and Cassie just shrugged.

"It's none of your business."

"Because it's about me."

She shrugged again. "Maybe. Maybe not."

"You're such a pain in my ass," Sean muttered. Cassie's grin didn't wane, but her eyes did come to me. They were sweetness and mischief all wrapped up in one, and a shiver ran up my spine. I wasn't one to feel intimidated, but as a woman of sarcasm and wit, I had a feeling I had a lot to learn at the comedic altar of Cassie Phillips.

"Preaching to the choir, dude," Thatch chimed in. "She's been a pain in my ass since the day I met her crazy ass."

"Yeah, but you love my crazy," she said with a wink, and then proceeded to reach out and twist her husband's nipple through the material of his shirt.

"Ow, fuck," he muttered. "You're an evil fluffing woman, Cassie Kelly."

She laughed and then pointed across the table toward my T-shirt. "Speaking of *fluffing*, I *need* to know where you got that shirt. I fluffing yell at my fluffing kids all the fluffing time, and my voice is tired. I feel like maybe, with that shirt, they'd get the message subliminally."

"It was just some random shop online." I smiled. "But I can definitely get the link for you. And, kids?" I asked.

Cassie's eyes glazed over as she waved me off. "Two little boys. Light of my lives and my ticket to prison all in one if they don't stop whipping out their little cocks like they're some kind of prized gems and pissing everywhere but inside the fluffing toilet."

A bark of a laugh bubbled out of me without prompting. Cassie and Thatch smiled.

"It's genetics," Thatch touted proudly. "I've got a superior amount of testosterone."

Sean's smile pulled my gaze, the light in his eyes dancing. I looked to his sister and brother-in-law briefly and then back again, and everything *clicked*.

Sean's cocksure attitude. His easy laughs and smiles. The way he made everyone feel at ease around him.

He had a team other than the Mavericks behind him, and they were built just like him.

Mesmerizing.

Without hesitation, Cassie pulled out her cell phone and proceeded to demand that we exchange phone numbers.

So, we did.

Sean's sister and me.

And then, Thatch joined in, and by the time three servers brought all ten plates of food that had been ordered for our table, I had everyone's phone number *but* Sean's.

The mere ridiculousness of it made me giggle.

But it lasted all of two seconds.

While Cassie and Thatch argued over who got to eat the rib eye, Sean snagged my phone out of my hands and added his number to my contacts. Then he sent himself a text before handing it back to me.

I glanced down at the screen and read the text he'd messaged himself from my phone.

Me: I love your big cock. Put it inside me again after dinner? Pretty please with whipped cream and my cherry-flavored pussy on top?

Then my phone vibrated with a message.

Sean: Okay, baby. But only because you asked so nicely.

I couldn't not laugh at that.

Nor could I really be upset.

Because, yeah, more sex with Sean? *Count me in.*

Chapter Eighteen

Sean

Inside the car I'd borrowed to drive Six to the airport, we'd sat idling in front of the entrance for a good twenty minutes, mostly due to her stubbornness.

I wanted to walk her in.

But she wasn't a fan of that plan.

"Let me come in with you," I begged for the fortieth time since we'd left the hotel that morning. The team bus would be coming in just under two hours to bring us back here, to the private plane entrance to fly home ourselves, but I'd been nearly apoplectic at the idea of putting Six in a cab and sending her on her way by herself.

She was headed home, back to California for a week, and the idea of not seeing her until she met us in Dallas for the next game was…unsettling.

It'd actually taken a special favor from the hotel's concierge—a big fan, thankfully—to acquire a car to bring her myself.

If the picture on the backside of the visor was anything to go by, I was pretty sure he'd given me his personal vehicle.

"No way."

"Six—"

"Sean, no." She cut me off, turning her small body in the tan leather seat to face me. Her eyes were serious, something rare for Six, as she appealed to my rational side earnestly. "Are you forgetting who you are?"

"Pretty sure *I* know exactly who I am," I argued, turning her words against her. I didn't want to think about all the other stupid shit. To me, I was Sean Phillips, brother to Cassie and son to Greg and Diane.

Six rolled her eyes. "To the public, Sean. You're one of the Mavericks' best players. You're utterly recognizable around here."

I couldn't help but smile at her words of praise. Six was never easy on me, and she rarely acknowledged me as anything other than an asshole. Getting a little peek into a side of secret admiration excited me. "I am, huh?"

"Oh God," she sighed with a laugh. "Does your ego ever stop needing to be stroked?"

I waggled my eyebrows, and a wayward hand reached out to love on the meat of her thigh. It was all its decision, though, not mine, and I would hold strongly to my stance in a court of law. "Stroking is *always* good."

"I walked right into that one," she admitted, turning to look at the busy sidewalk right outside her window. Pittsburgh airport wasn't as bad as my home airport, Newark International, a major hub in a populated state, but it wasn't a slouch either. There was an uncomfortable amount of people, and all of the crosswalks bustled with hordes of humanity each time the light switched over to allow for pedestrians.

The police patrolled the drop-off and pickup stations, and I could guarantee any vehicle that came in or out of here was on a rigorous amount of security film. Hank, the concierge, must have had pretty high confidence that I wouldn't get into too much trouble.

I shrugged. "Yep. Pretty much. Now, let me come in with you and help you from walking into other things. Like walls. People.

Men's locker rooms."

She rolled her eyes. "Pretty sure there are no locker rooms in an airport."

"Men's restrooms, then."

"No," she declared unequivocally, completely rejecting the good-natured bait I'd left in an attempt to inject some humor. "I'm not interested in having our picture everywhere."

"Embarrassed to be seen with me?"

"No." She shook her head. "Not normally. I mean, it's not *you*. But this is a once-in-a-lifetime opportunity that I earned by working hard and not by fucking one of the players. I'm not too keen to give that all away to tabloid fodder claiming otherwise. And yes, I am sure it would end up in a tabloid. I'm not stupid. There are cameras everywhere."

"All right," I finally conceded. I wanted to extend our time together, but not at the expense of her career. I wasn't that big of a dick. "I guess this is it, then."

I glanced in the rearview mirror and caught the familiar black of a full uniform. The officer was working his way up the line of cars, telling them to move on, and I knew I had to usher in a sense of urgency if this goodbye wasn't going to be a total letdown.

"Come on, baby. The cop is on his way. When he gets to us, he'll make me drive away whether you and your bag are out of the car or not."

Forward and without warning, Six leaned into my space and sealed her mouth to mine. The line of her lips was pliant and accommodating, so I sank my tongue into the deepest part of her mouth and savored the taste. With a flavor of apples and crisp water, Six tasted fresh and uncomplicated, unlike all of the other women I'd ever met. She didn't have a fancy flavored lip gloss, and her face wasn't overdone. She was natural beauty personified.

I watched achingly as she walked away, telling myself it was the fault of a sexual connection. The two of us fit, harmonized, and elevated one another.

But our fun would be brief, though a little longer than the rest, and when she was done filming us at the end of the year, I'd say my goodbye without hesitation.

It was imperative for my focus and relevant to what I wanted out of life. I didn't need distractions and bitter feelings clouding my game, and I didn't need a woman who lived on the opposite side of the country.

Still, the goodbye nagged at my insides as I pulled away, and I got lost in a series of daydreams. The sex we'd had and that we hadn't. I ran through every interaction I'd had with Six and then some. She was dynamic and bold and unchallenged by the idea of knowing how much she had to offer.

She forced me into humility on nearly every occasion she could manage, and yet, I still felt better about myself around her than I felt anywhere else.

I glanced up as I pulled inside the parking garage, startled to find that I hadn't exited the airport as intended.

Instead, I'd circled, finding the most convenient parking for short-term visitors and set about doing it.

Committed, I didn't give myself the chance to rethink before finding a spot, shutting off the engine, and speeding inside.

I scoured the ticket counters to no avail and immediately rerouted to the security line. Cognizant of her wishes, I pulled the ball cap lower over my eyes and stood to the side, waiting for her to weave back in my direction to get her attention.

I didn't think shouting her name would win any awards with her or airport security.

She finally noticed me ten minutes later, and when her eyes softened and the corners of her mouth turned up in a smile at my subtle wave, I knew it'd been worth it.

No words were spoken and, materially, nothing was gained. But that one moment had confirmed to me what she refused to make known—whether she wanted to or not, she liked me just as much as I liked her.

Six's face was vibrant and engaging as she interviewed each of the players for the opening segment of the Mavericks series on her YouCam channel. Since the first episode released this morning, it'd already seen over five hundred thousand views, and the comments were overwhelmingly positive—aside from the normal number of trolls.

I, however, was reliving the first day we'd really interacted with each other and thinking about how cute she'd been while giving me a hard time.

Backing out of the app on my phone where I'd been working on my latest architecture project, I moved into the messages and typed one out to her.

Me: I look fat.

Six: Um, what?

Me: On camera. The first episode of your series. My abs aren't being showcased properly.

Six: Why? Because I made you wear a shirt?

Me: Yes. I feel oppressed.

Six: Hey, I told you to do the segment in your underwear.

Me: No! You joked about it, but you shamed me with your eyes. I saw them. Judgy, chocolatey, shame eyes.

Six: Really? You could see all that through your pouting?

Me: You forgot about me!

Six: You're very forgettable.

Me: So you say. And yet, you keep sleeping with me.

Her response was nearly immediate.

Six: Convenience.

I laughed out loud. Even in text message form, she had a quick wit.

Me: There's an awful lot of B-roll in this episode featuring me, though.

Six: Joe has a crush on you.

I laughed out loud at her easy deflection and settled in to see how she was faring out in California without the important things. New York…and me.

Me: How's California treating you?

Six: Pretty well. I'm getting a lot of work done on my other segments that people expect from me. I went to Target this morning and did a dance video on overspending. Then I went to Toys R Us and sent them off with a Broadway-worthy We're Closing number.

Curiosity got the better of me, and I pushed.

Me: And your sex life? How's that?

Six: Busy. Hard to find a spot that's not filled.

I smiled despite her words, knowing something so brazen had to be a lie.

Me: You're cruel.

Six: Yeah, I am. And I'm sure you're celibate.

Me: I'll have you know I might as well be. Without your little pussy pal, I've been living the life of a recluse.

Six: Yeah, right. What are you doing right now?

Knowing she didn't believe me, and wouldn't via text, I backed out of the messages and dialed her number on FaceTime.

Her eyes were covered as she filled the screen. "What are you doing?" I asked with a laugh.

"I don't want to be blinded. Tell me there are no dirty things. Tell me I won't be scarred for life. Promise it and swear it and then maybe I'll look."

My teeth pushed into the soft flesh of my bottom lip as I smiled. "It's safe. You can look."

One finger moving cautiously away from the next, she made a slit and peeked through before uncovering all the way. I laughed at her theatrics and rolled my eyes as she scanned the sight of me.

"Wow," she remarked. "You're dressed and everything."

"Believe it or not, I don't usually sit around my house naked."

"Not. I do *not* believe it."

Her smile was bright as I flipped her off.

"So, what exactly are you doing?" she asked.

"I told you. I was watching the first episode on YouCam."

"That's it?" she asked suspiciously. I laughed again.

"What exactly do you think I am?"

"I have no idea," she mused. "A special creature with all kinds of dangerous secrets."

My scoff was audible. "Oh yeah, secrets. My biggest secret is the online architecture game I play."

Her chocolate eyes sparkled and danced. "Oh my God. Actually telling me your secrets? This is exciting! Hold on while I get a pen and pad. I want to write all of these down to use against you later." She moved out of the frame and grabbed a pen, licking at the tip dramatically and pretending to write.

"Give me a break."

Her smile was easy as she leaned into the camera of her phone and turned her eyes down at the corners to make them look sultry. She was a master of self-expression, that was for sure. "Tell me, Sean. Tell me all about this architecture app."

I fidgeted self-consciously as a wave of regret rolled over me. I didn't normally bring this up to anyone. "It's nothing."

"Oh, come on. You can't do that. Tell me about it."

"It's just an online competition. I design stuff on my phone, and people rate it. You advance if you beat the other people in your round."

"Have you always been interested in architecture?" she asked thoughtfully.

"I thought that was what I was going to do for my career," I admitted. "When I tore my ACL." I chuckled and shrugged. "I guess it's funny how things work out."

She nodded, a serene smile making her look gentle. "I went to school for finance. So yeah, I get it."

"Wow. That's a big change in career."

She nodded enthusiastically. "That was really more of my parents' plan, though. This was in my blood. I just never expected it to take off," she admitted self-consciously.

"If I'd known you before, I could have told you it would," I declared.

Her eyes widened in surprise. "You could have?"

"Yeah," I agreed, studying the undeniable likeability all over her. "You were made for this."

Chapter Nineteen

Six

My hip vibrated just as I sat down in my seat, and I pulled my phone out of my pocket to look at the screen.

Cassie: You at the game, girlfriend?

Crazy as it sounded, ever since I'd met Sean's sister Cassie in Pittsburgh, we'd somehow managed to become texting buddies. And to be honest, I really liked her. She was off her fucking rocker, but she was also a total sweetheart.

Me: Yep. Just sat down.

Cassie: How does he look? Is his knee bothering him?

Me: Well…I just sat down, so I'm not sure. But considering he hasn't complained about that knee all season, I think it's safe to say he's feeling just fine.

I'd caught on pretty quickly that Cassie was still freaked out over her brother's knee injury a few years back. But it didn't take a rocket scientist to deduce that information from the one thousand text messages I'd received from her over the past few weeks.

Cassie: Jesus, Six. You are no fluffing help.

Me: LOL. Sorry, dude.

Cassie: How did he look in practice this week?

Me: Like he's ready to kick some ass.

Cassie: Okay, good. :)

Sliding my phone back into my pocket, I took in the view that was Dallas's vast stadium. The atmosphere was electric and alive, and the guys were only halfway through their pregame warm-ups.

More than that, the stadium wasn't even filled yet.

The crowd hummed and vibrated as fans filtered inside in waves, some finding their seats right away, some making necessary pit stops at the concession stands and restrooms.

All the while, pregame entertainment commenced on opposite sides of the venue.

The Dallas cheerleaders performed while the Rodeo Drum Line provided the mesmerizing soundtrack for their sexy, sassy, and perfectly choreographed dance moves.

Tonight, I'd be filming footage and snippets for another episode of the Mavericks series. But I'd be doing things a little differently. Instead of being on the sidelines with Joe and Barry, I'd be in the stands, experiencing the game with the fans.

There was something magical about being one in the crowd.

The mere idea of it led to reminiscent thoughts of going to Lakers games with my dad.

Inside the venue, while our favorite professional basketball team played their opponent, it was impossible to feel alone. Everyone in the crowd acted the same, cheered at the same moment, and felt the same emotions together. And what I'd read on their faces during the game, I'd known was also written on mine. And in that, a true echo of humanity—where no matter which team we were rooting for, we would be as close as we could ever be.

At every Lakers game I'd gone to with my dad, because of that unity within the crowd, there had always been a feeling of freedom I could never really experience in other parts of my life.

Until I'd started my vlog.

And because I had friends in high New York places, I'd scored a kick-ass seat on the fifty-yard line. The Mavericks' bench was right in my viewpoint, and I could literally see everything on the field.

With my GoPro camera in hand, I took a few short clips of the guys during their warm-ups, the stadium, and the crowd, before turning the camera to my smiling face.

"Only ninety minutes until kickoff and this Texas crowd has brought their A game!" I exclaimed. "But I think our boys are ready for battle. Quinn Bailey is throwing rockets with the precision of a freaking cardiac surgeon, and Sean Phillips has yet to drop the ball or falter in his steps. Dallas might be ready to bring the heat, but I think our Mavericks are going to do what they do best. Win football games!"

I turned the camera and took a few more short clips of the expansive stadium, the crowd, and even the Dallas cheerleaders who were shaking their hips and asses in their notoriously skimpy uniforms.

They looked crazy good, and I thanked the Texas weather for them. Even though it was mid-November, it was a balmy seventy-something degrees. No doubt their eye-catching, sexy as hell cheerleading gear would be a "freeze their little dancing asses off" situation in New York.

When I'd boarded my flight from JFK—having been briefly in the city for a segment at Rockefeller Center—the temperature had been thirty-eight degrees.

Winter had arrived, but you wouldn't know that standing inside Dallas's stadium watching their cheerleaders bounce and twerk around in their booty shorts.

With the camera back on my smiling face, I added, "Who's ready to kick some Dallas ass!" Behind me, luckily, sat a boatload of New York fans who had made the long trek for the game.

They hooted and hollered and cheered their agreement.

I turned the camera toward them and gestured for more enthusiasm, and gladly, they obliged.

"Mavericks! Mavericks! Mavericks!" twenty or so people started to chant in our own little visitor's bubble inside the stadium.

And across the way, Dallas fans started to shout their disagreement.

"Dallas! Dallas! Dallas!"

I caught the battle on camera for a good three minutes or so, and thankfully, everyone managed to keep it PG and friendly. I had a feeling that had more to do with the fact that the game had yet to begin than anything else. Once the whistle blew and the beers started flowing, that friendly little battle could be an animal of a different, more aggressive color.

Die-hard football fans were known for getting rowdy.

And this was a big fucking game.

Both teams were going in with the same exact winning record.

A lot of sports analysts were predicting whoever won tonight's game would most likely win the championship.

Looking down at the sidelines and around the field, I caught sight of Barry's and Joe's positions. Joe was kneeling in the end zone catching footage of the Mavs' kicker warming up his leg. And Barry was on the sidelines, camera focused on the fifty-yard line where Quinn and Sean stood chatting with a few of Dallas's players.

Despite my mental prompting, I couldn't seem to pull my eyes away from Sean once my gaze had latched on to him.

I hadn't seen him in over a week, and damn, he looked good.

It should've been illegal for him to wear tight football pants.

Honestly, those formfitting spandex duds revealed a lot of the good things beneath his clothes—*ahem, his tight, firm ass and strong thighs*—and also hinted at other good things.

Big good things.

Penis kind of things.

Sure, he had on a jock strap, but still. It didn't take a perverted genius to figure out Sean Phillips was blessed with more than just talent.

Or good looks or an adorably cocky and charming personality or gorgeous eyes or a handsome smile or a sexy, raspy voice that makes my toes curl or...

Yeah. Okay. Pretty sure I could stop mentally ticking off all of his attributes.

My phone pinged again in my pocket, and I pulled it out again to check the screen.

Cassie: How does he look now?

I laughed quietly to myself once I read the message.

If there was one thing she had in spades, it was persistence.

When Cassie Kelly wanted an answer, she'd fucking find a way to get it.

Me: Like a man who is ready to kick some ass.

Cassie: What about his knee? How does it look?

Me: From my seat on the fifty-yard line, it looks just like a real-live, human knee. Well-rounded. Bendable. And connected to both the upper and lower leg.

Cassie: Smartass. And now, my stupid husband is losing his fluffing shit over your response. Like, full-on cackles. You now

owe me a vodka sacrifice and a trip to Barcelona Bar for Harry Potter shots next time you're in New York.

Me: I don't even know what half of that means, but okay. ☺

Me: But, seriously, I think he's good to go. You have nothing to worry about.

Cassie: Thanks, you little smartass. And don't you worry about your innocence. Georgia and I will rob you of it soon.

With a smile etched on my lips, I slid my phone back into my pocket.

I really liked Cassie, even when she was texting me incessantly about her brother's knee. She was hilarious and sweet and often said the craziest shit that had me laughing my ass off.

Hell, I even adored her husband, Thatch.

Getting close with Sean's family had never been my intention, but somehow, it just kind of happened.

His sister and brother-in-law aren't the only ones you're getting close with...

Refusing to give that train of thought any more fuel, I pushed my focus back to the field.

But when I caught sight of Sean standing on the fifty-yard line with a giggly, smiley Dallas cheerleader clinging to his side, it was pretty fucking hard to stop my mind from racing with thoughts. And doubts.

She touched his bicep and tossed her head back in laughter, her long blond locks creating a lush arc of silky strands.

And he smiled down at her.

My heart felt like an off-kilter elevator cart, whooshing from my chest to my goddamn toes in a matter of seconds.

I kind of hated how much it bothered me, seeing him chatting up another woman.

I mean, for all I knew, maybe he knew her? Maybe they were good friends?

Maybe they're fuck buddies?

I cringed at my own thoughts, and the biggest question on my mind played on a loop.

Am I getting too close to Sean Phillips?

Chapter Twenty

Sean

Cheers rang out in the locker room as everyone hollered and offered slaps and hits to the shoulder. Those might not seem like the signs of a good time, but I can assure you—to a bunch of overgrown boy-men, they were.

We'd been gnashing our teeth and shit-talking for hours on the field, and it was only natural some of that would transfer to a euphoric version in the locker room after a seemingly impossible win.

"Fuck yeah, Phillips!" Teeny congratulated, pounding me on the ass and then picking me up on his shoulder for a spin. "That fucker they put as your cover couldn't touch you with a ten-foot pole!"

I laughed and high-fived Quinn as Cam pulled me down, but inside, I was dying to be rid of these fuckers. I spent more hours than I could count in their company, and tonight, I could only think of one person I wanted to be around.

Under.

On top of.

I'd take any fucking position I could get.

"Get your ass in the shower," I advised, shoving Teeny away with a laugh. "Go stroke yourself or something."

"Oh! Kinky, Sean-y."

I laughed as Quinn shook his head.

"A bunch of two-year-olds, really."

"Oh, sorry," I cooed. "We can't all be as dignified as you, Southern boy."

Quinn laughed at that. "Yeah, well, you, I can forgive. Your sister is worse than you are, so I have a feeling your homelife didn't give you much of a choice."

"She's straightforward," I defended out of familial obligation.

Quinn didn't buy into it for a second. "Cassie is straight crazy, son. You know it, I know it, that big fucking husband of hers knows it."

"Yeah, but she's hot," Cam butted in.

I shoved him away and went back to putting my T-shirt on over my freshly showered skin and slipping my boxer briefs underneath my towel. When I pulled it off, I had them in place, so I reached for my jeans, eager to get the hell out of here.

"You going out with us?" Cam asked, and I shook my head.

"I don't know. Feeling like laying low tonight."

"Boringgggg!" Teeny shouted from the shower, having over-heard me.

I looked to Quinn as he laughed at me. "What? You're not going out with them either."

Quinn shrugged. "Yeah, I am. Cat's coming with."

"Wow. That's surprising."

Quinn flipped me off. "Dallas is a big win. We gotta celebrate." He looked across the room to Cam doing his best rendition of a scene from *Dirty Dancing* and shook his head. "Plus, someone has to keep these assholes out of trouble."

I raised my eyebrows in a nod and flicked out a hand in good-bye. Quinn called out as I was leaving, but I didn't turn back. "What are you doing?"

"Nothing," I lied. "Absolutely nothing."

A crowd of family and friends waited in the receiving area, and I scanned the faces for one I found familiar.

None stood out as the one I was after.

Too big. Too pointy. Not nearly delicate enough. They were all a smeared depiction of everything Six wasn't.

Disappointment settled in the pit of my stomach as I considered the possibility that she hadn't waited for me.

Disinterested in interacting with any of the guys again and explaining my change of heart, I headed for the side of the building where our bus would be waiting. We'd have to take it back to the hotel before going anywhere else anyway, and at this point, I wasn't even sure I'd do anything but go to my room.

Darkness faded as I walked out of the back tunnel, and little lights shone at the top of the wall next to the ceiling. This was Dallas's loading and unloading hub for visiting teams, and I'd been here for more than my fair share of games. It was kind of surreal, but the more times I did it, the more it seemed to become commonplace. I never wanted that for myself—to take the gifts I'd been given for granted—so I forced myself to study the magnitude of it all.

The halls were enormous and the space busy with employees. A stadium of incomparable size sat above us, and just an hour ago, it'd been filled to the brim with people who paid their hard-earned money to watch my teammates and me play a game against the players of Dallas.

I swore to myself then, no matter how hard I had to work to keep myself grounded, I'd never forget the details.

The bus in front of me, I focused my step and lengthened my stride. The smack of my feet on the concrete floor was mesmerizing, and I'd nearly lulled myself into a state of subconsciousness when the voice came at me from my side and startled me.

"Hey, stranger."

With wild hair and brown, beautiful eyes, Six was decked out in a criminally well-fitting pair of jeans and a leather jacket, and the boots on her feet were a girlie version of combat. Her tank top was

the color of mustard and low-cut, and the look of it against her cara-
mel skin made my cock jerk without permission.

"I thought you'd left," I said by way of greeting.

She shook her head tauntingly, a slow reminder of the feel of her
hair as it danced against my chest. I wanted to spend an hour taking
her in while we ate dinner, and then I wanted to spend the rest of the
night watching her take *me*.

"Come to dinner with me," I offered, going after what I wanted
without preamble. But a flash of her eyes made me reconsider the
state of my politeness. "Please."

She looked down the hall behind me, almost as if she could
summon more of the guys with her eyes. "We should go out with the
team."

Out with the team? God, that sounded awful.

"Why? They smell. Awful. Honestly, I was just in the locker room
with them, and I almost didn't survive."

Six laughed. "I've been the locker room with all of you before,
remember? The smell was potent, but the penises were a powerful
counteraction."

My smile was mischievous. "I could counteract your desire to go
out with them with *my* penis."

"That kind of power really only happens with multiple penises."

The image of her having a threesome—or God, a foursome—
popped into my mind unbidden. I swallowed thickly. "You have experience with multiple penises a lot? Like, is that a thing for you?"

Six winked, and my heartbeat shredded in an unexpected
rhythm.

"Wow. I don't know how to feel right now," I admitted. "All I
know is that it's a mix of arousal and fear."

"Scared of me, huh?" she taunted.

I shrugged. "I don't know. The more it settles, the more I dig it."

"Well, then," she said with a teasing lilt. "Use tonight to practice
sharing me."

On cue and without my invitation, the guys came pouring out

from the hall, headed for the bus.

They were just as rowdy as ever, but thankfully, now clothed.

Teeny barreled toward us at a run and scooped Six off her feet, dropping her into a groom's carry and swaying her back and forth. Just the sight of his hands on her made my temples pulse, but I tamped it down.

She wasn't mine to feel protective over.

"Thank God I found you, Sixy," Teeny sang. "Leaving women alone with Sean almost always leads to defilement."

"You're too late," Six teased, touching the tip of his nose and throwing her head back with abandon. "I'm completely besmirched."

Teeny laughed uproariously.

"Shoot, girl, you're funny. Can you imagine?"

I frowned hard, the lines of my mouth making my skin pull in ways I wasn't used to.

Why the hell was the idea of us together so fucking funny?

Chapter Twenty-One

Six

"Golfing? Whose idea was it to go fucking golfing?" Sean asked as we barreled down the highway in Cat's rental car. None of the guys had anything to drive here in Dallas, but apparently, Quinn was a real forward-thinker when Cat attended. If the hotel bar wasn't an option, or they came up with something to do, he knew they would be needing wheels.

And he'd rented her a Suburban.

He drove cautiously and calmly, the radio thumping quietly with nineties rap in the background, but the rest of the guys acted like lunatics. It was really no wonder they put Quinn in charge in group situations.

Sean glanced to Quinn and narrowed his eyes. "No doubt, this is all your doing."

"What? Why?" Quinn asked innocently as he steered us off an exit and reached out to capture Cat's hand. I watched with rapt attention, completely unable to look away while he planted his lips on the skin there and lingered.

God, they are so sweet.

"Southern money," Sean offered vaguely, and we all turned to look at him. It wasn't like him to be so vague, so obviously, he expected Quinn to know what he was talking about.

Turns out, Quinn was just as clueless as the rest of us.

"And what's that supposed to mean?"

Cat spun her upper body, her hand still in Quinn's grasp but now relegated to the top of his thigh. She made no moves to pull away, but she did roll her eyes at me—and never even hesitated as she ratted her boyfriend right out. "It *was* him."

I admired her ruthlessness.

"He's been wanting to go the Topgolf back home but had been struggling to find a captive audience, what with you all having your own lives," she explained further.

I thought back to the beginning of my time with the Mavericks, to my unplanned trip to the locker room and thoughts of a particular golf handicap—ten inches, to be exact—and blushed. Thank God my thoughts were private.

"Oh!" Cam yelled from his seat on the other side of Sean. "She sold you down the river, QB."

We were a threesome in the middle row, cramped with the size of their shoulders, even with the lack of mine. I'd offered magnanimously, as the smallest person in the car, to take the dreaded middle seat, but Sean had cut that off immediately and taken it himself. It was almost like he didn't want me to be that close to Cam.

Weird.

"What if I've never golfed?" I asked, eager to do my sisterly duty and take some of the heat off Cat. Not that she seemed all that concerned.

Quinn laughed, more than willing to focus on me rather than the ragging of his girlfriend, even if the person she'd sold out had been him. "That's actually more fun. I'll be sure to stand as far away as possible when you're up, though."

I pushed an elbow into Sean's ribs and lowered my voice to a whisper.

"What about you? Have you golfed?"

"Once," he admitted, a hard swallow making his throat bob. His eyes were manic as he glanced at me and then forward again. The eye contact was there but fleeting, and nowhere near consistent with the level of Sean's normal confidence.

My eyes narrowed as I asked, "Why was that word so filled with trauma?"

Sam Sheffield leaned forward from the seat behind us and surprised me. "He went with his brother-in-law and his friends, and he was awful. Thatch still hasn't let him live it down to this day."

The name Thatch stuck in my throat. I'd had firsthand experience with the guy now, and he was seriously irresistible. I wasn't about to tell Sam that, though.

I could only imagine the ragging he gave Sean on a daily basis. From what I'd witnessed of the guy, he didn't exactly seem like the quitting type. No, he seemed like he'd make you live in a hell of your own making until the day you died, just for his enjoyment.

I pulled my lips in on themselves and tried to say something positive. "Practice is good, then, right?"

Sam laughed. "It would be if he weren't banned from the course."

My eyes widened, and I coughed a startled laugh before I could stop it. "Banned?"

"It's a long story," Sean mumbled.

He couldn't be thinking this was the kind of thing he could leave at that, could he? I mean, I lived for these kinds of stories. Hell, I'd built most of my career as a YouCam blogger with similar ones of my own. "One you're going to tell me, right?"

"If he doesn't, I will," Cam offered, obviously listening in as well. I laughed at how cutthroat they were for being teammates and mused about doing a segment about it at some point. There had to be something to it.

Teammates on the field. Enemies at the after party.

Pretty sure that would land me a pretty healthy lawsuit from Wes Lancaster.

"I told you. We should have gone out ourselves," Sean insisted quietly. Not quietly enough. The quarters were close, and my, oh my, Grandma, the ears were large in this car.

Sam laughed. "Oh, come on, Sean. Six is smarter than that."

Sean's smile faded immediately, and a twinge of disquiet turned in my chest.

Sam's words were among the scariest I'd ever heard.

Because all I could do from that point on was study the planes of Sean's disappointed face. The heavy line of his brow. The sharp downturn of his eyes. The ragged misshape of his mouth.

A sadness clung to him and made me want to reach inside to find the root. Would it be deep and endlessly seated, or was it new growth?

And was there a way I could fix it?

Realizing how quickly my thoughts had fallen victim to the death nail in every woman's coffin—the fantasy of a man who needed her—I frowned.

I feared the truth with acute terror—I wasn't smart. When it came to Sean Phillips, I'd proven I wasn't smart at all.

Chapter Twenty-Two

Sean

"Control your club!" Sam cheered, two beers making him louder and much more direct. He went out a lot, but typically drank very little. But the victory against Dallas was a big occasion—apparently, big enough to imbibe fully—and it was funny to see such a big guy get drunk so quickly. "Line it up with your balls. That's very important for follow-through."

We'd been at Topgolf in Dallas, an establishment where droves of people flocked to hit golf balls on a high-tech driving range, drink, and eat for entertainment. Fuck if I could understand the appeal, but I didn't mind being out with Six.

She had been acting weird since we'd gotten out of the car, though.

Taking a seat at the back of our personal driving bay, I'd done my best to stay out of the action, instead laughing and talking as the other people in our party made fools of themselves.

Six had spent most of her time laughing and joking with Teeny, and she'd only recently ventured back to the end of the table I occupied.

I was just about to strike up a conversation with her when Quinn stole my mojo.

"Come on, Six," Quinn called. "I've been watching you up here, around the side, back there—everywhere to avoid taking a turn. Don't think I'm going to let you get away with it."

She widened her eyes innocently and shook her head, but Quinn wasn't born yesterday. As the most mature of the group, he had a general eye for bullshit and didn't usually tolerate it. I, on the other hand, swam in it. If nothing else, my sister's crazy ways had trained me to ride the wave. Whether she was tight-lipped or, to my utter dismay and personal disturbance, going free tit, Cassie could always find a way to take it further. She'd punched men in the balls on several occasions and danced with numerous strangers. She'd requested STD results in the DJ booth of a bar, danced with old men, done a Jell-O shot and thrown it up in the same breath, and I'd been a witness to it all. Anything I could say or do would be used against me, and as a result, I'd kind of adapted that approach with all women.

I wasn't sure it was right, but it was what I knew.

I smiled slightly at Six's uncomfortable laughter as she got to her feet, and unfortunately, Quinn noticed. With an active point and a face of steel, he swore me to my fate.

"You too, Sean. You're next."

I flipped him off, but he just laughed. It would take a hell of a lot more than a flying finger to effectively threaten Quinn Bailey into submission. I pondered briefly turning my torment to his girlfriend Cat, but it didn't take more than a moment to reconsider.

Quinn was a gentle soul, but if I riled the wrong side of his personality by taunting the one person he loved most, I could kiss my balls goodbye.

And they wouldn't be mutilated in a quick fashion either. No way, QB was too precise and calculated to do anything hurried.

Well, unless, he was in the pocket and had a linebacker driving toward him with the intention of taking his fucking head off.

"Which club should I use?" Six asked, rounding the table and surveying the tub of Topgolf-provided clubs.

"Mine's free," Cam volunteered, and I reached forward and slapped him on the back of the head.

Six's smile was gleefully thankful. The knot in my stomach eased just minutely.

"Any one you want," Quinn explained, glancing chidingly at us hoodlums. "Any with the blue on them are sized for women."

I watched as she pulled the biggest one out of the hole and then ran my mouth, unable to resist.

"Size matters to you, huh?"

Jesus, Sean, I mentally chastised. *One step forward and twenty steps back.* No wonder most women thought men were idiots. Most of the time, we fucking were.

Her voice was sweet, but her words were teasingly lethal. "Got to find it somewhere when it's lacking everywhere else."

Teeny's laugh was infectious—to everyone but me. I was busy picking my balls up from the ground where she'd left them.

"Whoa. Savage, little Six," Sam commented playfully as he took a swig of his beer.

Cam elbowed me. "Good thing we know she's not talking about us, huh?"

"Yeah," I forced out. "Good thing."

Good thing I had the rest of the evening to figure out a way to prove her wrong.

An hour and a half, two turns, and three beers later, I'd reached the edge of my limit.

Six was going again, adjusting her hips at the direction of Quinn for a better position with the club and wiggling her ass to settle into her feet.

She grasped at the grip, and my cock jerked in my pants.

I needed her hands on me, rough and unyielding in the way that she'd started to grip the club, and I needed them there soon.

My veins were larger than normal, and blood flow was at a dangerous level. I tried to redirect it from the fast track to my dick, but the more I watched her, the less control I had.

Her hips. Her perfect ass. I wanted it all in my hands as I sucked on her tits and drove her back into the wall with every thrust.

Glassy-eyed and happy, she'd allowed herself a drink or two tonight as well, and I knew better than to take her without permission.

She hit the ball with a laugh, turning and bending over at the waist as it dribbled two feet in front of her. The swing and the hit of the ball were a dud, but her ass was just about all a man could handle.

Jealousy raged and burned as I looked from myself to Cam and Sam to find their eyes on the same thing.

Teeny, bless him, was too busy having a good time to notice how fucking hot she was.

With a careful adjustment in my pants, I rose to my feet and moved to the side of the table where the club holder was, eager for her return. She laughed at something Cat said and danced my way, nearly bumping into me before she even realized I was out of my seat.

She startled, and my jaw flexed with the resistance it took to keep myself from picking her up and fucking her right there on the bay table in front of all of our friends—and everyone else.

Set up like a driving range, but with access to food, drinks, and seating, each group at Topgolf had their own "private bay." But what they meant by private—open air and right next to another group— and the kind of enclosed area I would need to fuck Six on the table were two different things.

"Come on," I ordered quietly, turning her away from the table and putting a hand to her back. With gentle pressure, I guided her in the direction of the bathrooms for lack of a better place.

"Where are we going?" she asked, her breaths already coming faster as she pictured exactly what I had been seeing for the last hour.

She was a smart girl. Intuitive, and she could tell by the raging testosterone bleeding out of my skin that she was about to get fucked.

Still, the circumstances were cute and the wording too fun not use as I leaned down to her ear and whispered, "I'm going to show you how skilled I am in wielding a different kind of club."

She shivered and sped up her steps without prompting.

My heart kicked in my chest, and my cock fought with my pants as we finally pushed through the bathroom door. Thankfully, it was empty, so I kicked the door shut behind us and locked it without pause.

Her breathing was ragged as I pushed her back against the wall without saying anything, but her body was pliant and willing. She was so ready, the swell of her breasts seeming to double in size as she thrust them forward.

Not one to disappoint, I grabbed her shirt at the hem and yanked it up and over her head without finesse. She worked to help me, but once it was over her breasts, I would have left her to do most of the rest on her own whether she'd volunteered or not.

I was too eager, too hungry. And her tits looked too good through the delicate lace of her pink bra.

"God," I groaned, leaning down to take one perfect nipple into my mouth. Brown and round, they were the perfect quarter-sized tasty treats.

I sucked and nipped, and she keened, getting louder as I went. I tugged down the cups with my teeth when the lace became too much of a barrier, and she reached for the belt on my pants.

Hands filling the role of my mouth, I squeezed the bare flesh at her chest and kissed my way down to her stomach until I got to her jeans. The button gave easily with the force of my teeth, and after a moan, she moved her hands down to shove her jeans from her hips so I could put my mouth directly on wet flesh.

It was everything I wanted it to be and then some, and I sucked and swallowed like a ravenous animal. She crowed wildly, scratching at the material of my shirt and climbing my body to give my mouth better access to her clit.

I licked and sucked and lapped my way through all the juice she had to offer until she finally broke.

"Enough!" she yelled. "I need you inside me. *Now*, Sean. *Right fucking now.*"

She nearly growled those last three words, and my dick all but did a fucking cartwheel in excitement.

Hot damn.

The feeling was mutual.

My smile was wicked as I climbed to my feet, undid my pants, and donned a condom, the glow of her arousal coating my mouth in taunt. "I thought you'd never ask, baby."

"You were waiting for me to ask?" she asked breathlessly, and I laughed.

"Beg, really," I clarified. "I really wanted you to beg."

She slapped weakly at my chest, but the feel of my cock sliding inside of her was kind of distracting.

To her, to me—it was a goddamn game changer for both of us.

Pleasure teased and tickled at my spine as I fought the urge to pound relentlessly until I came right from the first heavenly thrust inside. But after the night with her avoiding me, I wanted her to face me. I wanted her to look me in the eye and feel every goddamn stroke. I wanted her to *feel* us. "Look at me, Six," I ordered. "Look me in the eye."

"I am," she protested, but her focus was scattered. My eyes, my chest, my dick sliding in and out of her as I pushed her harder and deeper into the wall. All of it was fascinating, but I wanted her to *see* me.

"You're not. *Look* at me."

"Sean," she breathed, desperate and dying as everything she was afraid of built inside her. She licked her lips and tightened her legs at my hips.

"Feels good, doesn't it?" I asked on a growl, frantic and adamant to have her answer. I wanted her to say it. To get it out there in a way she couldn't take back. "The two of us together. Tell me you've never felt anything better."

She bit her lower lip but stayed silent.

"Tell me," I ordered again.

She shook her head, and the pleasure rush broke me. I didn't care if she said it anymore because I'd say it for the both of us. This was special. This was real. This was everything I never knew I god-damn wanted, and I'd wait for her to figure it out.

"Fine. I'll do the talking. Because I don't have any trouble saying it, Six. Your pussy is the best thing I've ever felt. Wrapped around me, under my hand, on the tip of my tongue. Any way I can get it. I'll take it and you and everything we're turning out to be together, and I'll take it until you won't give it anymore."

She came just as I finished the avowal, and I wasn't far behind.

Caught up in blinding stars and dark shadows, I danced in the space of euphoria and pledged never to come back.

Not from this, not from us—not from any of it.

Six could take her time. I'd do exactly what they taught me in football.

A pick six was an interception you took all the way to the end zone.

And I'd damn well use my training to steal her first, and then take her all the goddamn way until she was mine.

All. Fucking. Mine.

Chapter Twenty-Three

Six

L A traffic was a nightmare, as per usual, and I wasn't the only one in a rush. Horns honked and people yelled, and giving the finger was practically as normal as using a turn signal.

I'd only been back home for a couple of days since leaving Dallas, and everything about my home city of San Diego had felt entirely more foreign than ever.

The faces weren't familiar, the sun didn't warm me as deeply, and the breeze that blew through from the ocean didn't feel anything but cold.

I knew my stint with the Mavericks was intended to be short-lived from the beginning, but I still couldn't wrap my mind around the fact that it would all be ending soon.

The time with the guys during shoots, the raucous parties celebrating their victories with them, and perhaps most of all, the pseudo-relationship I'd formed with Sean Phillips.

I pinched at my skin as a force of habit, something I'd been doing over the last several weeks every time I thought of his name and my own in the same vicinity.

We'd been well acquainted with each other in ways I'd never imagined—emotionally, personally, and physically—but he was still a professional football player, and I was just a YouCam video blogger.

More than the whole life on opposite sides of the tracks factor, we'd still yet to say anything about our relationship to anyone. We snuck around and lied and fell into each other in the strangest of locations. Bathrooms and hotel beds and secret guest bedrooms and random closets, it was all the same to us, as long as we found a way inside each other.

My phone buzzed in the vent mount, and despite being behind the wheel, I couldn't stop myself from looking.

I took solace in the fact that the traffic was stopped at the moment, but I still knew it wasn't right.

No man's text was worth my life or the life of someone else behind the wheel, but…*Sean.*

Giving in to temptation, I touched the phone and lit up the screen to read the message. It was short and sweet, but the context made me smile.

Sean: I just watched an hour of news about a building fire in LA just hoping I'd get to see you drive by. What time is the conference?

I tapped out a quick response, occasionally glancing to find traffic doing absolutely nothing.

Me: In like five minutes, actually. But I'm in bumper-to-bumper traffic trying like hell to get there. I'm hoping being fashionably late qualifies as a topic in fashion.

Sean: Why exactly are you going to a fashion blog conference? You don't blog about fashion.

Me: I do. Occasionally. Okay…once. But I have a good friend who does. I met her online, but she seems to think it's worth my time. They do a lot of topics on branding and general audience marketing that's relevant no matter who my audience is.

Sean: Why don't they have one of these in New York?

Me: They probably do.

Sean: Okay. Why aren't you at that one? ☹

Me: Because I live in California.

Sean: Don't remind me.

Brake lights up ahead faded as the gridlock started to move, so I typed quicker to be ready to roll.

Me: Traffic is moving. I'll talk to you later, okay?

Sean: I'm pouting.

I rolled my eyes and smiled at the same time.
I wanted to text him back.
I wanted to call him.
Hell, I kind of wanted to skip this conference and head back to New York early.
But rationality, reality, and the now empty space in front of my vehicle demanded my attention.
I clicked off my phone and shifted back into drive.
My little Toyota Camry wasn't fancy, but it'd never done me any wrong no matter how many times I'd unknowingly tried to sabotage it. I guessed the Japanese could build one hell of an energizer motor.
And, apparently, there'd been something blocking the road because we were sailing now. I used my hand to fan myself, did a quick

smell of my pits, and put my foot to the floor. With any input from the Toyota gods, I'd be there in no time.

But even with my eyes focused on the road, I couldn't deny the urge to text him back was still strong. And more than that, even though I wasn't able to respond to his last message, my eyes kept glancing toward my stupid phone, hoping for another notification from him.

My heart felt like it was in a vise inside my chest.

And for the rest of my drive to the conference, all my brain fixated on was Sean. Memories of Sean. Fantasies of Sean. His perfect mouth. His laugh. The way his eyes looked when that sexy smile of his consumed his face.

Oh, sweet summer child, I was heading toward dangerous territory when it came to him, and if I weren't careful, I'd let myself fall straight past the point of no return.

Mary Jane was shaking her head before my ass even hit the chair as I snuck my way into the first seminar. She'd at least saved me a seat, even if it was in the middle of the row.

Doesn't she know notoriously late-arrivers preferred back row seats?

"Excuse me," I muttered, tripping over a lady's bag and landing on another woman's foot. She shot me a venomous glare, and I shrugged. It's not like I could take the stumble back.

"Always late and always in trouble," Mary Jane, or MJ as I called her, remarked softly while looking down at her notebook and taking a quick note about website pixels.

I rolled my eyes and took out an old envelope from my back pocket. "Do you have a pen I can borrow?"

MJ stopped writing, turned her head with a swirl and a twist, and I balked. Her eyes looked possessed, and I feared I'd poked the wrong bear.

"I can ask someone else," I mumbled, but her grumble was louder as she bent down to her purse.

It didn't take her long to find what she was after—she was a hell of a lot more organized than I was—and hand me a pen.

"Here. Now shut up and listen."

Somewhat childishly, I had to fight the urge to defy her, just because. I was proud to say I managed it, though.

When the talk finally ended and a round of applause broke out, I took my first full breath.

"Thank God," I muttered and silently prayed the speaker took the stick she'd had up her ass with her as she left.

MJ laughed. "Why do you come to these things if you hate them?"

"Because you're always telling me it's good for business. And I'm nothing if not interested in money. I want to make it. I want to spend it. I want to fucking bathe in it."

"You're ridiculous. But I'll admit it's good to see you."

"Obvi," I remarked. "I'm always a good time."

Her head's shake had to be permanent at this point as she led us out of the meeting room and down the hall of the hotel. We were headed for the lobby—and the lobby bar if I was really lucky—and the possibility of any of the above sounded amazing.

I needed a drink, and I needed to dish.

I had to spill to someone about all of the secret things I'd been filming with the Mavericks. It wasn't a condition of the contract to keep my mouth closed, but it was good practice. I didn't want to go blabbing to just anyone for fear they'd scoop my goddamn story.

But I trusted MJ. She was a fellow vlogger, a guru of fashion and makeup on the YouCam circuit, and she was a good person to her core. When you told MJ something and asked her to keep it to herself, she locked that shit up and threw away the key.

And, in this industry, that was a fucking rarity.

The vlogging community was notorious for being cutthroat and competitive.

With only bar-height tables available in the crowded lobby space, I hoisted myself up to a seat. Christmas was just around the corner, and the room looked like a pack of tiny elves had vomited up holiday cheer.

Lights and trees and tinsel and ornaments galore.

I sighed. "They take our drink orders at the table, right?"

MJ nodded. "Yes, relax. You'll be able to get drunk with as little effort expended as possible."

"Oh good," I breathed. "That's just how I like it."

"So what have you been working on lately? I saw a couple of episodes post about the Mavericks." She whistled. "That's a big fucking score. Are you planning to do any more with them?"

My mind soared and my mouth curled as I thought about the deal I'd gotten. MJ had actually been the one to encourage me to go after something with them in the first place.

She'd known I was an avid Mavericks fan, and she had just happened to be one of the lucky bitches on the Birmingham to New York flights that brought Quinn Bailey and his lady love Cat together.

"Yes! After you called me a few months ago and told me about all of the stuff that went down on the plane with Cat and Quinn and Sean and the spectacle the whole thing had made, I felt the need to go after it. I basically hounded their director of marketing until she got back to me."

MJ's nod was approving. "Good girl. And?"

"And they signed me for eight episodes! I have one more left to film before it's all over. I can't believe how fast it all went."

"They're having a pretty good season, though. Maybe they'll sign you for something postseason as a bonus?"

I thought about Wes and how much his head seemed to spin every time I was there. I didn't do anything, per se, but I had a feeling he'd be happy when I was finally gone.

"I don't know." I shrugged. "The owner seems pretty stressed with me there. I think this is going to be it."

"Well, that's a bummer."

"I know," I agreed. "But it's been great. All of the guys have been so much fun."

"All of the guys, huh? Any side business going on?"

My heart kicked and flipped in my chest as panic took hold. Had she seen something about Sean and me in a tabloid? I didn't think I was ready for that.

"No, why?"

She rolled her eyes. "Because Cam Mitchell is hot. Because I'd totally jump into bed with him if I got the chance."

I laughed. "Cam is nice."

"Boringggg."

I shrugged.

"Well, at least you didn't get caught up in Sean."

My throat constricted, and my chest got tight.

Is it hot in here, or are my hands just clammy?

"Sean?" I asked, throat thick and drier than the Sahara.

"Yeah. Sean Phillips. Total dog. Sleeps with anything that moves."

I rubbed my hands together, picked at the tablecloth, and tried for nonchalant. "I thought I'd heard that he changed."

"Oh, he changed all right," she said through a huge laugh. "Changed women. Whoever the poor girl is he's hooked on his line now is in trouble. Because there's another fish out there lurking, and it won't take much bait to convince him to throw her back."

Stomach nauseous and putrid, I did my best to keep a straight face.

But if I made it through the rest of the day, it wouldn't be without consequences.

The vast ocean seemed so appealing in all its colorful blue glory. Life ebbed and flowed, and new adventures were born. But there'd been one too many bad fishes in this conversation with MJ and me, and no matter how much my stupid heart longed for Sean, I had a feeling I'd never eat seafood again.

A server stopped by our table, and I ordered a glass of wine as a means of distraction.

And while MJ dove into what her current vlog plans were, I couldn't stop thinking about Sean and us and his reputation and my true feelings for him.

I was deeper than I should be; I knew that much. And soon, I'd be taking my last trip to New York to film the final episode of the Mavs series.

The reality of it all became more and more apparent.

When I boarded my flight to Newark, I needed to have a clear head and an expectation-less heart.

Chapter Twenty-Four

Sean

"Ho, ho, ho, it's Christmas at the Mavericks," Six explained to the camera, her red suit and big white wig ill-fitting in an entirely comical way.

I stared hard, trying to find the outline of her body underneath the baggy material, but it was a lost cause.

Luckily, I had the mental film reel to tap into when the physical recreation became faulty.

"We've been following these guys long enough to know they can expect something more than a lump of coal in their stockings, but what is it they actually want? Lamborghinis? A championship win? How about a pony? We don't know yet, but I'll tell you right now, I intend to find out!" A hearty, exaggeratedly jolly variety of a chuckle left her white beard-covered lips.

I positioned myself in the corner up against a wall but within reach of a table where a group of the guys had gathered. I couldn't help but be a little sad that the video blog series with Six was coming to an end, but I was trying to work through it.

Fuck. No one even knew we had anything more than a

professional relationship.

My tie felt tight around my neck as she came toward me, swaying her hips in a way unworthy of Santa or Mrs. Claus. The gleam in her eye was vivid and teasing, and I couldn't wait to hear what would come out of her mouth.

It was one thing to connect with her bodily, but I'd never met a funnier woman in my life—and Cassie Phillips, queen of the punch line, was my sister. As much as I'd miss having Six around for the sake of our physical relationship, I feared I'd miss my friend even more.

"Ho, ho, hello, Sean," she greeted, winking at the other guys as they laughed at her creative use of the Claus-ism. "Have you been a good boy this year?"

Sam Sheffield and Oran Wells taunted and howled their boos, but Six and I both did our best to ignore them. Instead, I turned on the charm and embraced my public persona. These videos were important to the success of Six's blog and good for the popularity of the Mavericks organization. If sounding like a cocksure asshole every now and then benefitted viewership, I was willing to make the sacrifice.

"I think my fans know I've been an excellent boy this year." I winked.

Cam hacked and coughed, dramatically faking the need to retch. The other guys laughed and high-fived behind his back, and I realized for not the first time that we might have a slight maturity problem. As I considered the possibility, Quinn found my eyes in the distance and nodded.

Yes, he confirmed nonverbally. *I've been trying to point this out for years.*

I laughed at the clarity of Quinn's Southern twang in my head and turned back to Six.

"Ah, yes," she mused. "Touchdowns, completions. Santa loves those things."

"If he's a Mavericks fan, he does."

She laughed, high and giggly, and then rolled it into a deep, throaty ending as she realized she was supposed to be playing the part of a man. I laughed at the irony of the womanliest female I'd ever met trying to come across as a man. She wasn't exactly trying that hard to be convincing, though. "He is. Especially, Quinn Bailey."

Six winked as my smile melted and stepped around me to talk to Quinn, who'd been moving closer slowly in feeble acceptance of joining the rowdy group.

"Quinn Bailey," she greeted. "I *know* you've been good this year."

"Always, Santa," the fucker replied dutifully, forming his hand into a Boy Scout's sign and crossing it over his heart or some shit. I'd never been a Boy Scout, instead playing in the woods with Cassie to the theme of straight-up survival games. So I couldn't be certain, but it sure seemed like something a do-gooder would do.

"And what is it you'd like as your reward?" Six asked, pointing the microphone in Quinn's face and winking back at the camera. Joe smiled behind it and bit his lip to suppress his laugh. I knew they'd known each other for a long time, but I wondered idly if he'd ever crushed on her. Six was the kind of woman I imagined most men lusted after. Hot and luscious in all of her petite curves, with bold, defined, goddess-like features and a mouth like a sailor, she was the ultimate prize to carry in your belt. She was fun and funny and she could hang with the guys, but she was also deliciously wild in bed.

I was completely mesmerized by her appeal, so I couldn't see a reason why someone else wouldn't be.

Especially someone who spent as much time with her as her cameraman did.

Quinn shrugged. "I've already got the perfect little kitten."

I rolled my eyes and the guys guffawed, but no doubt the sap was going to make the women who watched this series swoon.

I walked toward Six, and then I turned her attention back to me with a bold grab of her hips. She startled at the intimate contact but deflected it with a quick and cute reference to her costume.

"Oh, hello, Sean. Did you want to sit on Santa's lap?"

"I'd rather it be the other way around, and I think Santa would too," I suggested unabashedly. Quinn's eyebrows rose to his hairline and some of the other guys quieted, but I ignored the scrutiny.

Six had a harder time.

She smiled under the beard and played it off, though, using her good-nature as a veil. As far as Six would have them know, my lap was the same as any of the others in the room.

"Okay, then. Make a chair for me."

I sat and pulled her into my lap, and she wrapped her arms around my shoulders without thinking. I didn't dare call it into notice. The time was short where I could relish her closeness without uncertainty and waiting to see her again.

Would she be in the New York area at any point in the future, and would she want to see me if she were? What if I went to California? Would she be open to that?

Questions rose and raced in my mind, but I shut them all down as she asked one of her own.

"What is it you want for Christmas, Sean?"

The truth was ripe and real, and I didn't hold back as I let her have it. "Seems like I've got it right here."

Angels swooned and the stars aligned and everything worked out for the best.

At least, in my head, it did.

The reality was much harsher.

Freshly uncomfortable, Six climbed from my lap and parried my comment with one of her own. "Santa doesn't offer ego-protection plans," she teased, but her voice was both playful and annoyed. "Check with Manwhores 'R' Us."

Damn, that stung a little bit.

The other players may have heard her response, but they forgot about it as soon as she graced them with her undivided attention.

I headed for the bar and grabbed a drink, watching her across the room as I sucked it down. The taste of the whiskey was potent and unforgiving, but then again, her brush-off had been too.

Quinn was quiet as he took a place next to me, a soft, reflective sigh as deep as a crater.

I knew he'd watched us.

I knew he'd seen.

Quinn Bailey was a keen observer and a kind heart, and ultimately, he was the keeper of the team. He looked after us emotionally and physically, and right now, thankfully, he understood that I needed some space.

The silence lasted the depth of my glass and half of a second before Six moved to the front of the room and climbed up on a chair.

The crowd went wild for her, just like my heart, and I rubbed at my chest to ease the tightness.

"Guys, guys!" she yelled over the din of cheers. "Thank you so much. I couldn't have done this series without you, obviously." She winked. "But mostly, I couldn't have turned it into what it is without your willing and witty input. I'm going to miss all of you as I travel back to California, but I hope you'll all keep in touch." Her eyes moved to me, and my heart picked up so much it climbed into my throat.

"I've had the best time. And I'll remember it forever. Thank you!"

The guys cheered and hollered, but my jaw might as well have been sewn shut.

Quinn noticed, as he always did, and filled the space with much-needed chatter.

I felt his hand come down on my shoulder and squeeze as he told me some good news intended to distract me.

"I'm going to propose to Cat," he murmured softly. I nodded. "Think you can help me set it up?"

My jaw felt dangerously close to shattering, so I forced it open in order to answer.

"Of course," I agreed and then showed the ultimate return of trust by confirming his suspicions. "Now that Six is heading home, it seems like I'm going to have the time."

He offered a short, curt nod, but other than that, knew not to take it any further.

I moved my eyes across the room, and they latched on to Six like a magnet.

She laughed at Teeny, and her throat opened as her head went back. She was happiness and freedom and none of the crushing disappointment I felt embodying me.

I wished I could've been okay with her leaving.

I wished I could've been perfectly fine with saying goodbye.

I wished a lot of fucking things in that moment.

But, sadly, that didn't mean any of them would come true.

Chapter Twenty-Five

Six

The Christmas party had continued on well past midnight, and somehow, someway, even Wes Lancaster had turned a blind eye to the boisterous group of men that had taken over the large reception room inside the stadium.

And most of those men were more than just a few beers deep.

Then again, tomorrow was Christmas Eve and the very last week of their season. While most of the teams in the league would be playing their asses off to end their season with a play-off-worthy record, the Mavericks would be sitting pretty with the best damn record in the league *and* an easy game this weekend against the worst team in professional football.

"Speech! Speech! Speech!" Martinez yelled, beer raised high in the air.

First, Cam, then Quinn joined in, and next thing I knew, the team was all but demanding another speech from me.

I blushed. Which was ironic because I almost *never* blushed.

I was the girl who had no issues with making a fool of herself at comedy's expense. Hell, before I'd changed into a pair of jeans and long-sleeved red shirt, I'd spent the better part of the evening waltz-ing around in a Santa suit, badgering the guys to tell me what they wanted for Christmas.

Yet this, right now, it just felt different. But I guessed a room full of bigger-than-life men showering you with attention would have that effect.

"I already gave a speech, Teeny!" I shouted back, but he just shook his head and waved his beer around a little.

"That was the sugarcoated, professional version because you were surrounded by the stuck-up suits that make up the Mavs orga-nization. Now, it's time for you to give us your raw, real speech filled with your usual commentary and rambles fueled by f-bombs and feisty little attitude."

The f-bombs? Yeah, he had me there. But I strongly disagreed with the latter.

"Excuse me," I said, and with a hand to my hip, I pointed a defi-ant index finger straight in his direction. "I do *not* have a feisty little attitude."

Cam chuckled. "You might be pint-sized, but we've all seen you in action."

"Yeah, little lady," Martinez agreed. "Mitchell is right. You might be small enough to fit into my fucking pocket, but what you don't have in size, you make up for in sass and the ability to curse like a sailor, drunk and on leave."

I rolled my eyes, but then, I took in the sight that was a room full of Mavericks, looking toward me with nothing but acceptance.

Somehow, I'd done what felt impossible.

I'd filmed an entire vlog series with these football gods, and more than that, I'd managed to do it and walk away with several friend-ships in the process. My eyes briefly flitted back to Sean. I took in his handsome face, and I just felt *it*. All the way to my fucking toes.

And love. You totally fell in love.

I nearly cringed at the mental admission.

If there was one thing I shouldn't have done, it was *that*. I never should've let myself get so close to him. And most importantly, I never should've let my heart get involved.

I cleared my throat and forced my brain to focus on something less heavy.

And with my glass raised high in the air, I attempted to bring some levity to the situation.

"Even though every single one of you was a pain in my ass at times, I've had some serious fun with you guys," I stated proudly. "Now, I hope you all won't mind, but since this experience has been so wonderful, I've decided to accept Pittsburgh's offer."

"What Shitsburgh offer?" Mitchell yelled from the background, and I forced a neutral smile to my face.

"They want me to film a ten-episode series with their team."

"Are you fucking with us?" Sam Sheffield asked, his mouth paused right above the neck of his beer bottle.

"Why would I be fucking with you?" I questioned and bit back my smile. "They've offered me nearly double the amount of money, and they want two extra episodes. It's a fantastic opportunity."

"Say it isn't fucking so, Sixy," Teeny demanded.

"I thought you guys would be happy for me..."

"I'd be happier if you were heading to Miami... Hell, even Arizona," Sean said, and his words were a little too firm for my liking. "But Pittsburgh?" he questioned. "I'm not so sure I can let you go spend two months with that team of assholes."

Teeny looked at me, eyes narrowed. "Say it," he said. "Say you're just fucking with us."

Damn, who would've thought the Mavericks would be so territorial?

"All right. So, I might be fucking with you," I announced and held my index finger and thumb mere centimeters apart. "Just a little bit fucking with you."

"Just a little bit?" Quinn asked, and his lips crested into a grin. "Or is this like the time you pranked Sean about his propensity for posting pictures of his abs on social media?"

I shrugged. "Okay, maybe I'm fucking with you a lot."

Several of the guys started to laugh, and Martinez glared.

"You're an evil, evil woman."

"Oh, get the fuck over it, Teeny," I retorted and held my glass high in the air again. "I'd like to propose a toast to the Mavericks. The guys who have won my little heart and will forever be my favorite bunch of assholes in the league! Thank you for letting me film your every move, and sometimes, get away with a few little pranks in the meantime." I winked and took one last, long look at the group of men.

"So, tonight, I raise my glass with a smile on my face and gratefulness in my heart. Cheers to you guys!" I exclaimed, ending my toast, and then took a hearty drink of my beer.

The guys joined in, raising their glasses in the air toward me and then following my lead.

And before I knew it, Martinez had set his glass down on a table and started stalking toward me.

I attempted to escape him, but for a guy his size, he was too fucking quick. Into his arms and on top of his fucking thick shoulders I went.

With Marty, one of the defensive ends on the practice squad, playing DJ, the music was turned up as loud as it could go while Martinez attempted to moonwalk across the hardwood of the dance floor, with me on his shoulders.

"Teeny!" I shouted over the beat of "Get Lucky." "You've got some moves, my man, but fucking hell, I don't want an aerial view of it!"

"You like?" he shouted up toward me, and I could see his cheeks lift up in a smile.

"I'd like it a lot better if my feet were firmly on the fucking ground!"

He just laughed me off and proceeded to moonwalk and two-step his way around the dance floor for what felt like forever. By the time I slid my fingers into the hair on top of his head and pulled hard, the song had switched over to one of my favorite Rihanna songs and he was breathing heavy from exertion.

"Ow! Shit!" he groaned and finally got the point. With strong hands and even stronger arms, he lifted me off his shoulders and let my feet touch the ground again.

Thank God.

Before I could start dancing on my own, he wrapped me up tight in his arms and gave me a big old bear hug. "I'm gonna miss you, Sixy," he said and grinned down at me. "Keep in touch, okay?"

"Definitely." I nodded. "Bring home a championship?"

He smiled as wide as Texas. "You got it."

The beat and tempo of the song increased, and my body vibrated with the need to let loose. Between the lyrics of "This Is What You Came For" and Rihanna's sexy, sultry voice, I couldn't *not* dance around to it.

But my solo performance didn't last long. Another thirty seconds into the song and someone came up behind me, wrapping their arms around my waist and pulling me close to their chest. I leaned my head back to find Sean looking down at me.

"W-what are you doing?" I asked, shocked by his very public display of affection.

It wasn't the first time he'd been a little too touchy-feely with me at this party.

"I'm dancing with you," he whispered into my ear, and goose bumps rolled up my spine and down my arms. "I'm dancing with the sexiest woman on the fucking planet."

My traitorous heart pitter-pattered inside my chest at his words, and the realization of too much PDA between us in front of other people was long forgotten.

Next thing I knew, with hips swaying, I followed his rhythm.

He felt so good wrapped around me. And inside of his arms, I just felt safe; it just felt *right*.

And I didn't feel like thinking about saying goodbye.

I didn't feel like thinking or doing anything besides staying close to him.

So, I did. And we danced until one song bled into the next song and the next.

But my momentary bliss started to fade away as I started to look around the room, and eventually, the reality of our situation began to grow heavy on my shoulders.

No one knew Sean and I had been hooking up.

No one knew we'd had sex or that something had grown between us.

We'd hid it. From *everyone.*

None of that really mattered, though, because whatever we'd started would come to a screeching halt.

My chest started to grow tight with anxiety, and the inside of my mouth felt dry and scratchy like sandpaper. I needed a drink. And I needed space. And I needed not to feel so many fucking things for Sean.

His dating record had proven he wasn't the relationship kind of guy, yet I was the relationship kind of girl.

And more than that, I wouldn't be here anymore, following the team around. I wouldn't see him on a daily basis, nor would we have hotel rooms and secret doors to hide behind.

Filming was done, and I'd be headed back to San Diego in the morning.

I could fantasize and dream and wish all I wanted, but the facts were pretty clear-cut. The odds of Sean wanting to be in some sort of long-distance relationship were a big fat fucking zero. And sadly, I knew to my core I wouldn't be able to continue whatever it was we were doing with the reality of understanding that monogamy wasn't a possibility on his end.

My thoughts had gotten away from me, and I hated myself for even thinking about Sean and relationships in the same sentence.

Rationally, I knew better than that. But my stupid heart seemed to have a hell of a time understanding the certainty of the situation.

I disentangled myself from his arms, and he looked down at me, brow raised.

"I'm going to grab a drink," I said and didn't stick around any longer.

I needed to put some distance between us, but I didn't go to the table where all of the drinks and snacks were located. Straight out of the entrance of the reception room, I found a quiet spot down one of the long corridors that had a gorgeous floor-to-ceiling view of New York City's skyline.

The lights glimmered and shone, and I just stared off into the distance, taking in the tall skyscrapers and wondering what the hustle and bustle of the city that never sleeps looked like at half past one in the morning on a Saturday night.

"Everything okay?"

Instantly, I froze in my spot. I knew that voice like the back of my hand.

And my traitorous heart, well, she knew the man behind that voice all too well. Hell, she all but jumped out of my chest at his first word.

I just nodded and kept my eyes trained on the cityscape view. "Just needed to cool down for a little bit."

Sean moved toward me and wrapped his arm around my shoulder, tucking me into his side.

And I liked it, too fucking much. He felt too good. This felt too good. And quickly, it became more than I could handle.

My heart responded with an ache and pound and twist inside my chest.

God, I liked him. Way, way too much.

Like him? You've fallen *for him.*

Fuck.

The mere idea of not seeing him on a daily basis was already hard enough. But when I calculated in the fact that whatever had grown between us would now come to a sudden end, it was too much pain for me to physically tolerate.

I disentangled myself from him, and he stared down at me like I'd grown two heads.

"Are you sure you're okay?" he asked, and the concern in his voice made my throat constrict.

"I'm good," I said and forced a phony-ass smile on my lips. "I'm a little sad to leave you guys, but I'm really excited to finally go back home to California. It's way more my speed."

Lies. Lies. Lies.

"Look, Six," he started, and I watched the way his Adam's apple bobbed as he swallowed. "We really need to talk."

I waited for more. But he didn't offer more. He just stared down at me, his brow furrowed and his full lips fixed into a firm line.

He's probably just trying to find a way to let you down easy, my mind taunted.

I mean, this *was* Sean Phillips. The playboy. The famous football player who avoided labels and relationships and commitment. The man most women knew as the manwhore with the big cock.

I mentally grimaced at that thought.

God, I had to get out of here.

I had to find reprieve away from this stadium, away from my thoughts, away from him.

I needed to woman up and just save him the time and hassle of trying to find the right way to end this, whatever the fuck it was.

Forcing a deep inhale into my lungs and long, quiet exhale through my mouth, I steeled myself for what I was about to do.

Up on my tippy toes, I pressed a soft kiss to his cheek, and it took all of my strength not to let my lips linger against his skin.

"This has been a lot of fun," I said and locked my gaze with his. "But I guess it's time to get back to real life, huh?"

"Get back to real life?" he questioned, and his full, soft, fucking kissable lips turned down at the corners.

God, I'll miss those lips.

Sorrow pricked behind my eyes, and I had to swallow past the thick emotion lodging itself in my throat.

Just fucking focus, Six.

"You know," I said and cleared my throat. "*Get back to real life.*"

He didn't respond, instead just stared down at me.

"I mean, we both knew whatever was going on between us couldn't last forever, right?" I tried to lighten the situation, but stiff and stilted and strained, my words felt all wrong.

He looked out through the floor-to-ceiling windows, and I watched the way the lines of his face hardened beneath the shadowed light of the night's sky. "So, this is goodbye?" he asked and brought his gaze back to mine.

Goodbye.

God, it hurt my heart.

Especially when I had to hear that word leave his lips.

It was much easier to handle coming from my mouth or when it was locked tight inside my head.

"Yeah," I said, pushing my words past the growing tightness in my throat and chest. "I guess this is goodbye."

"Take care of yourself, Six," he said soft as a whisper and wrapped me up in a tight hug.

But the embrace ended quicker than it started. And before I knew it, Sean gave me his official goodbye.

He let me go, and without another word, walked away from me.

A sob threatened to bubble up my throat, but I swallowed hard against the emotional onslaught and held a hand to my lips.

I stared at the skyline for God knows how long. But eventually, the tears pricking behind my eyes became too thick, and I headed in the opposite direction he'd gone and found reprieve inside of a women's restroom.

Locking myself inside one of the stalls and with my head in my hands, I did the only thing I could do. I cried.

Big fat fucking pathetic tears.

They were there because I would miss him.

They were there because saying goodbye to Sean felt like the hardest thing I'd ever done.

And mostly, they were there because I was a stupid, stupid girl who had let herself fall for a man who never fell for anyone.

Chapter Twenty-Six

Sean

"Dude," QB yelled toward me just as Coach Bennett blew his whistle. "What's going on?"

"I'm just having a shit day," I muttered, but deep down, I fucking knew why.

Ever since Six had so easily said goodbye to me a few days ago, and basically written us and what we'd shared together off as some emotionless *just having fun* situation, I'd been completely fucked in the head.

This was new territory for me.

I'd never, in my whole life, been mindfucked by a woman.

I couldn't scrub our last conversation from my brain. Couldn't distract my mind enough not to keep hearing her final words on a loop inside my head. And more than that, I couldn't erase the memory of what she'd looked like when she'd said it.

She'd looked sad. Like something was off. Like she hadn't wanted to say the words that had left her lips.

But still, she'd said them.

Maybe I'd just been imagining her despondence? Maybe I'd just wanted her to be sad about it? But, in reality, she was back home in California and had already found a new fuck buddy?

Dude, she's not the fuck buddy type, my mind whispered.

If that was the truth, she sure as fuck seemed fine with it when it came to me.

"Phillips!" Coach B shouted from the sideline, and I jogged toward him.

I'd been playing like shit since I stepped onto the field this morning. Surely, his current plans revolved around shoving his foot up my ass or kicking me straight in the dick.

When it came to a pissed-off Coach Bennett, both were pretty viable options.

"What the fuck is going on?" he spat toward me once I stopped in front of him. "Are you trying to play that fucking bad? Or did you get your goddamn period and need a fucking tampon?"

Yeah. He was pissed.

"Sorry, Coach," I said dutifully. Honestly, when Bennett was on this big of a tirade, there wasn't much more you could do besides sit there and take it until he'd cleansed himself of anger.

"You're sorry?" he exclaimed and tossed his clipboard onto the ground. "Oh, man! Well, that makes every-fucking-thing better!"

And then, even though he stood a good few inches below me, he reached up and grabbed me by the face mask and got directly in my face.

"Listen up," he spat toward me, and I fought the urge to flinch when his fucking saliva hit me directly on the cheek. "You're going to go home and figure out whatever the fuck is making you play like you can't tell the difference between your head and your ass. And by next practice, you're going to be back to the Sean Phillips I know. The man who plays his fucking ass off and never drops the goddamn ball. Got it?"

I nodded. "Yes, sir."

He stared at me for a long moment before letting go of my helmet and striding toward the center of the field.

"All right!" he shouted and blew his whistle again. "Nice work, everyone besides Phillips!"

Damn, he was really reading me the riot act today.

Unfortunately, I more than deserved his diatribe.

"Hit the showers! And since you all have an off day from practice tomorrow, I expect to hear that every single one of you came in for weights and cardio. That understood?"

"Yes, sir!" everyone, including me, responded in synchrony.

"All right! Hit the showers!"

Most of the team headed toward the inside of the stadium to clean up and get some much-wanted time away from the field.

But I, on the other hand... Well, I wasn't in any rush to get home to an empty house where my mind could get the best of me and race with ongoing thoughts of a woman who made ending things with me look easy.

I wasn't proud of it, but I'd spent the better part of last night watching her YouCam vlogs, both the ones that were part of our series *and* her own personal content that she posted on a daily basis.

It was all pretty fucking sad, to be honest.

And for most of it, I'd been so tempted to text her, call her, do anything just to have some sort of direct contact with her. Fucking anything to hear her sexy, raspy voice speaking directly to me.

Luckily, I'd stayed strong and avoided making a fool of myself by showing her just how pathetic I'd become since she'd dropped me like a bad habit.

I slid my helmet off my head and grabbed a bottle of water from one of the coolers on the sidelines. I chugged it down in practically four hearty gulps and swiped a hand across my face once I finished it off.

"Yo! Phillips!" Cam's voice filled my ears, and I turned to find him slowly walking off the field. "You okay, bud?"

I shrugged. "Besides playing like shit, I'm good."

He just grinned. "Yeah, you definitely weren't on top of your game today, huh?" he questioned, and I shook my head.

"Not in the fucking least," I muttered, but I didn't add any fuel to the fire.

Only Quinn knew the truth about my pathetic mood. For all Mitchell could probably surmise, I was just having a few off days. Which, for a lot of ballers in this league, happened from time to time. Generally, not to me, but yeah, other guys had experienced it.

"You know what I think you need?" he said, and his eyes lit up.

"What's that?"

He grinned like the devil. "A fucking night out."

A night out? It sure as fuck couldn't hurt my game at this point. Hell, it might even be good for my mental health.

"Where you heading?"

He shrugged and took a long drink from a cup of red Gatorade. "I was thinking about heading into the city and hitting up one of the bars in SoHo."

I thought it over for all of thirty seconds. "Count me in."

Two hours, *possibly three hours*, into the evening and I was thoroughly buzzed.

Sitting cozy in VIP of whatever the fuck bar Cam had led us to, I sat back and took in the sights while he schmoozed it up with some blonde on the dance floor.

The flashing neon lights, bumping music, and pretty cocktail waitresses striding around the room in negligible black skirts and tank tops served as a nice mental distraction.

Also, alcohol. That was good too.

"Hey there, Sean," someone purred behind me, her voice just barely rising over the heavy, pounding bass coming from the speakers.

I looked over my shoulder and furrowed my brow as I tried to put a name to this chick's face. She looked familiar, but my half-buzzed brain might as well have been trying to solve an advanced calculus equation.

She pushed her full, round, very fake tits up and toward my face, smiled, and fluttered her lashes. Apparently, she knew me. Or she *wanted* to know me.

"Hey," I responded for lack of anything else to say.

She put a little hand to her hip and narrowed her eyes. "Do you even remember me?"

"Am I supposed to remember you?"

Giggling, she shoved a hand toward my shoulder. "You're such a dick," she said. I couldn't stand the way her voice went nasal at her teasing words. It was nothing like Six's rasp.

God, stop thinking about Six.

Miniskirt. Half-shirt. This chick's body was toned and firm and curvy in all the right places, and she wanted everyone in this club to see it. I stared hard, trying to let arousal numb my thoughts.

Too bad your dick couldn't be any more flaccid at the sight of her...

She walked around the long booth until she stood in front of me, and then, she just up and chose to make herself comfortable in my lap. I flinched as the bones in her ass slammed into my thighs.

"I'm Aria," she whispered into my ear, and my brow rose to my forehead.

"Aria?" I repeated out loud and racked my brain over the familiarity of her name. "Wait...Aria, the pop singer?" I questioned, and she nodded. "And we've met before?"

Because, fuck, I honestly couldn't remember meeting her.

She giggled. "I swear to God, do you, like, have amnesia or something?"

Apparently, when it came to her, I did.

"We met at the ESPY's after party last year," she finally explained, but it still didn't ring any bells.

I nodded my head anyway. Women never reacted positively to the words *I don't have one fucking clue who you are.* "Oh yeah, that's right."

Silently, I wondered if our little meet-and-greet had turned into something more physical than just a friendly exchange of words.

Instantly, my chest ached at the thought.

It was weird and so out of character for me.

Normally, I wouldn't have given a shit about who I'd fucked or who I couldn't remember fucking or who I'd forgotten about fucking, but now, after Six, it just felt different.

Because it feels wrong.

Fuck, I wanted to hate her for that, but as hard as I tried, I couldn't hate her.

I liked Six too much. Way too fucking much, actually.

You more than like her, you idiot.

My head swam, and the chick in my lap wiggled her ass, which did absolutely nothing for me. It had the exact opposite effect she was probably hoping for. If anything, my dick was half tempted to crawl up inside of my body and hibernate.

Goddammit, Six. You've totally messed with my fucking head! I mentally cursed her even though I knew she couldn't hear me. Nor would it fix anything.

"You know..." Aria smirked at me and slid her hand up my chest. "I wanted you to come home with me that night..." She paused and pushed out her lipstick-covered mouth into a pout.

Those nearly blood-red lips of hers were such a turn-off.

I didn't want those lips. I wanted different lips.

Soft, pink, full, pliant lips.

Six's lips.

"But...you turned me down," she purred like a fucking cat. "Isn't that sad?"

Sad? The only thing sad right now is me.

She stared at me with knowing eyes and pouty lips and leaned herself in a little closer to press those stupid lips of hers to my cheek. Her strong, flowery as fuck perfume hit me like a Mack truck, and I had the strong urge to shove her off my lap.

"Don't you think we should remedy that tonight, Sean?"

Fuck, is she still talking?

She pressed her fake tits into my chest and fluttered her eyelashes in what I guessed was her sultry and seductive face.

Her tits, her face, her body, it all had about the same effect as her lips.

A total fucking turn-off.

God, what was wrong with me?

She's not Six.

"No shit," I said, and honestly, I couldn't even really remember what I was responding to or what she'd just said. I also didn't really give a fuck.

I looked around the room and then down at the table in front of me. I counted the empty glasses and quickly surmised I'd had at least six vodka and tonics, possibly eight, but I wasn't sure if those were actual extra glasses or if I was just seeing double.

Basically, it was too much, and I needed to get the hell out of here.

Without thinking twice, I stood up and removed Arielle or Aerosol, fuck whatever her name was, from my lap and started looking for Mitchell.

"Oh my God," the chick muttered, and I looked down.

Instantly, I offered her a hand when I realized I'd nearly dumped her off my lap and straight onto the floor.

"Sorry about that," I apologized, and with a strong hand, I made sure she was steady on her sky-high stilettos before I let go. "Look, it was great chatting with you, but I'm gonna call it a night."

"What? Seriously?" she questioned, and I nodded.

"See ya around, er..." *Fuck, what is her name?* "Yeah...see ya around!" I called over my shoulder as I strode out of the VIP section and headed straight for the dance floor.

The instant I spotted Cam in the center, dancing with some random blonde, I pushed through the sea of people until I stood beside him.

"Dude, I need to go," I said directly into his ear, and he nodded, honoring the bro code like a fucking soldier.

"Sorry, sweetheart," he said to the girl who was currently grinding her ass into his crotch. "Gotta go."

And that was that.

We paid our tab and got the hell out of there before I drank more alcohol or ended up hooking up with a chick named after a hair spray can.

Or is it Ariel? Like that fucking Disney mermaid?

Fuck if I knew. Fuck if I cared.

I just wanted to go home and pass out in my bed.

But first, I'd pound a jug of water and eat some carbs to avoid a soul-crushing hangover in the morning. Lord knows, Coach B would be pissed to see me hunched over and hurling in the weight room tomorrow.

After tonight, the only certainty I knew was that I needed to find a way to get the fuck over Six Malone or else I might as well just sell my cock on the black market and become a goddamn monk in the off-season.

Yeah, good luck with that, asshole.

Chapter Twenty-Seven

Six

I'd been home in San Diego for all of four days.

You'd think, after being on the East Coast where the temperatures rarely hit above freezing this time of year, I'd be out savoring the California sun.

But instead, I was locked up inside my apartment, staring at the television as reruns of *Jersey Shore* filled the screen.

Snooki was drunk again, and honestly, I was jealous of her ability to gain access to alcohol.

I'd yet to go to the grocery store since I'd gotten home, and besides responding to work-related emails and posting a few videos to my public YouCam profile—videos I'd luckily had as backup for days that I just needed a fucking break—I'd done nothing else.

Which explained the bare fridge, the various empty takeout containers scattered across my kitchen counter, and my vagabond-like appearance.

Ugly blue robe wrapped around my gravely unshowered body and dirty, Pebbles-style ponytail, I was a total hot mess.

I truly wondered if people who passed by my apartment could

smell the aroma of pathetic seeping out from beneath my front door.

I was sad for a million different reasons, but the one that had me the most fucked up revolved around a name I didn't even want to think, much less verbalize out loud.

Because once I said it or even thought it, that would make it real.

And if it was real, it meant I actually had to deal with it.

Avoidance felt like the better option at this point.

Deep down, I knew that no matter how real my feelings for him were and how hard it had been saying goodbye and how much I missed him, it didn't matter.

It wouldn't change anything.

Right before I found the strength to sit up and grab the remote control from my coffee table, my phone started ringing and vibrating across the couch cushion beside me.

Heart in my throat, I waited with bated breath as I picked it up and looked down at the screen.

Incoming Call: Everly

My heart almost dropped to my feet once I saw who the call *wasn't* from.

God, why did I still hold out hope he'd call me?

I mean, why did my brain even think that was a possibility?

With a heavy sigh, I pushed out the ridiculous thoughts that would never come true and answered Everly's call with a quick tap to the green phone icon.

"Hey," I greeted. I tried to be cheery and happy and shit, but I just sounded like a monotone robot.

"Six?" she questioned. "Is that you?"

"Of course it's me," I muttered. "Why wouldn't it be me?"

"Because you sound like someone just killed your cat."

"I don't have a cat."

"Thank God. I can't stand those little fuckers."

I sighed. "Everly."

"God. What in the hell is going on?" she demanded. "You sound terrible, and you know I can't stand it when people don't laugh at my jokes."

"I'm just feeling a little under the weather," I lied.

"Please hold," she said, and next thing I knew, she'd managed to conference Sammy into our call. "Okay, now, please resume your bull-shit lies, but just know, both Sammy and I are now listening and ready to call you out on it."

"Fucking hell," I muttered. "I'm not lying."

"Oh, come on, Six," Everly retorted. "Just tell us what's wrong before we have to come all the way there. You know if you see me in person, I'm going to make you watch *General Hospital* every day."

"No more soaps!" I shouted, the trauma of Everly's detailed fantasies about Sonny and Jason playing behind my eyelids. God, half of my high school experience had been robbed by her talks about sex swings and whips.

"Honey," Sammy chimed in. "What's going on? Are you okay?"

I sighed…again. "I'm fine."

"Are you sure?" Sammy's much calmer and less aggressive voice filled my ears. She was always the mother hen who could carefully reassure anyone into admitting the truth. Everly, on the other hand, was more of metaphorically grab you by the back of your hair and force you into admission kind of gal.

"You know we're just worried about you, sweetie," Sammy added, and her sympathy and concern were too much.

Silence consumed the line, and the instant tears started to prick at my eyes, I couldn't hold it back.

"I think I fell for the manwhore," I half whispered, half sobbed.

"You fell for the manwhore?" Everly questioned, voice laced with confusion.

"Sean Phillips," I responded through shaky tears, and the mere admission of his name felt like a dagger to my heart. "I was just sup-posed to fuck him, but I fucking fell for him."

"Wait… You hooked up with Sean Phillips?" Sammy questioned, and I could literally picture her pretty blue eyes damn near bugging out of her head as she asked it.

"Multiple times," I muttered. "In his car. At Topgolf. In hotel rooms. All over the fucking place, to be honest."

"Ho-lee shit," Everly said, and I couldn't agree more.

Holy shit was right. I'd stupidly let my heart get involved with a man who didn't ever let his heart get involved with any-fucking-one.

"So…you guys just had sex or…?" Sammy paused, and I knew exactly what she was trying to get at. Always the romantic, she was secretly hoping there was some kind of budding love story developing between Sean and me. And in her hopeful, romanticizing brain, we'd eventually reunite and live out our happily ever after with Snow White's fucking birds chirping around us and shit.

But there were no birds here. Or happily ever afters. Or Sean.

Just four days' worth of oil in my hair and a fort of empty Chinese takeout containers.

"We definitely had sex…*a lot of sex*…and I was the stupid girl who let herself get too attached to him."

"What about him? Surely, he's tangled in your wild mane of hair," Everly asserted, and I rolled my eyes.

God, I wish.

"Sean Phillips is not the type of guy who settles down," I denied. "He's a brilliant fuck buddy. A terrific one-night stand. But boyfriend? Hell to the no. He'd rather cut off his big dick than commit."

"Are you sure about that?" Sammy's naïve question filled my ears, and I scrubbed at my face, roughly wiping the tears away from my cheeks and eyes.

"Trust me, I'm sure," I answered. "So, you two can go ahead and stop filling your heads with daydreams about Sean and me getting together and having some kind of fairy tale happily ever after. That will never happen."

"Damn, girl," Everly muttered, all of her normal humor officially snuffed out by the sound of my tears. "I'm so sorry."

"Me too," Sammy agreed. "Is there anything we can do for you? Do you want me to try to get some time off work and visit   this weekend?"

Considering she only lived a few hours away in Palm Springs, the idea was tempting, but I still needed a little more time to wallow in my own pit of self-pity and despair.

"I really appreciate the offer, but I have a lot of work to get done over the next few weeks, but how about next month?" I suggested. "How about both of you come out next month, and we can have a girls' weekend?"

"Count me in," Everly said, and Sammy quickly agreed.

"All right," I said. "It's settled. Next month we'll drink wine, catch up, and maybe eat at that expensive Mexican restaurant in Beverly Hills you both love so much."

"Hell yes! Take me to El Padre, and I'll put a temporary hold on my threesome with Sonny and Jason for the weekend."

I grinned at Everly's excitement, despite her overzealous expression of detail, and honestly, I think it was the first time I'd smiled in like five days.

Which was really flipping sad.

I ended the call a few minutes later, and both Everly and Sammy urged me to call them if I needed anything or wanted to make the girls' trip sooner.

God, I really needed to get it together. I couldn't just sit around and be sad about a man who didn't see our time together as anything more than a fun way to pass a few weeks.

Grabbing my laptop off the coffee table, I fired up my internet browser and decided I'd attempt to get some work done.

I logged in to my email and started to scroll through the pages upon pages of unanswered messages. Some were from fans. Some were from sponsors trying to get me to promote their products. And some weren't even work-related, just various websites and newsletters I subscribed to.

Before I'd even managed to get through page four of unread emails, I froze in my spot, and my fingers dropped away from my laptop trackpad as my jaw plummeted toward my lap.

Sean Phillips has a hot night out with pop sensation Aria!

The subject of the email from *Gossip!* grabbed my attention instantly.

Like a full-fledged masochist, I clicked it open.

I didn't waste any time reading the article. Instead, I scrolled down to the bottom and took in the collage of photos.

Aria sitting in Sean's lap.

Sean smiling up at her as she stood behind him, her hand on his shoulder.

Her lips pressed to Sean's cheek.

Picture after picture after picture filled my eyes, and my poor little heart felt like someone had carved it with a rusted-out butcher's knife.

It'd been all of a week, and already, he was out having a grand old time with Aria—the pop sensation who was so popular she only needed one goddamn name like Madonna.

And while he was out partying his ass off and most likely hooking up with celebrities, what was I doing?

Wallowing in my sadness and missing him.

Fuck that. Fuck this. Fuck *him*.

I didn't want to be that girl.

Hell, I *refused* to be that girl. I refused to let myself fall into some sort of depression over a man.

No way.

And just like that, I felt renewed. Validated.

I peeled myself off of the couch and stretched out the creaks in my joints and muscles.

First step, a goddamn shower.

Next step, move the hell on and stop thinking about the motherfucker who could give zero fucks about you.

Obviously, ending things with him had been the smartest thing I'd ever done.

My brain was on board. Rational and realistic and ready.

But my heart said otherwise, whispering, *Yeah, keep telling yourself that, you stupid, stupid girl.*

Chapter Twenty-Eight

Sean

"You all right?" Quinn asked from his spot beside me at the bar, and I couldn't miss the way his eyes scrutinized me.

We were supposed to be out celebrating our big postseason win against Baltimore.

One more game and we'd be a shoo-in for the championship game.

This was the furthest we'd even gotten in the play-offs, and it should've been a fantastic fucking night.

But Quinn was obviously trying to put a damper on my fun. And, most likely, put an end to one of the biggest reasons for my fun. Alcohol.

"Of course I'm good," I muttered and took a long swig of beer. "Why wouldn't I be all right?"

"Because you almost never drink during the season, and for the past few weeks, you've done just that."

Bingo.

I sighed. "Just calm down, Mom. I'm just having a little fun. No need to get your panties in a fucking bunch."

He stood up from his barstool and looked down at me with a firm jaw. "Listen," he said, his voice a near whisper. "I can tell you're going through some shit and I know it has everything to do with a certain little vlogger, but for now, I'm going to let you be."

"And what about later?" I questioned, sarcasm dripping from my voice. "What are you going to do later, Mom?"

Internally, I grimaced. I knew I shouldn't have been taking my anger out on him. He was one of my best friends. And he never failed to be someone I could count on.

But, fuck, I couldn't stop myself.

He stared at me for a long moment, concern embedded within his steely gaze, but eventually, he just decided I wasn't worth the time.

"Don't fucking worry about it," he muttered, and just like that, he walked away, leaving me sitting at the bar by myself.

We'd just arrived back home in New Jersey a few hours ago, and now, most of our team was partying inside our regular hole-in-the-wall of an establishment, Doolan's. We came here a lot, but it wasn't without purpose. It was one of the only places we could go without being overly hounded by fans. Apparently hungry for our business, the owner saw to it personally. Hell, half the time, if it got too busy or if too many people started showing up to get autographs, he would just shut the place down and let us hang out in peace.

It was a good thirty-minute drive from the stadium but one hundred percent worth the time and distance.

Tonight, we blended in to the crowd.

And the only people who really even noticed us were the women who tended to follow the team around.

The groupies.

The fangirls.

The chicks who did everything in their power to fuck a Maverick.

Somehow, they were well-versed in our whereabouts and always made it so fucking easy for any one of us to take them home.

Maybe that's what I need, I thought to myself. Maybe I just needed a random night of fucking to cleanse myself of *her.*

Fucking Six.

She was in my thoughts. In my dreams. Hell, sometimes, when I woke up in the middle of the night, I swore I could smell her perfume on my fucking pillow.

I missed her. And I hated that the most.

I hated that I missed the woman who'd so easily walked away from me, who didn't even want to try to give us a shot.

But it's not like you told her you wanted to give it a shot, my mind taunted, but I fucking ignored it. With my lips to the bottle, I chugged the rest of my beer and gestured toward the bartender to bring me another.

Before I knew it, I was six beers deep and making eyes at some blond chick across the bar.

I raised my beer toward her and winked.

She took that as the opening I intended and slid off her barstool, sashaying her ass directly toward me and not once breaking eye contact.

"Is this seat open?" she asked, and I shrugged.

"Looks that way."

"Mind if I join you?"

I raised my beer toward the bartender and gestured for him to bring two more. One for me and one for my new friend with the generous rack. Which, with the way her tits were nearly shoved to her chin, she obviously wanted me to be aware of. I silently wondered if it was a push-up bra or an actual boob job.

It was hard to tell, and I hated that I started thinking about Six's body.

God, I loved her body. Subtle curves that fit so perfectly into my hands. I loved every inch of her curvy, petite, fucking mind-blowing little frame.

Fuck, get it together, I coached myself. *Stop thinking about her and focus on the blond chick who keeps rubbing her hand up and down your thigh.*

It was all pretty fucking sad, really.

The fact that I was thinking about Six while another woman was all but shoving her hand into my pants and getting my dick out.

I couldn't keep living like this, though. I needed to move on.

Eyes focused…well, focused enough, I looked directly at the blonde sitting beside me. "What's your name, sweetheart?" I asked, and her scarlet red lips crested into a smile.

Her lips were all wrong, but I fought past the turn-off.

"Kimberly."

"Kimberly, I'm Sean," I introduced myself, and she just giggled.

"I know who you are."

"Is that right?" I questioned, grinning, and wrapped my arm around her shoulders. "You a big Mavericks fan?"

"I'm a big Sean Phillips fan," she whispered and punctuated that statement by sliding her hand up my thigh until it sat just centimeters below my dick.

She was pretty in an overdone kind of way, but at this point, I didn't really care.

All I wanted to do was fuck Six out of my system.

And Kimberly seemed like the perfect option. Hell, she was already trying her damnedest to seduce me.

No patience for talking and no desire to actually get to know her, I decided then and there to put my plan into action.

"You want to get out of here?" I asked her, and she nodded.

"I'd love to."

I threw a handful of cash onto the bar and waved goodbye toward the bartender.

With my arm wrapped around Kimberly's shoulders, I led us toward the front of the bar and out the doors.

The cold New Jersey air hit me straight in the face, so fucking frigid it nearly sobered me up completely.

But I kept my focus and tried to stick with the plan.

I led us toward an outside awning, and the blond chick on my arm nibbled at my earlobe and kissed along my neck while we waited for a cab.

It took all of thirty seconds for me to grow tired of the fake little fucking moans she kept forcing past her lips.

I tried to ignore it. I tried not to be annoyed with her. I tried to focus on the task at hand—fucking Six Malone out of my goddamn system.

But when Quinn strode out of the bar and met my eyes, his own shining cold, defiant, and judgmental, I felt like he'd managed to dump a bucket of cold water over my head, even though he was standing like fifty feet away.

Fuck. What am I doing?

I looked down at the overzealous woman, and instead of being aroused, all I felt was fucking nauseated. And disappointed. Not in her, but in myself.

I wanted to go back to the way I'd been before Six had walked into my life, but I couldn't. As much as I didn't want to admit it to myself, she'd changed me. She'd opened my eyes. And most importantly, she'd shown me that I wanted more than just a random fuck.

I wanted more than that.

I wanted *her*.

"You need a ride?" Quinn asked loudly, and I nodded.

"We going with him?" the blonde asked me, eyes excited.

I shook my head and started to guide her back toward the bar entrance. "Listen, honey, I'm going to have to take a rain check."

"What?" she questioned and stopped just before I could get her back inside. "But I thought—"

I cut her off. "I'm sorry, but I just can't," I answered honestly. "I wanted to, but I can't."

"You can't?"

"No. I can't." I shook my head. "Why don't you go back inside, have a few more drinks, and tell the bartender to put your drinks on my tab?"

Her smoky eyes stared up at me in confusion. "You're not staying?"

"No," I stated firmly. "I'm going home."

Eventually, she shrugged, and without a second thought, walked back inside the bar.

And I did the walk of shame toward Quinn's truck.

He didn't say a word, though, and we both climbed inside, only silence, the click of the engine, and the soft hum of the radio filling up the space between us.

Once he pulled out of the parking lot and drove for a good five minutes on the main road, he couldn't hold it back any longer.

He smirked at me and shot me a look out of the corner of his eye. "So, I was right, huh?"

"Right about what?"

"The reason you've been in a shit mood the past few weeks," he said, and I looked over at him just as he said the one name that hit me right in the fucking chest every time I heard it. "Six."

He had a small idea that something had happened between Six and me, but I'd never opened up and told him the real details.

I sighed, but instead of lying or brushing it off, I decided to tell him the truth. Hell, maybe telling him what had really gone down between Six and me would make me fucking feel better.

"Yeah," I finally responded. "You were right."

"I fucking knew it!" he exclaimed with a soft chuckle.

"Well," I said through a sigh. "There really isn't much to know besides the fact that I was starting to fall for her and she pretty much wrote us off as fuck buddies."

Quinn grimaced. *"Fuck."*

"Yeah."

"I'm sorry, dude."

"Me too, man," I responded. "Me fucking too."

The open road stretched long and far in front of us, and I settled into my seat and let my misery consume me.

There was no use avoiding it.

No use trying to fight it or trying to find ways to get past it.

Obviously, Six Malone had done a real fucking number on my heart.

Chapter Twenty-Nine

Six

Georgia: Call me. I have an exciting proposition for you.

I stared down at the text message and sighed. Unless she'd started a new job, her exciting proposition had something to do with the Mavericks. And the Mavericks meant the one man I was valiantly trying to scrub from my brain would be involved.

It'd been a few weeks now, but still, Sean Phillips was all up in my goddamn thoughts like a sticky vat of jam.

Mothersmucker.

With a heavy heart and anxiety clawing at my throat, I tapped her number and called her.

She answered by the second ring.

"Six! How are you?" Georgia greeted, voice cheerier than Santa Claus on Christmas Eve.

Even though it felt like my entire world was crashing down and I was on day one of my period and I was certain my uterus was plotting an exit route from my body and my traitorous brain couldn't stop thinking about Sean, per societal norms, there was only one appropriate response to her question.

"I'm good." It was a bullshit response on my end, but I didn't make the rules for proper social interactions. "How are you?"

"Well, considering the Mavericks are getting ready for the championship game, I'm fantastic."

I already knew the news. I'd watched the game. I'd seen Sean score two glorious touchdowns. Hell, I'd even watched the live aftershow where they celebrated and interviewed nearly half of the team.

Well, they'd interviewed nearly everyone but Sean.

Which, pathetically, had only made me feel sad.

Even if he'd moved on, even if he'd long forgotten about me, I still wanted to see him. Hear his voice. Take in the handsome lines of his face and the way his eyes lit up when he was happy and excited about something.

Obviously, I was a masochist.

"That's a huge deal," I responded. Because it was. The Mavs could very well end their postseason with a big-ass championship trophy in their hands and bragging rights for the rest of their lives.

"A huge deal that we want you to be a part of," she added, and I could hear the giddy smile in her voice. "We want you there for the big game. We want to add an additional episode to the series."

Shit. Sadly, it was all of my worst fears realized.

It was one thing to see Sean's handsome face on my television, but it was a whole other ball game to have to witness it in person.

My sad little heart could only handle so much.

I knew my reaction to her news was crazy stupid. I should have been ecstatic. I should've been jumping up and down like a lunatic. But all I felt was anxiety. Throat-clawing, chest-tightening, *vomit all over myself* unease.

"Six? Are you still there?"

"Yeah. Sorry about that." I cleared my throat and swallowed down what felt like an entire bread loaf's worth of apprehension. I knew I shouldn't have eaten an entire baguette. "I guess I'm just a little bit shocked."

"I hope it's a good shocked…"

"Of course." I pushed the two words past my lips. "Of course, it's a good shocked. This is an incredible opportunity."

"Well, it's well deserved," she said. "The response to the series has been overwhelming, and ever since that first episode posted several weeks ago, my players have received several endorsements. Because of you, the Mavericks are becoming a household name to nearly everyone in America."

"Wow. That's fantastic." The incredible nature of it all was amazing to me.

"So, you'll do it?" she asked. "You'll let us fly you out to Minnesota for the championship game next week?"

I wished I could say no. I wished I already had some sort of obligation that would make me unable to commit.

But I had nothing. Not even the self-sabotaging stupidity it would take to turn down an offer like this. Obviously, my parents were to blame here, helping me pursue an education and all.

"Count me in."

"Fantastic!" she exclaimed. "We'll get our lawyers to draw up a contract and send it your way. In relation to the terms, almost everything will stay the same as the first eight episodes in the series. The only difference is that we would like this to be an hour-long episode instead of thirty minutes. And because of that, the compensation is higher."

If one thing could be said about Georgia Brooks, it was that she was fair. She could negotiate the hell out of a deal, but she never faltered at being honest. It was a rarity inside her profession.

I was sure it also helped that the Mavericks' marketing budget wasn't a pocket full of peanuts.

"Sounds good to me," I said. "I can't wait to get started."

Liar. You're totally dreading this.

"Fantastic. I'll have a contract for you by the end of the day," she said. "See you soon, Six!"

I ended the call with a feigned excited goodbye.

The irony of the situation wasn't lost on me.

Basically, everything I had ever hoped for and dreamed about in terms of my career was coming true. And all I felt was melancholy.

Which then made me angry.

I should've been celebrating. I should've been calling everyone I knew and letting them know I'd be at the fucking championship game.

But what was I doing? Grabbing my keys, hopping in my car, and stopping at the goddamn grocery store to pick up a cheap-ass bottle of wine and more tampons.

And what did I do after purchasing the wine? I went the fuck home, threw on some yoga pants and a tank top, and started to drink it.

One glass. Two glasses. Three glasses.

Down the hatch, it all went.

By the time the bottle didn't have a single drop left, I sat in the living room of my apartment buzzed—*more like drunk*—rewatching *Game of Thrones*.

I'd already finished all seven seasons, but I was addicted, and I wanted to see my two favorite characters together again.

Khal Drogo looked at his Khaleesi like she held all the power, like she was the most beautiful, perfect creature he'd ever seen, and I started to feel the emotion build up behind my eyes.

And then, he said it. One of my favorite quotes from the series where Drogo professes his undying love for his Khalessi and calls her the moon of his life.

My emotional dam burst, and tears starting flowing like water down my cheeks.

God, I wanted that. I wanted a man to look at me like I was his whole fucking world.

And I wanted to feel the same about him.

You have felt the same.

That thought only made me more emotional.

I didn't want to think about *him*.

I didn't want to think about Sean's smile or his laugh or his gorgeous eyes. And I sure as fuck didn't want to think about how he was probably out fucking other women while I was at home on my period, drinking my sadness away.

I hated how much it all hurt.

I hated that I wasn't really over him.

I hated that I'd let myself fall for him and still hadn't found the ability to move the fuck on.

I decided to blame it all on my period. No doubt, hormones held the power to make you a lunatic. And day one was always like being on an emotional roller coaster ride straight to hell. I could cry about anything and everything. Car commercials. Pictures of mini pigs in rain boots Sean's sister Cassie sent me. Running out of cookies. *Thoughts about Sean.*

The far too sensitive struggle was real.

Although, the whole bottle of wine I just drank probably isn't helping either...

A truer thought had never occurred.

With the sleeve of my shirt, I scrubbed the tears and snot away and took a long, deep inhale.

I needed to get it together.

But more importantly, I needed to chat. I needed to vent. I needed to ramble. I needed to get all of these thoughts off of my chest.

Without hesitation, I grabbed my phone, pulled up the YouCam app, and logged in to my private account. My long-distance besties, Everly and Sammy, would be the perfect audience for my emotional tirade.

"Guys," I said, skipping the greeting and diving right into the meat and potatoes of my pseudo-breakdown. "Buckle up and prepare for a ramble."

I stared into the camera and sighed.

"I'm on my period and my mental health status is in question. *Fuck* periods!" I bellowed. "Being a girl is so hard. So, so, so hard, right?" I questioned, but I didn't need a response. The constant sensation of a knife repeatedly stabbing my uterus was answer enough. "My uterus is plotting murder against me. Like, don't be surprised if you have to attend my funeral next week. If you do, it was my uterus. She finally killed me. She's a real bitch and a plotter, you know? Month after month, she makes her move, but this time, *this time*," I shouted, "she's really done it."

I picked up the camera and walked into my kitchen to grab a bag of Doritos.

Once the bag was open and I'd shoved a few chips into my mouth, I talked to the camera over a mouthful of nacho cheese.

"Wouldn't it be easier if we were men? I mean, if I had a penis, then I wouldn't have to deal with a period."

The word penis filled my head, and then visuals of Sean's penis followed.

"I has no penis," I said…well, slurred…into the camera. Obviously, I was drunk, but Everly and Sammy would understand.

Tears started to form behind my eyes again, and I let them fall unchecked down my cheeks.

"I have no penis at all," I announced. "But I had the best penis once. Seriously. The. Best. Penis. I've. Ever. Seen."

My lip trembled from the sad penis-less thoughts, and I tried to busy myself by licking the nacho cheese dust off my fingers.

And eventually, I found the strength to forge forward into another ramble.

"I was best friends with that penis. But it's been so long since I've seen him. It's been so long, practically as long as he is, and I'm so sad. I wish I could talk to him. I wish I could kiss him. I wish I could tell him I didn't mean any of the things I said on the last day of filming and that he's got the perfect rounded head. I wish I could tell him that I *do* want to be with him. That I want to be together. That I want to try to make it work. But I-I got scared. I got so scared, guys." Tears blurred my vision, so I took my hand out of the chip bag and scrubbed at my eyes. "I fell for the penis that never falls for anyone. The rod that never sets its reel. The shaft that never ever closes down its elevator for the night. That thing goes *up*, guys. It's like poetry. But you only need poems when you're in a relationship!"

I sighed and sighed again and then blew some of the curls out of my face with a long, upward puff of air from my lips.

"But now it's too late. He's moved on. He's found other girls."

Other girls. Sean and his penis were probably out fucking other girls right now.

A soft sob escaped my lips. "I wish I had more wine right now. Even though I think I'm really drunk. Like, right now, it looks like there are two cameras. But I'm pretty sure I only started with one camera."

I wiggled one finger in front of my face, but there appeared to be so many it was bordering on disorienting. So, I refocused on the bag of Doritos on the kitchen counter.

"And there's also two bags of Doritos, but I think that's a good thing because I love Doritos. You know what else I love?" I asked, and instantly, fresh tears formed behind my eyes and started to fall in big fat waves down my cheeks.

I scrubbed away the liquid emotion with my hand, and then quickly realized I still had Doritos on my hand, so I wiped it all away again with my shirt.

"What was I just saying?" I looked up at the camera and then at the ceiling, and then I remembered. "I love Sean Phillips, guys. I love Sean and his penis, which used to be my penis. It was all veiny and thick and really and truly perfect. It was warm without a turtleneck, and the circumcision really looked good on him. I don't think I want to love him—Sean, him, not penis him—because he isn't the kind of guy who settles down, but I can't help it. I love him."

Another little sob. Another sniffle. More tears.

"God, I miss him. I miss him so much. And I'm going to have to see him again soon, and it's going to hurt so bad. Almost as bad as this *gremlin* in my *uterus*. I'm tired of my heart hurting because of Sean Phillips and his perfect penis. It's a really big penis. But, like, not overwhelming big. Just, like, perfect big."

Fuck, I had to stop thinking about him.

I had to stop thinking about his penis.

"I think I'm gonna go now, guys," I announced through a half whimper and half yawn. "I'm feeling really sleepy. And I'm feeling kind of drunk. Or really drunk. I'm not sure. But I'm gonna go to bed."

I didn't even say bye. I just logged out of my live video feed and locked the screen of my phone.

By the time my feet had reached the couch, I let myself fall like a sack of potatoes onto the cushions and allowed sleep to take over.

In the too near distance, my phone kept on ringing and pinging and fucking vibrating, and I groaned my irritation into the pillow currently covering my face.

Eventually, silence took over, but it was fucking brief. And what felt like a minute later, my stupid phone started blowing up with notifications again.

With a groan and a muttered fuck from my lips, I removed the pillow from my face and opened my eyes.

What time is it?

It took several blinks of my eyes to clear my vision enough to check the clock below the television.

10:32 a.m.

Jesus, Mary, and Joseph, it felt earlier than that. But the late-morning California sun blinding me through the windows of my living room said otherwise.

I sat up on the couch, and instantly, my head throbbed and pulsed and swam with discomfort until it formed into a persistent ache behind my temples.

"*Holy shitola,*" I mumbled and rested my head in my hands.

Although my memory wasn't too clear on why I felt like

someone had shoved cotton balls down my throat and hit me over the head with a sledgehammer, I knew, without a doubt, I was hungover as a motherfucker.

Swallowing past the discomfort and with the constant annoyance of my phone chiming its presence somewhere in the kitchen, I stood up from the couch and shuffled my way toward its sounds.

Right there, on the kitchen counter, beside an empty bottle of wine and a half-eaten bag of Doritos, I spotted it.

And the little bastard just kept on vibrating and pinging and lighting up before my very eyes.

Jesus. Is the world ending? I mean, what could be so important right now?

I snagged it from the counter and stared down at what felt like one million notifications scrolling across the screen.

With one quick tap of my thumb, I unlocked it and proceeded to turn it on silent before I tried to decode why it felt like Armageddon had occurred while I was asleep.

Twenty missed text messages.

Twelve missed calls.

Too many YouCam notifications to count.

And several hundred missed emails.

What the hell?

I decided to start with the text messages.

The first one I opened was a group message with Everly and Sammy.

Everly: Holy shit. I thought Mexico was bad. What did you do last night?

Everly: For the love of God, tell me you meant to post that video last night...

Sammy: Uh...Six? What is happening?

Everly: Dear God, do you think we need to head to San Diego to make sure she's okay?

Sammy: Maybe? I mean, let's give her like another hour or so. But if we don't hear anything by then, we probably need to start planning an SOS mission.

What video? I wondered. And then an onslaught of memories hit me like a freight train. I'd posted a video to my private YouCam account last night, a full-on tirade about God only knew what, but I had a sneaking suspicion it most likely revolved around a certain man I couldn't seem to remove from my brain.

Me: What are you guys talking about? The video I sent you last night? Was it that bad?

Everly: Sent us? Uh...you didn't just send that to us.

Me: Huh?

Sammy: Sweetie, you posted that video to your public YouCam account.

What?
My stomach pretty much fell straight out of my body as I tapped out of the group chat and opened up the YouCam app.

I didn't even need to log in because I was already fucking logged in. And right there, on the screen of my *public* profile, stood a still shot of my face covered in Dorito crumbs, which just so happened to be the image for the latest video I'd posted.

Last fucking night, apparently.

I didn't want to, but I did. I clicked on the video and proceeded to watch a drunken, wine-stained lips, and Dorito-crusted version of myself ramble on and on into the camera.

It started out as a diatribe about my period.

Okay, no big deal...

Surely, I'd done more ridiculous things than this before.

But then, it took a real abrupt turn down Nightmare Lane when drunk me somehow found a slurred segue from talking about wishing I had a penis to missing *Sean's* penis.

Oh God.

"No! No! No! Stop talking!" I shouted at the fucking lunatic of a woman rambling on and on into the camera, which, unfortunately, just so happened to be me.

And then, it all went up in flames.

"I love Sean Phillips, guys," I slurred on the video.

The fucking public, viewable to millions and millions of people, video.

If I hadn't been holding myself up with a hand firmly secured on the kitchen counter, I most likely would have collapsed to my knees.

I'd just accidentally told the entire world I was in love with Sean Phillips. And more than that, I'd even waxed poetic about his penis and how much I loved his penis and missed his penis and...*fuck.*

As quick as my fingers could move, I tapped across the screen until that god-awful, embarrassing, fucking terrible video was deleted from my profile.

But I knew it didn't matter.

I'd posted it several hours ago.

Which was more than enough time for pretty much anyone and everyone to record the evidence of my wine- and period-fueled mental breakdown.

I was so fucked.

So fucking fucked.

I stared down at the screen of my phone, jaw resting on my goddamn toes, and eyes wide from what I assumed was post-traumatic stress.

And just before I threw my phone across the room, a text message notification from Cassie lit up across the screen.

Oh, please, for the love of God, tell me his freaking sister hasn't seen it...

I clicked open her message with very little hope and pretty much just braced for impact.

Cassie: Hot damn, girl. I think I'm in love with you. Although I could've used a little less commentary about my brother's dick, I loved every second of your video. You fluffing owned that shit and let your crazy flag fly motherfluffing high in the sky. Hell, even Thatch pretty much has a boner for you at this point. (Obviously, he's a sucker for crazy chicks.) See? Thatch is basically your number one fangirl now.

And following that text was a picture.

Of Thatch.

He was smiling wide, with a bag of Doritos in one hand, a thumbs-up raised high on the other hand, and his huge chest covered in a replica of the cat T-shirt I'd worn to dinner the first time I'd met them.

And all I could think was, *Has Sean seen the video?*

But, deep down, I already knew the answer to that question.

Help. Me.

Chapter Thirty

Sean

With the last empty box in my hands, I tossed it into the hallway with the rest of the cardboard that needed to be taken out to the trash.

Today was a big day for my best friend.

I stood outside of the room watching Quinn put the final, finishing touches on what would be Cat's new home office.

A picture frame on her new desk.

Paintbrushes near the art easel by the window.

The final heartfelt, thoughtful details that proved his love.

A perfectionist to his core, he had spared no detail *or* expense. Everything inside of this room had been thoughtfully chosen and planned out.

And he'd done it all with Cat in mind.

If that wasn't love, I didn't know what was.

"You think she's going to like it?" he asked, walking toward the doorway where I stood. He turned to take in the finally finished room, and I didn't miss the big-ass, love-inspired smile on his face.

He was a goner. A total fucking goner for his girl.

"Well, I hope so considering we've spent the last God knows how many fucking hours getting it ready," I teased and he chuckled.

"True story."

I gave him a hearty pat to the shoulder. "Don't worry, QB, she's going to love it."

I'd watched Quinn and Cat's relationship blossom and grow over the past several months, and today, together, they were taking a huge step. It was official move-in day, and from here on out, Quinn and Cat would be living together.

Not to mention, my best friend had another huge surprise up his sleeve.

One that included a diamond engagement ring.

It was all part of his big plan.

And I'd spent the past few days helping him execute it.

"Fuck," he muttered and looked over at me. "I'm nervous."

That made me grin. "I think that's pretty normal, dude. You're about to ask her to marry you."

"Yeah," he said, and his eyes turned soft. "She's the one, Sean. She's the one I want to spend the rest of my life with."

I hated that his words made my chest hurt.

I was happy for him, obviously, but that happiness didn't make it any easier to watch.

If anything, it made it even more real that all of the things he had with Cat were what I had wanted with Six.

Still want with Six.

Internally, I grimaced.

You'd think I'd be over it by now.

You'd think I would have long since moved on.

You'd think that I, the guy who had been nicknamed the playboy manwhore, would have had at least one fucking hookup since Six had ended things.

You'd fucking think that would be the case.

But, sadly, it wasn't.

Hell, I'd given it the old college try. I'd even attempted to find a random fuck for the night, but I couldn't follow through.

And more than that, my dick couldn't even get hard.

What a fucking mess.

"You have nothing to worry about, QB. She'll say yes. And you'll get your happily ever after with the fucking mansion and white picket fence and future quarterback kids. And you know what?"

"What?"

Another hearty pat to his shoulder. "I'm happy for you."

The words shouldn't have felt heavy on my tongue, but they were.

He was a man who'd found the woman of his dreams and didn't have a care in the world, and I wanted that.

I wanted that so bad I could fucking taste it.

Before Six, I hadn't realized I needed that.

But I did. I needed it.

And even though I was happy for my best friend, I was miserable too. Miserable that I was pining for a woman who didn't want anything more than a fucking fling with me, *the fucking manwhore.*

The irony of that situation wasn't lost on me.

"Thanks, man. That means a lot." Quinn grinned. "And thanks for helping me."

"Anytime," I responded. "I know you'd do the same for me."

"Honestly, I never thought I'd see the day when Sean Phillips would help me get everything ready to propose to my girlfriend. Even offering up some swoony fucking suggestions in the process. I had no idea you had it in you, to be honest."

"Huh?" I questioned and furrowed my brow. "What do you mean by that?"

His grin grew wider. "Let's face it, before a certain someone, you would have already been MIA by now. But here you are, making sure everything is perfect. Hell, I probably would've had to beg Teeny to bring his big ass over here and help carry that huge desk in. Which, no doubt, with his giant, clumsy self, would've ended up leaving holes in the drywall."

He had a point about Teeny. The man had the strength of ten

men, but goddamn was he like a bull in a fucking china shop. There was nothing gentle or easy about him.

But everything else Quinn had said felt like total bullshit.

"A certain someone?" I questioned, and those three stupid words provided visuals of a gorgeous brown gaze and wild hair flashing behind my eyes.

Or maybe it wasn't that his words were bullshit, but they revolved around the one thing, *the one fucking person*, I was trying so goddamn hard not to think about.

"You know exactly who I'm talking about," Quinn answered instantly, and I waved him off with a disagreeing hand.

"Oh, come on," I responded, and I couldn't hide the annoyance in my voice. "She has nothing to do with this—or anything else, for that matter."

He raised an eyebrow in my direction. "Are you sure about that?"

No, I wasn't, but that didn't mean he had to know that.

"How about you focus on getting Cat to say yes, and I'll handle my own shit, okay?" I tossed back, and he just smiled knowingly.

Fuck, I knew he was only teasing me, but it was striking a nerve.

A big-ass nerve, at that.

Instead of getting into a verbal pissing match with him, I chose to take the high road, the smart road, and distract myself.

"I'm going to take those boxes down to the garage," I said by way of ending the conversation. "I'm assuming Cat will be here soon."

Considering I'd just heard him talk to her no less than fifteen minutes ago, and she had been en route, it was safe to say she'd be here soon.

He glanced at his watch and nodded. "Any minute now."

"All right," I said and walked into the hallway. "I'll work on getting all the cardboard and trash out of the hallway and spare bedroom."

"And what am I supposed to do?" he asked, and I couldn't not smirk at him over my shoulder.

"Get your fucking game face on, son," I said. "It's almost proposal time. And then, once she says yes, it's motherfucking championship time."

We were only a few days out from the big game against Dallas, and I was ready to get back on the field. It was the one place I still felt in control of my life

A man on a mission, I walked into the hallway, grabbed the stack of cardboard, and proceeded to carry it into the garage.

By the time I came back into the house and was inside the spare bedroom gathering the rest of the empty boxes, I heard Cat's arrival.

Even though I was trying to give them their privacy, their voices echoed throughout the big house and made it impossible for my ears not to hear their every word.

Cat sounded happy, excited, and well, like a woman who was desperately in love with Quinn. I heard the love in her voice when she said hello, and I didn't miss the very same thing in his when he started to take her through the house and show her all of the personal touches he'd added.

When they reached the upstairs, I heard her gasp of surprise, and I knew she'd finally seen her new office.

"Did you do all of this?" she asked, and her voice carried straight to my ears.

"I did," Quinn responded, and pride rang loud and clear in his voice. "Without any help either."

What a dick. I'd been helping him for what felt like the past week getting all of this shit together.

"Fuck that!" I shouted toward the hallway. "I helped!" I added, and I couldn't hold back my raucous laughter.

And then, as I stared down at the pile of cardboard in the center of the spare bedroom, I decided the credit-stealing bastard could finish cleaning up his own mess.

I'd more than done my share.

Not to mention, I wasn't sure how much lovey-dovey bullshit I could tolerate with thoughts of Six attempting to consume my brain like a wildfire.

Without a second thought, I strode out of the room, jogged down the steps, and marched out the front door, pulling it closed with a loud bang behind me.

I hopped into my Jeep, clicked on the engine, and turned out of Quinn's driveway in the direction of my house.

But I didn't even reach the gated entrance before a text notification pinged.

"Text message from Teeny," Siri announced through the speakers.

I clicked the accept button on the steering wheel and let Siri read the message to me through the speakers of the Jeep.

"Dude. You need to watch the latest live video Six posted on her vlog," Siri stated robotically. "Homegirl is talking about you."

What?

Before I even knew what I was doing, I slammed on my brakes and pulled off to the side of the road.

With uncharacteristically fumbling hands, I grabbed my phone from the dock and pulled up Teeny's message to read it with my own eyes. Surely, Siri had fucked it up somehow.

Teeny: Dude. You need to watch the latest live video Six posted on her vlog. Homegirl is talking about you.

My phone pinged again in my hands.

With a follow-up text, he even provided a direct link to the video in question.

My heart started racing inside my chest, and I had no idea why.

Hell, my lungs even joined in and grew tight with anxiety.

I had no idea what was in the video, but I had to find out.

With one quick click to the link, my phone's screen rerouted to some random gossip website, and there, on my screen, was Six's face. Apparently, per the now-viral article, she had posted this video last night. And although she had recently deleted it from her YouCam profile, it had stayed live for a good ten hours.

Jesus. What in the fuck is in this thing?

I tapped play and braced myself for the unknown.

Wild curls messily piled on top of her head, eyes red-rimmed and highlighted by shadowed remnants of mascara, she looked like a beautiful fucking disaster.

And after hearing all of four words come out of her pretty little mouth, I knew she was drunk, too.

She started into a ramble, talking to no one in particular, and honestly, hardly even looking at the screen.

First, it was about her period.

Then, she switched to penises.

And at one point, while rambling about a combination of the two, she started shoving Doritos into her mouth, crunching loudly into the camera.

But then…the mood shifted.

"I love Sean Phillips, guys," Six said, her voice a half slur, half whimper. *"I love Sean Phillips. And his penis, which used to be my penis. I don't think I want to love him because he isn't the kind of guy who settles down, but I can't help it. I love him."*

My heart started pounding wildly at her words.

I had thought she was done with me, but mere hours ago, she had said she loved me.

She loves me?

I couldn't take my eyes off her. She was an adorable fucking mess. And my heart grew ten sizes inside my chest.

God, I miss her.

With big, huge tears streaming down her cheeks, she continued, "I miss him, you guys. I miss him so much. And I'm going to have to see him again soon, and it's going to hurt so bad. I'm tired of my heart hurting because of Sean Phillips and his perfect penis."

The video didn't last much longer. But I watched until the very end, which was basically a point where Six got too tired and abruptly hit stop on her video.

Holy fucking shit.

Eyes wide and jaw damn near in my lap, I stared out the

windshield of my Jeep trying to process what I'd just seen.

I had an underlying feeling she hadn't really meant to record that video, but accident or not, thank fuck she had.

Now that I knew... Now that I'd heard her say that four-letter word, I'd do everything in my power to get her back.

Because not only did she love me, I loved her too.

I wanted her.

I needed her.

And we fucking belonged together.

I silently thanked everything for the fact that the Mavericks organization had hired her back to create one final episode of the series. We'd gotten the notification via an email from Georgia late last night with the news that Six would be joining us for a finale piece at the championship game, and at the time, I'd felt nothing but dread.

But now...now, it felt like fate. Destiny.

With a deep breath, I put the Jeep back into drive, and all the while, I started to mentally prepare myself for the two biggest games of my life.

The championship.

And Six.

The first was important—hell, it was the most important game of my career thus far. But the second, well, it meant the most. It would make or break me.

Even though my heart was about to be on the line and I didn't have any fucking control over the end result, I knew what I needed to do.

I pick Six.

All day, every day, for the rest of fucking time, I pick her.

Chapter Thirty-One

Six

Only a few minutes behind schedule, I walked as fast as I could past the various media sources and cameras hanging out in front of the hotel lobby.

"Six! Over here, Six!"

"Do you really love Sean Phillips?"

"Were you guys dating during filming?"

"Have you spoken to him since you posted that video?"

"Why did you delete it from your account?"

They shouted questions at me from every angle, but with the help of hotel security, I kept my head down, ignored them, and hopped into the limo provided by the Mavericks organization that waited idly at the curb.

The instant I found the sweet sound of silence in the backseat, I let out a long, exasperated breath I hadn't even realized I'd been holding.

It'd been a rough last couple of days.

Ever since I'd accidentally posted that stupid, ridiculous video on YouCam, my phone hadn't stopped ringing. It felt like everyone and their goddamn mother wanted some insider information about

Sean and me.

Which was why I'd kept my lips shut tighter than Fort Knox, and it appeared, even if he'd seen the video, Sean had done the same.

Setting the wheels to rolling, the driver headed in the direction of Minnesota's stadium.

Tonight, the Mavericks would play Dallas in the championship game, a rematch against the absolute toughest team the Mavericks had faced this season, and I'd be filming an episode to capture it all.

With kickoff only four hours away, the anxiety that had seemed to develop into some sort of permanent appendage on my body took up residence inside my chest and started to clench tighter by the second.

I was going to have to see Sean again. In fucking person. After I'd pretty much made a fool out of myself in front of the entire world.

If I have an actual heart attack tonight, it should not come as a surprise.

God, it felt like a million knots filled my stomach, and I fidgeted on the black leather seats of the limo.

I directed my gaze forward, and honestly, I felt ridiculous to be the only person riding in a vehicle made to fit at least ten people.

I stared at the tinted glass windows and watched the traffic speed by while silently wishing I would've told Joe and Barry to wait to go to the stadium until now.

At least then I would have had someone to talk to.

But they'd left a good hour or so before me, focused on getting cameras set up and making sure they didn't have any issues getting all our equipment past security.

And now, sitting all by my lonesome in the back of this limo, all I could do was think. And think. And think some fucking more.

I wonder if Sean is nervous.

I wonder how Sean looks.

Will it be weird when I see him tonight?

What am I going to say to him?

What if I have to see him at an after party, and he has a girl on his arm?

Maybe I should try to put on some sort of disguise so he doesn't even recognize me?

Jesus. I had to stop these incessant thoughts.

Without giving myself time to overthink it, I moved toward the front of the limo and tapped on the sliding glass that separated me from the driver.

His name was Sal, and he had one of the friendliest smiles I'd ever seen.

Surely, that smile of his could provide some comfort to my nearly frayed nerves.

He opened the window with a simple tap to a black button on the center console and looked at me in the rearview mirror. "Everything okay, Miss Malone?"

"Everything is good, Sal." I nodded. "How far away from the stadium are we?"

He glanced at the clock and then focused his eyes back on the road. "Probably about fifteen minutes."

"Oh, okay. That's not too bad," I said and searched my brain for something else to talk to him about. Because fuck, making small talk with my driver was better than driving myself crazy with these fucking thoughts about Sean. "So…where are you from, Sal?"

"I'm actually from New York, but I moved out to Minnesota a few years ago."

"That's awesome," I said, and he just shrugged.

Come on, Sal. Give me something to work with here.

"So…" I paused, racking my brain for conversation topics. "How are the taxes here compared to New York?"

Taxes? Was I really asking him about fucking taxes right now?

"Uh… New York's are definitely a little bit higher."

"Taxes are the worst."

"Yep."

It was safe to say this conversation wasn't winning any fucking awards.

Change the subject. Talk about something else. Just not taxes.

Anything but fucking taxes, you weirdo. Even fucking accountants hate talking about taxes, and it's their goddamn job to talk about them.

"Are you married, Sal?" I asked

Jesus, first taxes, and now, he probably thinks you're hitting on him.

I glanced down at his fingers that were wrapped around the steering wheel. A gold wedding band shimmered beneath the rays of the sun.

"Been married for twenty years to my high school sweetheart."

"That's awesome."

"Best decision I ever made was getting down on one knee to convince my Sara to marry me." He grinned, his smile proud and warm and every bit of a man who truly loved his wife. "What about you, Miss Malone? Got a husband?"

"Nope."

"What about a boyfriend? Someone special in your life?"

Damn, Sal. Nosy much?

"No," I answered. "No one special at the moment."

"You'll find that person," he said. "And it will happen when you least expect it."

"I hope you're right," I answered, but on the inside, I was thinking, *What if I did already find him, and he just isn't the kind of man who gets married or falls in love?*

Heart now aching, I patted Sal on the shoulder gently before moving to the very back seat where I gave in to the madness and let my mind race with thoughts of Sean until we arrived at the stadium.

Son of a motherless goat. This is going to be a lot harder than I thought.

Time ran off the clock until it was all zeros, and the whistles blew loud and clear. Halftime was officially upon us.

The crowd cheered and shouted and bellowed for their respective team as the players filed off the field and into the tunnel where they'd regroup in the locker rooms and prepare for the second half of the game.

From the sidelines, I looked up at the scoreboard and noted the score.

Mavericks: 14

Dallas: 14

The first two quarters of the game had been an all-out battle. Both teams had fought for every yard, every fucking inch, every down. And still, they'd both ended the half tied.

If I had any nails left by the end of this game, it'd be a damn miracle.

I glanced down the sidelines and noted that Joe and Barry were already busy rearranging their cameras to capture the big halftime show.

Every year, during the championship game, people around the world tuned in to watch this fifteen-minute performance.

It was a big fucking deal.

And just as the lights of the stadium dimmed and the crowd settled down into a calmed hush, I walked in front of Joe's camera, and he gave me a thumbs-up.

"All right, guys! It's time," I said into the camera, a giant smile consuming my lips. "We're about to give you an up close and personal view of one of the biggest shows in the world! Any second, you're going to see international pop sensation Aria waltz onto the big stage and most likely give you the performance of a lifetime."

Externally, I was smiling, but internally, my heart ached at just the mention of that name from my lips.

What were the fucking odds I would be announcing her performance?

I mean, out of all of the musicians in the world, it had to be the one I'd seen splashed all over the tabloids while smiling like the fucking sun on Sean's lap.

Fuck, now is not the time to think about that.

I mentally shook off those thoughts and forced my brain to focus on the task at hand.

Just as the initial beats of her chart-topping song "You're Mine" started to vibrate through the stadium speakers, I found my zone and grinned toward the camera.

"It's showtime, guys!" I announced and then slowly removed myself from the camera's frame and watched Aria take the stage.

The crowd went wild, and I just felt like puking.

Like a knife straight to the heart, her appearance generated a stabbing pain inside my chest.

God, I hated the way my heart still responded to anything and everything related to Sean. I hated watching the woman he'd most likely fucked after we'd broken up dance around in a sexy, barely there costume while her voice sounded like a goddamn angel.

And mostly, I hated that I hated things.

Hate was such a strong word that I never liked using, but yet, there I was, hating on everything, including a female pop star with a million-dollar smile.

No doubt this venture, filming another Mavs' series episode, was turning out to be a lot harder than I thought it would be when I'd told Georgia I'd do it.

But, goddammit, I would get through this. And I would make sure that this championship game episode would be the best one yet.

Aria belted out the lyrics to her popular song, and before I knew it, I was singing right along with her.

Stupid catchy pop songs.

They sure knew how to burrow themselves into your brain until they could never ever be forgotten. It'd been a while since I'd heard Britney Spears's "Hit Me Baby One More Time," but I could guarantee if it came on the radio, I'd be able to sing every single lyric as if I'd actually written the guilty pleasure.

Hell, even when I was ninety, I'd probably still be able to sing that song from memory.

Two songs in and Aria closed out her performance by doing a seductive, choreographed routine that ended with her dancers carrying her off stage, her body held high above their heads. She waved goodbye to the crowd, blew them kisses, and the audience responded with fervor. Chanting her name. Cheering their enthusiasm. Some die-hard fans holding glitter-embellished signs and sporting her merch were highlighted on the big jumbotron screen. They waved and bounced up and down excitedly as Aria exited the stage.

Then the lights dimmed again, and just before the next performer took the stage, a giant screen in the center of the stage flashed with the entire Mavericks squad.

A montage of the players I knew so well flitted across the screen.

Videos of them laughing, smiling, and saying hello passed by at a rapid-fire pace with the beat of Rihanna's "Work" providing the soundtrack.

And then, Rihanna was there, filling the screen and standing in the center of the Mavericks' stadium, a half-shirt Mavericks jersey on her cute little frame.

"Wait a minute," she said toward the camera, and the music stopped. "Are we in the middle of the halftime show?" she asked, and the camera actually nodded, moving up and down gently. "Really?" The camera nodded again.

"Yo, Mavs!" she called over her shoulder. "Did you know it's halftime?"

The camera zoomed in on Quinn, who paused mid-throw and looked over. "Then why are we here?" he asked, and then pointed knowingly toward the camera with a little smirk. "Shouldn't we be there?"

"Yeah, I think that's exactly where you're supposed to be." She grinned. "But first, I think we need a game plan, boys. I mean, Dallas is a tough team. You need to be ready."

"Dallas ain't got shi—*nothing* on us!" Martinez bellowed and jogged toward the camera.

Within seconds, the entire team and Rihanna huddled together with the camera in the center.

"What's the game plan, boys?" she asked.

"Score touchdowns!" Mitchell yelled. "Lots of f-udging touchdowns!"

She rolled her eyes. "Some actual *plays*, Cam."

"What about a Pick Six?" Teeny asked and grinned into the camera. "I'd totally pick Six."

"No way." Sam chimed in, shoving his shoulder into Martinez's stomach. "*I* pick Six."

"No way, dude," Cam interjected, winking toward the camera. "*I* pick Six."

What the what? Are they fucking talking about me?

I looked over at Joe, and that was when I noticed that not only were both he and Barry smiling at me, one of the cameras was pointed directly at me.

Before I could ask them what the hell was happening, an all-too-familiar voice filled my ears.

"Hell to the no, son. *I* pick Six."

I looked back toward the stage, and right on the screen was Sean.

Smiling the biggest fucking smile I'd ever seen cover his handsome face.

My heart made an effort to jump into my throat at the sight.

"Not only do I pick Six," he said, his eyes brightening with his words, "but I *love* Six."

Jaw nearly resting on the ground, I stared at the screen with my eyes so damn wide I thought they might actually be touching my hairline.

"You love Six?" Rihanna asked, grinning.

"I love Six," Sean said, and the sincerity in his voice urged a rush of tears to form behind my eyes.

"Aw, did you hear that, Six?" Rihanna smiled into the camera. "He thinks you da one, girl." After she shot one last wink toward the camera, the screen went black, and the lights on the stage turned neon bright as Rihanna walked out onto the actual stage singing

"You Da One."

The crowd went crazy.

Screaming. Chanting her name. Singing right along with her.

And all I could do was stand there, shell-shocked and feet fro-zen to the goddamn sidelines, wondering what in the hell had just happened.

Sean Phillips loves me?

Had he really said that? On a freaking video in the middle of the halftime show of the championship game?

Holy. Fucking. Shit.

Chapter Thirty-Two

Sean

Huddled around Coach Bennett, I glanced up at the scoreboard.

Fourth Quarter. Five seconds left on the clock.

Mavericks: 21

Dallas: 27

We needed a touchdown.

This was our last time-out, and not only that, we had thirty yards to go before we reached the end zone.

"Everything we've trained for. Everything you've worked so hard for. It all comes down to these five seconds. These last seconds will decide if you're going home with that championship trophy or not," Coach Bennett said, his voice firm and his eyes serious.

He looked each and every one of us in the eyes.

"Now, I know you can fucking pull this one out. You've done more in less time. But you need to go out there and play these last five seconds like it is the very last game of your fucking career, and once the clock hits zero, you'll never have the opportunity to step onto that field again."

"We got this, boys!" Sam Sheffield bellowed. "We fucking got this!"

We responded with fervor, hooting and hollering and pumping each other up.

"All right. All right," Coach said and raised both arms in the air, gesturing for us to settle down. "Martinez, I need you to hold your fucking ground and give QB time in the pocket."

Teeny nodded, jaw stern. "Got it, Coach."

"And, Bailey," Coach instructed, looking up from his crouched position in the center of our huddle to meet Quinn's steady gaze. "We're going to set up for Razzle Dazzle because we know their defense is looking for you to get the ball into Sean's hands, but instead, I want you to find Mitchell." Coach's eyes locked with Cam's. "You got it?" he asked, and Cam nodded.

"Yes, sir."

"All right," Coach said. "Get out there and show Dallas how we win games."

Hyped up and ready, we jogged back onto the field, and before we lined up, I grabbed Mitchell by the helmet and stared him straight in the eyes.

"You got this," I said and smacked the top of his helmet a few times. "You fucking got this, son!"

Toes to the line and only five seconds on the clock, we were ready.

The instant Quinn called for the ball, we jumped into action.

With two defensive backs on my fucking balls, I did my best to keep their attention. And by the time I hit the twenty-yard line, I moved in the opposite direction of Mitchell and prayed to everything holy—*God, Jesus, Buddha, fucking Mother Teresa*—that I'd pulled the defense enough to give QB room to complete the pass.

Just as I glanced over my shoulder, Bailey let the ball soar out of his fingertips.

High into the air, the pigskin flew like a fucking spiral rocket until it landed directly on Cam's fingertips.

He snagged it from the sky and pulled it to his chest.

Ten yards.

Five yards.

Three yards.

One yard.

He ran until he couldn't run anymore, until Dallas's defense stopped his progression, and all he could do was fall to his knees. But the entire time, that fucking ball stayed cradled in his arms.

The game clock hit zero.

Referees blew their whistles.

More defense piled on top of Mitchell until he wasn't even visible, and the refs blew their whistles some more as they jogged toward the mountain of players.

Adrenaline pumping hot and heavy into my veins, I ran toward the end zone, praying to God Mitchell had managed to get the ball over the line.

The instant the refs were able to get Dallas's defense off of Mitchell, my battered, bloody heart damn near fell out of my chest and onto the field.

There it sat.

The ball, just outside the fucking end zone.

The refs blew their whistles and waved their arms in the air, signaling no touchdown, and then, it was over.

Zero seconds on the clock.

And barely an inch outside of the goddamn end zone.

We'd lost.

We'd lost the fucking championship game.

While Dallas's team cheered and fireworks and confetti guns went off like rockets and the crowd inside the stadium went wild, I fell to my knees.

Straight to my fucking knees, right outside the end zone.

Fuck!

I stared up toward the sky and sighed the heaviest, saddest breath that had ever left my lungs.

God, I wanted that win.

I wanted that win so bad I could taste it.

I wanted to walk away tonight with a championship ring on my finger, and I wanted what we'd all spent years working toward to come to fruition. Quinn's jaw was hard as he battled against the emotion, and Cam gave him a commiserating slap to the helmet. Teeny's walk was subdued, weighted, no doubt, by the same lead in my chest.

It looked like what I wanted and what was reality were two goddamn different things.

I shut my eyes and took another deep breath, trying to come to terms with the loss.

Fuck. Fuck. Fuck.

It hurt. It fucking killed. Hours upon hours of work and weeks of fantasizing right down the drain.

I breathed through the disappointment, readying myself to start all over again. There'd be another season next year. Another championship game. Another chance to have it all.

I wasn't sure I was fully convinced, such was the sting of frustration, but when I opened my eyes, there she stood, her body mere inches from mine and her big brown eyes looking down at me.

Six. *My* Six. The only woman to ever hold my heart.

She was a mess of wild and beauty. Tears stained her beautiful cheeks, and a worried little smile covered her lips.

The crowd, the field, the fucking stadium, everything around us faded away, and we just stared at one another for the longest time.

Until her perfect voice broke our silence and took all the pain away.

"You pick Six?" she asked, and more tears spilled from her eyes.

"No." I shook my head. "Didn't you watch the video, baby? I more than pick Six. I *love* Six."

She was better than a fucking championship. She was better than one win in a bucket full of games. She was the ultimate season, the neverending championship, the tiniest, most perfect trophy of all.

She was *everything*.

A little gasp left her lips, and I hopped back to my feet.

With love and want and deep, deep need coursing through my veins, I moved toward her, and before she could even respond, I had her in my arms.

"I'm so sorry," she whispered and buried her tear-stained face into my chest. "I'm sorry I ended things the way I did. I was just so scared. God, I was so afraid of getting hurt. I had fallen for you, Sean, and I just didn't think it was possible for you to fall for anyone."

"It wasn't," I agreed, but I didn't hesitate to speak my truth. "Until you, baby." I leaned back and put my finger underneath her chin and lifted her gaze to mine.

And when those big brown eyes of hers looked up at me, my heart pretty much melted.

"You changed all the rules," I said. "You changed everything. And fuck, I'm so happy you did. I love you, Six. I really fucking love you."

She didn't hesitate to respond. "I love you too."

"I know you do, baby." I grinned, and she raised a curious brow.

"Wait a minute…what do you mean, you know?"

I shrugged. "Well, you kind of let everyone know you loved me when you posted that amazing ramble of a video…"

"Oh God," she muttered. "I swear I'm never going to live that video down."

"You had a lot of wonderful things to say," I teased, and she grimaced.

"Oh yeah, especially the part where I waxed poetic about your penis. That was real wonderful."

I nodded and chuckled softly. "The best damn poetry I've ever heard."

She shoved me playfully in the chest. "Of course it is, you cocky bastard."

I laughed again, but I did it while I wrapped her up tightly in my arms again. "God, I've missed you," I whispered into her ear.

"I've missed you too."

I leaned back and stared deep into her gorgeous eyes. "You're mine."

She quirked a brow, but I didn't let it stop me.

"I'm yours," I added. "And now, we're going to get the fuck out of this stadium and spend the rest of the night making up for lost time."

A beautiful smile kissed her lips. "Count. Me. In." Mischief colored her chocolate eyes with a creamy swirl and settled as she winked. "You could use the practice."

My laughter was a roar.

For a man who'd just lost the game of his life, I felt victorious.

I'd won more than just a championship or a trophy or a ring.

I'd won the fucking girl.

Without a second thought, I leaned down and tossed her pint-sized, curvy little body over my shoulder and proceeded to carry her off the field.

She laughed and giggled and swatted at my shoulders the entire way, but I didn't give a shit. I was taking her, my girl, back to my hotel room caveman-style, and not anyone or anything was going to stand in my way.

When several cameras and journalists tried to grab our attention, I ignored every single one of them.

Now wasn't the time for an interview.

Now wasn't the time for anything but Six.

Epilogue

Six

Three months later.

"**S**ix," Sean's voice singsonged into my ear. "Wake up, baby."

"Go away." I groaned and turned away from the handsome bastard who seemed insistent on ruining my delicious sleep.

"Nuh-uh," he said, and I could hear the grin in his voice. "It's time to wake up."

Actually seeing that grin was tempting as hell, but *sleep*. I fucking loved sleep.

"What time is it?" I asked, voice raspy and groggy and eyes still firmly shut.

"A little after nine."

"Oh my God!" I exclaimed and swatted at him over my shoulder. "It's too early. Go away! Let me be, you crazy person!"

He laughed and proceeded to pick me up from my cozy spot and place me on top of his chest.

I blinked my eyes open and found us nose-to-nose. Sean gazed at me, a smirk etched across his full lips. And instantly, I knew something was up. He looked too damn mischievous. Sexy as hell, but way too playful.

I quirked a brow and then narrowed my eyes. "Why are you looking at me like that?"

That smirk only got bigger. "Like what?"

"Like you're up to no good."

He offered a shrug of one meaty, muscular, bare shoulder, and when I glanced out of the corner of my eye, I quickly realized the reason.

My GoPro camera sat firmly in his grasp, pointing directly at us, and the little red light indicated it was recording. *Everything.*

Including, my messy, just-woken-up state.

I wasn't Snow White or Cinderella. I didn't just roll out of bed fresh-faced and skin glowing like the sun. That shit took time. It took coffee and, at the very least, washing my face and running a brush through the rat's nest eight hours of sleep tended to create on top of my head.

I could only imagine the disaster that camera was currently catching on film.

"You're such a bastard!" I exclaimed and shoved my face into the firm skin of his bare chest. "Turn it off!"

"No way," he said. "You promised I'd get to handle today's *Pick Six* content."

Over the past month or so, Sean had been badgering me about handling one of my daily vlog videos, and last night, after he'd gifted me with several orgasms and I was nearly incoherent from pleasure overload, I'd agreed.

"Yeah, but you were supposed to let me wake up and, like, brush my freaking hair before you started recording shit," I muttered against his skin. "My subscribers don't want to see this hot mess with morning breath and crazy eyes."

"You're crazy, baby," he said, and I looked up at him with narrowed eyes. But the charming bastard went all swoony and added, "I want your subscribers to see how fucking beautiful you look when you first wake up. Most beautiful girl in the world." He waggled his eyebrows. "*My* girl."

I rolled my eyes and blushed at the same time.

He didn't miss either one and grinned down at me as he gently ran the fingers of his free hand across the now rouged skin of my cheek. "I love how you can be so damn feisty, yet my words still have the power to get past your little tough girl exterior and make you blush every once in a while."

"I'm not blushing," I muttered. "I'm just angry."

"Liar." He dug his fingers into my ribs and tickled my skin.

"Ah! Stop it!" I shouted and quickly rolled off of his big, muscular body—which was deliciously on display other a pair of shorts—and hopped off the bed.

All the while, Sean never faltered to keep the camera pointed in my direction.

"Jesus," I muttered. "Is that thing going to be in my face all day?"

He nodded.

I glanced down at my current state—braless in a tank top and a little pair of boy short underwear.

An exasperated sigh escaped my lips as I stared at my boyfriend. "You realize you're actually filming me in my underwear right now, right?" I punctuated that question with a hand to my hip and narrowed eyes.

He nodded again, unfazed.

"I'm in my underwear, Sean. I also have no bra on. My nipples might as well be waving hello to the camera." I shimmied my chest a little and glanced down at my boobs. "Say hello and smile for the camera, girls!"

He grinned at my antics. "So, some of this footage might just be for my viewing pleasure."

"You're a pervert."

He smirked like the devil from behind the camera. "For you, I am."

"I never should have agreed to this."

"It's too late to reconsider," he teased and waggled his brows. "You already agreed last night before we went to bed."

"Yeah, but I was cockdrunk at the time."

"Cockdrunk," he repeated. "You sure do have a way with words, baby."

I just rolled my eyes and walked into the master bathroom of the new house we'd purchased a few weeks ago.

Malibu. Oceanfront. Only three hours from San Diego. And even the goddamn bathroom had a view of the water. Basically, it was a dream.

And more than that, *he* was a fucking dream. Even when Sean was being a big, persistent, sexy as hell idiot who was determined to shove my own camera in my face and record my crazy morning hair, he was the most perfect man for me.

My guy. My fella. My person.

Somehow, someway, we'd found our way together.

Over the past few months, we'd grown as a couple. And the more time we spent together, the more we realized we didn't want to be apart for more than a few days here and there.

Which explained the awesome home purchase.

During the off-season, we'd live in Malibu. And when Sean was busy with the Mavericks, we'd live in his New Jersey house, which was only thirty or so minutes from the stadium and another thirty away from the center of NYC.

Despite the fact that my boyfriend had woken me up with a camera in my face, I couldn't have been happier. Hell, most days, I had to pinch myself to believe it was all real.

"What are the plans for today?" I called over my shoulder as I added a strip of toothpaste to my toothbrush.

"It's a surprise!"

"Can you at least give me a hint so I know what to wear?"

"Nope."

"You're an asshole!" I yelled through a mouthful of

mint-flavored paste.

He just laughed. Big, hearty, annoying as hell chuckles. "I love you too, baby!"

I guessed I should just be thankful he wasn't in the bathroom trying to get footage of me peeing. Although, I wasn't putting that past him either.

Hell, I kept glancing over my shoulder just to make sure he hadn't snuck himself inside.

My reflection stared back at me as I brushed my teeth, and even though I was still one hundred percent annoyed with Sean's version of a morning wake-up call, I couldn't overlook the underlying glow of happiness that, over the past few months, had become a permanent fixture on my face.

That cocky bastard had turned my world upside down in the very best way.

And just a few months ago, during the Mavericks' championship game against Dallas, he'd gone out on the ultimate limb and told the whole damn world he loved me.

It was swooniest, most perfect, sweetest, most fucking thoughtful thing anyone had ever done for me. Hell, my toes still curled and my heart fluttered whenever I thought about that night.

Damn, I love that man.

We'd come along way, that was for damn sure.

Over the past three months, we'd blossomed and grown and just enjoyed the amazing thing that was us together.

Sure, we had our tense moments and our occasional little fights, but always, at the end of the day, we were a team. A couple. He was mine and I was his. And there wasn't a damn thing that could ever get in the way of that.

Not the media hounding us with a million questions about our relationship.

Not overzealous fans.

Not the paparazzi following us around and trying to capture photographs.

Not anything or anyone.

And trust me, since he'd professed his love for me during the freaking halftime show of the biggest game of the year, we'd become the apple of the public's eye.

They wanted to know us. They wanted to meet us. They wanted anything they could get from us.

We'd done interviews on the *Today Show* and *Ellen* and *E!* and *Jimmy Fallon*.

And we'd had a plethora of offers for a reality series of our own.

But we both decided, that while it was all very flattering, we wanted to keep our private life mostly private. And if there were things that we wanted to share with the public, we'd do it on our terms.

Obviously, I still posted daily content on my YouCam channel, which lately had included a lot of Sean, but that felt different. I was in control of it and always had the final say.

With a quick brush of my hair, I finished up in the bathroom and walked back out into our bedroom to find Sean grinning up at me from his cozy spot on our bed.

And, no surprise, the camera was still recording.

"So, should I get dressed or…?"

"Come here, baby," he said and gestured for me to sit beside him with a pat of his free hand to the mattress.

I listened, mostly out of curiosity, and crawled back onto the bed.

Kneeling beside him, I quirked an eyebrow in his direction. "All right, what are we doing today?"

But he didn't offer an explanation.

Instead, he set the camera down on the nightstand, and once he made sure it was situated perfectly and still capturing our every damn move, he slid off the bed.

"I have something I want to give you."

"You do?" I asked and teasingly glanced down at the crotch of his shorts.

He smirked. "It's not my cock, baby."

I pouted.

"Don't worry, that comes later."

"That's what she said."

"Nice one." An amused laugh left his lips.

"Okay…so are you going to tell me what's happening, or do I have to guess?"

"Come a little closer." He reached out his hand and led me toward the very edge of the bed.

"Is this good?" I asked, still kneeling and looking up at him.

"Perfect."

And before I even knew what was happening, Sean was down on one knee and looking up at me with sexiest, sweetest, most perfect smile I'd ever seen in my life.

"Before I give you what I want to give you, I need to ask you something really important."

Down on one knee?

Need to ask me something really important?

This isn't what I think it is…is it?

My eyes grew wide, and I stared down at him. "W-what? What? What are you doing?" I asked and covered my mouth with my hand.

He just smiled and reached into his pocket.

And before I knew it, inside the palm of his hand sat a sparkly, gorgeous, way too big diamond ring.

Literally, a diamond freaking ring stared up at me.

"Sean? What is happening?"

"Six." He looked up at me with his whole damn heart in his eyes. "I love you, baby. I love you more than I've ever loved anyone or anything. You're my best friend. My lover. My perfect match. And I know, without a doubt, I want and need to spend the rest of my life with you. Will you make me the luckiest man on the planet and marry me?"

"Oh my God," I muttered and just continued to stare down at him in complete shock. "Are you being serious right now?"

He nodded.

"This isn't like some sort of comedy bit for my YouCam channel?"

He shook his head, and his grin grew wider. "No bit, baby. This is one hundred percent the real deal."

"The real deal?"

He nodded again. "Marry me."

"You're crazy," I said because, honestly, he was. I mean, we'd only officially been together for all of three months, and he was freaking asking me to marry him?

"For you," he said. "I'm fucking crazy for you."

I took in the earnest lines of his face. The way his eyes shone with more love than I even knew was possible. And all I could think was, *God, I love him.*

He was my person.

The only person I wanted and needed to spend the rest of my life with.

When I looked toward the future, I saw him, and us, together.

I saw us being playful and traveling and exploring the world together.

I saw us making love and stealing kisses and cuddling on the couch rewatching episodes from *Game of Thrones* for the fiftieth time.

I saw us having babies and growing old together.

I saw everything I had ever wanted and all of the things I didn't even know I'd needed.

Until now.

Until Sean.

Marry him? I didn't even need to think about it.

In a bumbling rush, I hopped off the bed and threw myself into his arms. He nearly fell to his ass, but somehow managed to keep us both from hitting the hardwood floor of our bedroom.

"Yes! Yes! Yes!" I shouted in between placing crazy, erratic kisses all over his face. "Yes, you crazy bastard! Let's get married!"

He chuckled and wrapped both arms around me, embracing me tightly to his chest.

"You'll marry me?" he whispered into my ear, and I nodded like a lunatic.

"Yes!"

He pressed a long, soft, delicious kiss to my lips, and I pretty much just melted into his arms.

But before he let the kiss get out of hand, he lifted me back onto the bed, sitting my giddy ass back onto the mattress, and then, with him still on his knees and his gaze firmly locked with mine, he slid the ring onto my finger.

He kissed the top of the ring with his full lips and smiled up at me.

"Are you ready to get married, soon-to-be Mrs. Phillips?"

"I'm ready."

"Like, how ready are you?"

"Uh…" I scrunched up my face in confusion, and a confused laugh left my lips. "I just said yes, so I think it's safe to say I'm very ready."

"Good," he said and hopped to his feet. "Let's head out, then."

"Head out?"

He nodded and stepped out into the hallway to wheel two suit-cases into our bedroom. "The car should be here any minute. And I hope you don't mind, but for time purposes, I went ahead and packed your shit."

"What car? And you packed my shit?" I asked and glanced down at my favorite pink suitcase, which apparently, was already set to go. The only issue was, I didn't have a fucking clue where it was going. Or where I was going, for that matter. "Sean Phillips, what is happening right now?"

"Vegas, baby," he said, grinning. "You're ready. I'm ready. And I sure as shit don't want to wait another fucking day before I can call you my wife."

"We're going to Vegas? To get married?"

"Yep." He glanced at his watch. "Our flight leaves in about three hours."

"Have you lost your goddamn mind?"

He shook his head. "I've never been so clear or sure of anything in my fucking life."

He was crazy.

This was crazy.

But, good God, I was crazy too.

I jumped off the bed and into his arms. "I fucking love you!"

"I love you too," he said through a few chuckles and pressed a soft kiss to my lips. "Now, go get dressed so I can take you to Vegas and marry you."

I started to walk back into the bathroom, but I only managed two steps before he grabbed my wrist and turned me back toward him.

"Hold on," he said. "There's just one thing I have to do before we leave."

I quirked a brow, but when Sean started sliding my panties down my legs and doing the same with his shorts, I didn't even need to ask.

Before I knew it, my legs were wrapped around his waist and my back was pressed against the wall.

"So…you needed to do *me* before we leave?" I asked cheekily, but he just responded by sliding his thick cock inside of me.

"You do realize that camera is still rolling right?" I asked, but then I started to moan as he pushed himself deeper.

"Our first sex tape. I bet your YouCam followers will love this," he teased, and I wanted to laugh or smack him or maybe a combination of both, but his cock…

Holy moly, it felt so good.

His heady gaze locked with mine. "*Soon-to-be Mrs. Phillips*," he said, and his big hands gripped my ass. "I hope you don't mind, but I just had to be inside of you. I couldn't wait another fucking second."

I pressed my mouth to his, and the instant his lips parted, I dove my tongue inside to take a taste.

Soon-to-be Mrs. Phillips? Yeah, I could definitely get used to that.

And *this*.

God, I could get used to this, being all wrapped up in my soon-to-be husband.

Forever and ever and ever.

"Yes, okay!" Six yelled as I pulled her into the elevator at the Wynn Hotel in Las Vegas. "This *is* Sean Phillips, and I *am* the woman you saw ranting about his cock veins! Stare a little harder, why don't you!"

"Okay, baby," I hushed her with a laugh, wrapping a hand around her mouth as the doors finally closed. "Time to be quiet now."

"I'm sorry," she apologized with a stamp of her foot. "I broke, okay? Six straight hours of people staring at us in the airport and on the plane and in the other airport and in the lobby, and I fucking broke."

I laughed and shook my head, pulling her into a hug to place a kiss at the top of her head. She was the love of my life, and comforting her in her time of craziness was the least I could do.

Plus, when she found out I'd secretly had her camera running to capture audio for the last hour and a half, she was going to need this really romantic gesture of mine to look back on.

Especially since she'd gotten lost in the Las Vegas airport, and I'd been too busy capturing the hysteria on camera to help.

"I know. But we're on our way up to our room now. We'll shower—possibly together—and then we'll go get married. You can relax."

She had been holding it together pretty well, but people had been relentless and I hadn't prepared her for it. Since we'd lost the championship game, the two of us had done a superior job at living low-key. Paparazzi had hunted us for a while, but they'd eventually given up when we hadn't produced anything else noteworthy. Of course, that only made getting a shot of us now more coveted.

"I can't relax," she protested, jerking out of my arms. "And I can't do sexy time with you, so put your perfect penis back in his hidey hole."

I laughed and pouted. "Why can't you do sexy time with me?"

The snap of her eyebrows as they came together was comical. "Uh, because I'll be too busy making you a costume?" she suggested with an air of snobbery. Clearly, I should have been able to guess.

"What costume?"

She shook her head. "Disguise. I should have said disguise."

"Are we going on some top-secret mission I should know about?"

"We're getting married! In Las Vegas! And everyone knows we're here now thanks to my yelling about your cock veins. So, yes, we are going on a top-secret mission. I hope you're comfortable in spandex."

"If we're trying to avoid people recognizing me, shouldn't we be trying harder to disguise my penis? I mean, that's the part they're most familiar with, thanks to you. Spandex is hardly going to do anything to hide it."

"You'd better disguise your penis right now. Word on the street is that my fist is looking for it."

I bobbed and weaved with a laugh, covering the goods with a splayed hand. "Easy, Sixy. You're going to have to use a little care if you want kids one day."

"Kids?" she shrieked. "Can we just focus on getting married for now?"

The elevator dinged, and I ushered her out the doors and onto our floor. We passed a couple in the hall, but they were too busy canoodling to pay any attention to us.

"Trust me, baby. I'm completely focused on marrying you," I whispered sweetly into her ear.

She turned with a jerk, and I laughed as her hair smacked me in the face. "No sexy time!"

I gathered her closer, stepping out to the side of her body to walk as we hugged. "Okay, baby," I agreed easily. "You need to save your sexy-time energy for after the wedding anyway."

Her arms lined mine right under her breasts, and I could feel her smile as it warmed the hall outside our door. "Yeah," she whispered. "You better start planning now. We both know you have to put in a little extra effort to make it good."

God, she was a ballbuster.

I fucking love her.

"Are you sure this is the way you want to do it?" I asked, one last time, as we made the turn into the drive.

Six's nod was absolute, just as it had been the moment she'd come out of our hotel bathroom with fire in her eyes and a smartphone in her hand. Nothing good could come of internet surfing about your wedding in the room you peed, I had feared, and it didn't take her long to prove me right.

"Yes. I had no yarn and no time, so knitting you a disguise got eliminated pretty quickly."

"But our wedding in the *drive-thru*?" I asked again with a laugh.

Didn't she want the aisle? The flowers?

"Yes. It'll be just as special as if we did it inside—and a whole lot more private. This way, you don't even have to get out of the car."

"Ah, yes," I murmured sarcastically. "Staying in the car was my *number one* priority for my wedding day."

"Shut up. And pull up to the window. And flash them your abs so they'll give us a discount."

I laughed. "We don't need a discount. I'd say we're already getting a fucking bargain on our wedding by doing it this way." My pockets weren't being emptied by any pomp and circumstance.

"Discounts aren't always about need, Sean. Gah. Who am I even marrying right now?" she asked teasingly.

I stopped the car in the Tunnel of Love, behind a car in front of us at the Little White Wedding Chapel in Las Vegas, and leaned over to the woman of my dreams to touch my lips to hers.

They were soft and sweet and melted under my own as I whispered Six's truth. "The love of your life."

"Yeah," she agreed easily, melting into the momentous feel of what we were about to do. "Something like that."

The car in front of us started up, the people inside cheering in celebration of their nuptials, so I put the shifter back into drive and pulled forward to the window. With the infamous pink Cadillac next to our rental Chevy Malibu, I was feeling a little inferior.

"Maybe we should have rented something a little cooler."

Six narrowed her eyes. "Flashy cars aren't discreet, Sean."

"Neither is yelling about my cock in the Wynn lobby, Six," I challenged back.

She nodded. "Fair point, well made."

I rolled down the window on my side as a woman came to the window, our laughter still rolling as we mooned at one another.

"Well, well. That's what I love to see. A truly happy couple who can't even stop looking at one another long enough to look at me," the woman greeted.

My smile deepened, and so did Six's.

I knew in that moment that this was so much more than a crazy decision made out of lust and new love. This was *life*.

Six made me happier than anyone I'd ever met, and she did it all the time. Anytime we were together, my face ached. No matter the years spent as a happy guy, or the years hanging out with my crazy sister, or the many years I'd spent dominating on the football field, I'd never smiled as much as I did when Six was with me.

Making me laugh or turning me on, making fun of me or screaming in lobbies about my dick, Six was always finding a way to burrow a little deeper under my skin.

Keeping my eyes on the sparkling amber in her brown ones, I lifted a hand to push some of her wild hair out of her face.

The woman in the window would wait, but the words I had to

say wouldn't.

"I love you."

I wanted her to know forever and I wanted her to know always and I wanted her to know *right then*, right before I made her my wife.

"I think I fell in love with you the moment I met you," I admitted, thinking about staring down at her at the front of the team meeting room that day.

She laughed then. "Me too. Every *part* of you," she emphasized, glancing over my shoulder to the woman playing third wheel to our conversation.

I knew instantly she was referring to her moment in the locker room, and I pulled her in for a kiss.

Deep, wet, and real, this kiss was worthy of a beginning. Worthy of the start of the rest of our lives.

And apparently, I wasn't the only one who felt that way.

A throat cleared as I pulled away, and Six and I both shifted to look at the woman in the window. Her smile was wide, and her gray hair blew in the gentle breeze.

"Not too often couples do my whole job for me," she said with a laugh. "I say, the two of you tell me right now that you take each other to be husband and wife, and we seal this deal officially."

Six leaned forward to bring her head in line with mine and glanced over to meet my eyes. Hers were sparkling and sure, and I'd never been more captivated.

"I definitely do," she said.

My smile stretched from ear to ear. "I've never been more sure of anything in my life. I do."

"Well, then," the nameless woman we hadn't even bothered to introduce ourselves to declared. "By the power invested in me by the State of Nevada, I pronounce you husband and wife."

A drive-thru window, a Chevy Malibu, and a nameless officiant—it wasn't the normal dream. But it sure as hell felt like mine.

Cassie

"Aaaahhhhh bleeee blahhhhhh," Ace yelled as he tore through the house like a fluffing maniac, Gunner chasing after him like a rabid dog.

"No running in the house!" I yelled to the two of them, but then I quickly went back to focusing on the blinking cursor in front of me.

Writing romance novels, my new hobby, was no fluffing joke, and doing it with kids in the house was my own version of waterboarding.

Shut off the fluffing valve already! I'll talk!

I glanced at the clock, knowing my giant ogre of a husband would be walking through the door any minute and praying to all that was holy that Gunner would give him a shot in the balls as soon as he stepped over the threshold.

Both for old times' sake and practicality.

I was still crazy about Thatch—and crazy in general—and he was still hard all the time thinking about how gorgeous I was.

But I was in the middle of this fucking chapter, and the last thing I needed was him coming in the door and trying to rut all over me immediately.

An attack from Gunner would buy me testicle-recovery time and set Thatch's sights directly on our fluffing hoodlums.

Win-win.

I chewed at my lip, considering the different ways I could describe Regenald's hardening penis. It could be a bulging member or maybe a stiff rod. Or maybe I just needed to go all out and cock drop.

It was always such a hard decision.

I right-clicked the cursor to bring up the thesaurus for "penis," but I didn't get even a moment to explore before my phone rang beside me.

My brother Sean's smiling face taunted me. I answered with a sigh.

"This had better be good, Sean. I was right in the middle of researching all the different things to call a penis."

"Jesus Christ," he muttered, and all of a sudden, the interruption felt worth it. If there was anything I loved more than almost anything in the world—my kids and Thatch's Supercock took the top spots—it was skeeving out my brother with oversharing.

I smiled. "No dear, brother. Jesusina Christina, maybe, but I am not Jesus Christ. Is there a reason you're calling?"

He laughed in my ear, and I could fully imagine him giving me the finger. "Yes, Jesusina Christina. In fact, I was calling to tell you that I'm *married*. How's that? A good enough reason to interrupt the cock research?"

I screamed just as the door opened, and Thatcher came running before Gunner could give him a ball shot.

Still, this was worth it.

Winning bets with Thatcher was always worth it.

Ignoring Sean completely, I smacked at Thatcher's chest and then twisted his nipple. He shrieked, and my smile grew with my evil glee.

"What?" he asked, "What is it, Crazy?"

"I win the bet!" I told him victoriously.

"What bet?" Sean questioned in my ear.

Thatch frowned and groaned, but his disappointment was my gain. I smiled, large and proud, as I explained to Sean. "I told him the moment I met Six. I told him she was the one."

THE END.

Love Sean, Six, and the rest of the hunky Mavericks?
Don't worry, we're going make sure all of our favorite Mavericks
Tackle Love. ;)
Next up, Cam Mitchell in Trick Play.
Release Date: August 14th, 2018
Preorder Trick Play today!
#TrickPlay #MaxMonroeRomCom #MavericksTackleLove

Trick Play: A football play that uses unorthodox tactics to fool the
opposing team.

Playing Trix: A method employed by a bad*ss woman to bring
someone down.

Cameron Mitchell's strong presence as a tight end makes him one
of the New York Mavericks' key players. He is a man who can't be
outsmarted or outmatched.

But Lana Simone has more than the usual plays in her book.
Can Cam go the distance when a different kind of pressure is on?

After Cam, get ready for Leo!
Preorder 4th & Girl.

2018 has been the start of ALL THE FUN THINGS.
Find out why everyone is laughing their ass off every Monday
morning with us.
Max Monroe's Monday Morning Distraction.
It's hilarity and entertainment in newsletter form.
Trust us, you don't want to miss it.
Stay up-to-date with our characters, us, and get your own copy of
Monday Morning Distraction by signing up for our newsletter:
www.authormaxmonroe.com/#!contact/c1kcz

You may live to regret much, but we promise it won't be this.
If you're already signed up, consider sending us a message to tell us
how much you love us. We really like that. ;)

You don't want to miss sexy Cam Mitchell, do you?
#TrickPlay #Mavericks
Trust us, it's about to get a whole lot sexy and brooding bad boy and
mysterious real soon. ;)

Follow us online:

Website: www.authormaxmonroe.com

Facebook: www.facebook.com/authormaxmonroe

Reader Group: www.facebook.com/groups/1561640154166388

Twitter: www.twitter.com/authormaxmonroe

Instagram: www.instagram.com/authormaxmonroe

Goodreads: goo.gl/8VUIz2

Bookbub: www.bookbub.com/authors/max-monroe

Acknowledgments

First of all, THANK YOU for reading. That goes for anyone who's bought a copy, read an ARC, helped us beta, edited, or found time in their busy schedule to help us out in any way.

Thank you for supporting us, for talking about our books, and for just being so unbelievably loving and supportive of our characters. You've made this our MOST favorite adventure thus far.

Thank you to Basil and Banana for always being there to keep us in order!

THANK YOU to our amazing readers. Without you guys, none of this would be possible.

THANK YOU to all of the awesome and supportive bloggers. You're like the sparkling unicorns of the literary world, and we'd love to take you for a ride… Wait…what?

THANK YOU to our editor, Lisa. These deadlines, man. They just zoom right past us, huh? God, what would we do without you? Not publish 4 books in 2 months, that's for damn sure. We love you. Like, a lot. More than Thatch loves himself.

THANK YOU to our agent, Amy. We heart you hard.

THANK YOU to our Camp Members. You gals are the best-best-best. #CLY Say whaaaat? ;)

And last, but certainly not least, THANK YOU to our family. We love you guys. Thanks for putting up with us and our moments of creative crazy. Not to mention what feels like a constant state of us looking like hot messes and always on a deadline. Maybe we should stop writing so many books?

Monroe: [singing] Can't stop. Won't stop.

Max: [singing] Roc-A-Fella Records.

Monroe: [singing] 'Cause we get down, baby. We get down, baby.

Max: [singing] The girls, the girls, they love—

Monroe: Wait, should that be readers instead of girls?

Max: Aren't most of our readers women?

Monroe: True.

Max: And I'm pretty sure we have no affiliation with Roc-A-Fella Records so, basically, this song has absolutely nothing to do with anything right now.

Monroe: Damn. And usually, I'm so good at picking out songs.

Max: For playlists. But now, you've got us singing in our acknowledgments.

Monroe: I thought it was a nice change of pace. Because we stay fresh to death, we the best, nothing less.

Max: You realize that just because you're now speaking the lyrics, it's still the same as singing them?

Monroe: [shrugs and smiles] So, is there anything else we wanted to say here?

Thatch: You should probably mention me. And the fact that the three of us have been talking about books again, and I'm about to be in another—

Max: [looks at Monroe] How? Just…how?

Monroe [shrugs again] Because he's more parasite than book boyfriend these days.

Thatch: [smirks] But a sexy as fluff parasite whom you're currently writing—

Max and Monroe: Shut up, Thatch!

Thatch: [winks] Fine. Fine. Your secret is safe with me…for now.

Thank you for reading!
We love you tons and tons and tons!
XOXO,
Max Monroe

Printed in Great Britain
by Amazon

23212975R00154